The Canvas Prison

 Published in the United States of America by Germinal Press.

ISBN 0-918064-06-6 (cloth)
ISBN 0-918064-07-4 (paper)

First edition September 1982

Manufactured in the United States of America

Germinal Press
209 Prospect
San Francisco, Cal 94110

for **Ivo**

Special thanks to David Olson and Diana Dillaway, Steve Zeltzer and Kazumi Torii, Bill Snyder and Ann Nore, Sol and Dorothy Zeltzer, Pat Russell, Gordon and Dorothy DeMarco, Patty Weissman and Mark Marziale and Alvah Bessie for their financial and/or spiritual support.

And a special tip of the old snap-brim to Larry Duncan, proofreader, editor, typesetter, literary cerebalist and myth-maker for his incomprable labors to put Riley Kovachs back on the streets.

Cover by Clarissa An Matthews,55 Goodhue Dr. Akron, Ohio 44313

The Canvas Prison

Gordon DeMarco

Germinal Press San Francisco

The Canvas Prison is the second "hard-boiled" Riley Kovachs detective novel. Set in Hollywood (1949), Kovachs takes the reader on a political odyssey through the movie world, torn apart by HUAC witch hunters, while he looks for screen writer Dalton Trumbo.

From a slim lead provided by Trumbo, Kovachs is able to put together a plan to rescue FRANCES FARMER, the real-life rebel-actress, who is locked away in a mental asylum in Washington where she is scheduled to go under the knife of the nation's foremost lobotomist.

> Gordon DeMarco has created something new in the field of detective fiction. Although Hammet was a political radical, he apparently never thought of creating a progressive private eye . . . DeMarco has supplied this character in his creation of Riley Kovachs, who is not only as hard-boiled as the genre calls for, but is also onto the temper of the times, the era in which he works and the history of the working-class and radical movements in America.
>
> Alvah Bessie, ***Men in Battle***, member of the Hollywood Ten

> Sure, the detective novel is the form. But the substance is rare and precious. Frances Farmer has put her life and her mind on the line in a struggle for survival that is as relevant today as it was 30 years ago. ***The Canvas Prison*** is riveting reading to the last page.
>
> Anna DeLeon, Director — Berkeley, California School Board

> ***The Canvas Prison*** is not only a good read, but also a highly revealing tale of modern psychiatric terrorism. A left-leaning, San Francisco-based private-eye tries to rescue film star Frances Farmer from "Auschwitz on the Puget Sound" — a lunatic asylum. Along the way, he uncovers some harsh truths about the American mental health system — which radicals, together with practically everyone else, have too long ignored.
>
> Leonard Frank, ***The History of Electric Shock Treatment***, co-founder, Network Against Psychiatric Assault (NAPA)

> With this tidy package of history and fiction wrapped in a fast-paced detective thriller, DeMarco offers a distinctively candid view of Hollywood's turbulent post-war years. The characters are so alive it makes one wonder where they are now. ***The Canvas Prison*** leaves one thirsty for more.
>
> Marcello Rodriguez, ***San Francisco Bay Guardian***

CHAPTER 1

There must have been 250 people jammed elbow-to-cuff link into the upstairs room at Dovre Hall. The organizers were suprised, jubilant, and said so several times during the evening. They had expected maybe half that number at best.

So the sweat and hot, stale air, made hotter and staler by cigarette and cigar smoke, was tolerated by most. Even by me, and I was surrounded and suffocating in the front third of the room. The aisles disappeared twenty minutes into the meeting.

It was half past nine when Dalton Trumbo, the featured speaker, rose to address the gathering. Everyone in the hall who had been sitting on chair, floor or window seat rose with him and burst into a spontaneous ovation that lasted a full two minutes. Feet stomped on a bare wood floor, shrieking whistles carromed wildly from wall to wall like ricocheting bullets and voices called through cupped hands, "Give 'em hell, Dalton," "We support you," and "Long live the Hollywood Ten."

Trumbo raised his outstretched arms and a moment later, following a few throat-clearing coughs, order obtained. Trumbo was wearing a wrinkled white shirt, turned soaking dishrag by the human heat in the stuffed room. He had removed his coat and bow tie more than an hour ago. As he stood before us, he demonstrably reached up and unfastened the second and third buttons of his shirt.

"It sure is hot in here," he said with a smile. "Almost as hot as it was under those lights in Washington." The audience giggled. "But at least here," he continued, kicking his voice up an octave, "I am surrounded by friends, men and women of conscience, and not that pack of proto-fascist rats!"

The charged crowd ignited once more, whistling, stamping their collective feet, clapping their hands and yelling supportive slogans. Their faces dripped with a claustrophobic perspiration, but no one seemed to mind. All eyes were glued on the small man standing behind an improvised speaker's table. When the crescendo went away, Trumbo plunged into the text of a speech he delivered with only an occasional reference to small note cards he had spread out on the table in front of him:

Some time before he became involved in the Dreyfus Affair, Emile Zola wrote an article called "The Toad." It purported to be his advice to a young writer who could not stomach the aggressive mendacity of the press which in 1890 was determined to plunge the citizens of the French Republic into disaster.

Zola explained to the young man his own method of inuring himself against newspaper columns. Each morning, over a period of time, he bought a toad in the market place and devoured it alive and whole. The toads cost only three sous each, and after such a steady matutinal diet one could face almost any newspaper with a tranquil stomach, recognize and swallow the toad contained therein, and actually relish that which to healthy men not similarly immunized would be a lethal poison.

All nations in the course of their histories have

passed through a period which, to extend Zola's figure of speech, might be called 'The Time of the Toad': an epoch long or short as the temper of the people may permit, fatal or merely debilitating as the vitality of the people may determine, in which the nation turns upon itself in a kind of compulsive madness to deny all in its tradition that is clean, to exalt all that is vile, and to destroy any heretical minority which asserts toad meat not to be the delicacy which governmental edict declares it. Triple heralds of the Time of the Toad are the loyalty oath, the compulsory revelation of faith, and the secret police.

In four tumultuous days — October 27 to October 30, 1947 — the committee cited ten men for contempt of Congress, charging them with refusal to divulge their trade union and political affiliations. The indicted men had been refused the right of cross-examination; they had been denied the opportunity accorded to others to make statements; they had been refused the right to introduce as evidence those scripts which the committee had charged carried subversive propaganda; they had been refused the right to examine the evidence against them.

The ten men, like those who went before them in history, stood in solitude between the Constitution and those who would destroy it. They had the choice — surrender or fight: assert their rights or answer the questions.

The question of compulsory revelation of trade union affiliation is not complex. The whole history of organized labor demands that no precedent be set which may, under the compulsion of authority, weaken the right of secret membership. There have been times in the past when compulsory disclosure led to death: there are in the South even now instan-

ces of men lynched for trade union activities: and we have no assurance there may not in the future be other times when violence once more will attend the path of the organized worker . . .

The screenwriter continued, sketching in the most recent details of the contempt of Congress indictments of the case everyone calls the Hollywood Ten. Trumbo was one of the "unfriendly witnesses" to appear before the House Committee on Un-American Activities which was investigating communist subversion in the motion picture industry. What he said most of the supporters already knew, but wanted to hear again straight from the horse's shoulder.

Trumbo concluded his remarks with a chilling forecast of what we could expect in the mother country, if, as he said, "this obscene **wehrmacht** that calls itself a Congressional committee is allowed to rape and plunder our sacred democratic institutions. Ladies and gentlemen," he said, pounding the table with his fist, "this is Poland, summer of 1939. We don't have much time. We must act now! Today! Tonight!"

Following Trumbo's talk a hat was passed to raise money for the legal defense of the Ten and a sheet of paper was circulated for those who wanted to sign up for volunteer work with the Committee to Defend the Bill of Rights. A fellow with a guitar started singing "This Land Is Your Land" and the audience joined in. I threw a couple of bucks into the hat, but, being one who is short on vocal ability and at that time even shorter on fresh air, I took the opportunity to make my exit.

Though the February night was typically cold and drizzly, the rush of unused oxygen was exhilarating as it filled my lungs. The light rain cleared the sweat from my face. I reached into my coat for a Chesterfield. I lit it and began walking toward my car.

It was only half past ten, but the street was as deserted as Paris in August. That made it easy for me to hear the sound of shoe leather on the sidewalk behind me. As I approached the corner of 19th and Valencia I turned to take a gander at my tail. The man stopped in his tracks and turned toward the window of the nearest storefront. Since the only shop on the block sold trusses, he wasn't fooling anybody.

I continued down the block to 20th, stopping every ten steps or so to look back at my shadow. And each time he stopped and turned like he was doing some serious window shopping.

When I reached the intersection at 20th I crossed and stood on the south side of the street and waited for the light to change again. My lead-footed friend stood on the opposite corner staring at his collar. When the light changed I recrossed the street and joined him on the corner. The startled gum heel looked away from me and pulled a smoke from his pocket. I beat him with the light.

"Going my way?" I said with a store-bought smile.

He hesitated a moment. Then, not knowing what else to do, bent over and put his tobacco to my fire. "What're ya talkin' about, mister?"

"You've been seeing too many movies, pal. Cut out the goose liver and we'll get along famously."

Whether the man was naturally nervous, or simply uncomfortable at being caught in the act, I couldn't tell. He stood a half-dozen inches under six feet. Two small, dark eyes hid out like half-planted begonia bulbs among the many furrows of a leathery face that looked like it spent a lot of time out in the rain. Both his topcoat and snap brim were cut for a much larger man. He could have passed for Elisha Cook, Jr.'s older brother.

"You're talkin' crazy, mister," he continued, trying to cover a bad job of shadowing with an even worse job of play acting.

"Look, pal," I said, "you've been tailing me for two blocks. I want to know why." I grabbed his elbow and raised it unnaturally behind his back to punctuate my words.

"Ow! Okay! Okay! Yeah, I was shadowin' you. So what? I was tryin' to decide whether or not to trust you."

"Trust me?"

"Yeah. You were at the meetin' tonight, weren't you?"

"So?"

"Your name's Kovachs, ain't it?"

"Again, so?"

"Well, I might want to hire you for a job. But I got to be sure you ain't no fink."

"And tagging after me like a little brown doggie is going to tell you that?"

"Look, mac, you do things your way and I'll do 'em mine. I can't be too careful, you know. I've got a big black X painted on my back. They're ready to pull my plug, send me west, you know what I mean? I know too much. I can blow the lid off their can of beans sky high and they know it. Believe me, they know it. That's why I'm a candidate for a Chicago overcoat. Man, I'm no better than poured concrete on a one way trip to the bone orchard. They've got blasters everywhere just waiting for the right moment to pour hot lead down my bazoo."

"Stop the music!" I said, holding up my hand. "You lost me somewhere after your plug was sent west.

What are you talking about? Are you skunked?"

His eyes darted from side to side as rapidly as the words spit from his thin, cracked lips. Beads of moisture ringed his forehead like mosquito bites and the frightened look in his eyes told me they weren't raindrops.

"Look," he said, slowing down a little. "I know your name is Kovachs. I've been keepin' tabs on you since yesterday. I got the sheet on you from way back an' it says you're okay. Your goin' to the meetin' tonight proves it. I was followin' you to make double sure. You might think I've got the klanks, but I'm as sober as a bank president. I'm in the business, just like you. I do my peepin' outta Seattle. But I've been on the lam since I found out about them. Pal, I've been sleepin' in a different doorway every night. They're on to me, though. You can't stiff **them**. They know my every move. They were at the meetin' tonight. That's why I couldn't talk to Trumbo. They're closin' in for the kill, alright. The rope is gettin' tighter. Time's runnin' out. I'm a gonner. I'm . . ."

"Stop with the cliches, already," I said over his welling hysteria.

He clasped his hands together in front of him in an attempt to put on the brakes. He bit his lip just to make sure.

"Okay, okay. But I'm not off my chump. You gotta believe me. What I got lifts my own hair. Scares the livin' Jesus outta me. Kovachs, you gotta help me. Help her."

He looked around the edge of the brim of his skimmer to survey the intersection at 20th and Valencia. The traffic light winked amber. He took it personally.

"Look, let's get off the street," he said impatiently. "Is there a place where we can get a pick-me-up and talk?"

I suggested McCarthy's on Mission, a block away. He nodded and took my elbow, nudging me toward Mission's "Miracle Mile".

On the way he told me his name was Jake Diltz and he was a private investigator working out of Seattle. Or at least he had been once upon a time. He wasn't too specific on the difference between then and now.

We ordered a couple whiskeys at McCarthy's and took a table off the far end of the long mahogany-colored bar.

"It's like this, Kovachs," he said, gulping his shot of hard water. It seemed to calm him some. "I used to work for Marion Zioncheck. You know about Zioncheck, don't ya?"

I nodded. I knew the case of the rebel Washington Congressman, who, a dozen years ago, plunged to his death from a fifth floor window.

"I was his overcoat when he was in D.C.," Jake Diltz continued. "His bodyguard. The power boys in Seattle hated him from the git-go, you know, because he was a radical and represented skid row drunks. That was okay, though. Most of the flak they gave him was balloon juice and he handled it himself. Then in 1936 he took on Mr. Hard John himself."

"Who?" I interrupted, not even being sure what balloon juice was.

"Mr. Hard John! J. Edgar Hoover! Zioncheck blasted his cookies right on the floor of the House. It was in all the papers. That's when things began to happen."

I stopped Jake Diltz long enough to order us round two of what was shaping up to be a main event. He threw the alcohol down his throat like he was trying to put out a fire in his stomach. He wiped his mouth with the sleeve of a trench coat that looked like it came from a real trench, cleared his throat and continued with his story.

"Yeah, funny things began to happen to him. Not funny ha-ha; funny weird. Like almost bein' run over by a car twice in the same day. Like a piece of scaffoldin' fallin' from ten stories, missin' him by an inch. Like the electric lamp in his office blowin' up in his face when he turned it on. Like people takin' pictures of him every time he scratched a freckle.

"The man became worried because no one would do a damn thing about it. They told him he was paranoid. And when he told the Congress that the FBI had sent out its little hard johns to bring him down they figured he was ready for the feather farm."

Jake Diltz told me of personally catching someone booby-trapping Zioncheck's office one day and hearing from a squeal that someone connected with the government had put out feelers to the mob to cancel the Congressman's ticket.

"In less than a month after all this starts happenin'," he said, resuming his story, "head doctors are swarmin' all over Zioncheck. One day they take him away. Three days later I find out he's crochetin' doilies in a nut house in Arlington. They have him in whacko stir, but he busts out. Only when he comes out I don't know him. Like he is always goofed up on hokus or somethin'. They done somethin' to his mind, Kovachs. I know that as sure as I'm sittin' here." Broken red lines ran like tiny roots through the whites of his eyes. His voice wavered slightly as it rose in pitch.

"A month later, he goes back to Seattle and takes a

dive out a high window." Jake Diltz stopped momentarily to absorb a tear from the corner of a reddened eye with a thumb and forefinger. He compensated for his second of emotion by banging the table top with a clenched fist. The two empty shot glasses hopped and a salt shaker fell over on its side.

"I knew Marion Zioncheck and I know there is no way in hell he would ever blow out his own candle. No way at all! The F.B.I. and the Nazi doctors iced him and made it look like suicide. And now they're after me because I'm on to them. They want to make a hari-hari victim outta me, Kovachs. And they're goin' to do it, too. I can't stop them. That's where you come in."

"I was afraid of that," I said, feeling very much like the intended fall guy to this story.

"Look, Kovachs, I'm serious. I got a whole lot more than the Zioncheck thing stuffed in my cronk. I mean you don't think he was the only one they put away, do ya? You read about that guy from the State Department. Dived into a snow bank from the 16th floor of the Institute of International Education. There's a whole plot to eighty-six people with big yaps, especially if they're pink, if ya know what I mean. And they're not usin' the old droopy-lip goon boy tactics either. They're gettin' them knocked away in looney bins where they carve their straw."

"Their what?"

"Their straw! Humpty, cupola, brain, man, brain! They fix their brains. Electrocute it an' cut parts of it out. They turn people into dough balls. That's what happened to Zioncheck and that's what's goin' to happen to Frances Farmer if we don't head 'em off."

"Frances Farmer!" I uttered with an obvious degree of astonishment. I would be the first to admit my contribution to the conversation, other than ordering the drinks, had been severely limited. I wouldn't have taken a court room oath that I believed everything Jake Diltz had been pitching at me, but I knew for a fact some of it to be true. And he was acting less and less like a hop head and more and more like a man with something serious on his mind. Bringing the name of the former movie actress into the picture whetted both my curiosity and thirst. I went to the bar and ordered us two more bracers.

"Yeah," said Jake Diltz when I returned with the goods, lowering his voice until one of the all day patrons wobbled past us on his way to the powder room, "I've been followin' the Farmer case ever since she had her first run in with the law in '42. Hell, I knew a lot about her before that. Everyone in Seattle did. She was rat poison up there since before she took that trip to Russia in '35. The highups were out to get her then, just like they were out to shut up Zioncheck.

"So she had a pretty bad rep even before she made it to Hollywood. Besides bein' painted red she was a real Garbo, if you know what I mean. Didn't pal around with nobody and was a nose-thumber when it came to curtseyin' before the baggy pants muckety-mucks in Hollywood. She was a real counter-puncher, too, and the gossip cracklers would slobber a load of rubbish on her head every time she forgot to brush her teeth."

Jake told me that Frances Farmer was picked up by a Santa Monica cop one October night in '42 for driving with her lights on in a dim-out zone. The cop took her for a drunk and she took him for a creep. A real brannigan followed, the bottom line being Miss Farmer was cuffed off to the clink. She got six months probation, but folks like Lolly Parsons made sure she paid for it in spades. In fact, according to Jake Diltz, just about the only moral crime she wasn't accused of by the tongue-waggers in wonderland was gassing the Jews.

Jake had parts of his story down cold. At least he was producing names, places and dates like he had been keeping serious book on them.

"About three months later," he continued, "she gets into a row with a dame at the studio and socks her in the puss. She goes back to her hotel, has a few drinks, cries a little over a lot of things and hits the silk. Then what do ya suppose happens? The cops come bust down her door, followed by a platoon of flashbulbs from the local papers. The cops haul her off hell-west-and-crooked to jail, I mean she's a fighter, right, and she don't go easy. The next day, the judge revokes her probation. Says she hadn't been reportin' for the dim-out crime. She tells the judge he's a blowhard in a Halloween costume, and that she was never told she had to report to a leash in the first place. Then she is dragged kickin' and scratchin' from the court room. But she gets in her licks alright. It took two of them big screws to wrestle her to the ground and haul her away.

"Okay, you say. Might not sound as fair as an English cricket match. Just a case of tough luck. Maybe, if she had been stuffed in a six-by-ten at the county. But where do you think she goes?"

I shook my head, but the question, such as it was, was only rhetorical.

"Crescentview! That's where. In the psycho ward of a suburban walnut farm. From there she gets sent to Steilacoom near Tacoma. That place would give the shivers to a Nazi bully. She's been there twice and permanently since May 6, 1945. That's almost four years, Kovachs, four years in that concentration camp for droolers. Only she ain't no drooler. They got her there on a political rap and because she didn't like to wear polka dot dresses with big bows in the back."

Jake Diltz went into some detail about her commitment and the judge who signed her papers. He said the judge was a leader in a right-wing vigilante organization and had been personally denouncing the movie actress since she was a fifteen-year-old writer of a prize-winning essay on atheism. It was at that point I had to ask Jake Diltz what was becoming an obvious question. "What's your stake in this Farmer thing?"

Jake Diltz didn't drop a beat. "Like I said, I knew about Frances Farmer since 1935 and after Zioncheck's murder I followed her case once she got her feet stuck with the law. But I was only readin' the papers an' talkin' to a few people. Then, about a month ago, I'm down in L.A. and drop a few comments to some people about the Farmer case. Nothin' hard, just loose talk. Next day this screenwriter digs me up in a Santa Monica gin mill. He's an old friend of the Farmer dame an' he says he heard the sawbones at Steilacoom were gettin' ready to cut Frances' lid an' would I try an' stop them."

"You mean to tell me they're going to perform a lobotomy on her?"

"Yeah, an' the way I heard it, even her family, which ain't no band of angels in this thing, told the hospital to get lost. But there's still talk about cuttin' her up."

"Then we're talking about criminal activity. Operations can't be performed without the consent of the next of kin."

"Yeah, that an' a nickel'll get you a local phone call.

Look, Kovachs, these boys don't care nothin' about the law. All I know is what they do turns your head into salad fixins."

"How did this screenwriter think you could stop the operation?"

"He didn't say. I mean that's the tricky part, right. Who do you go to? To tell you the truth, I haven't had a whole lot of time to noodle it. The day after this movie guy gets me in touch with a head shrinker friend of his, a mug who knows a lot of the same things as me, my world starts gettin' crowded, if you know what I mean. Suddenly, I've got more tails than Fred Astaire has black coats. And I get phone calls, only no one is on the other end. And last night I'm stayin' in a flopper on Turk Street and what do you think happens? The goddamn table lamp blows up in my pan. Just like Zioncheck! I mean I'm walkin' in his footsteps and it's got me wound tighter than a two-dollar watch."

There was apprehension written all over Jake Diltz's face. Perhaps it was just plain fear. That much I knew about him to be real. There was no faking a thing like that. It was a mortal kind of fear I saw staring back at me. Not the kind of fright you get when your roller coaster car begins its descent from a high track, or even the kind of fear when a mug twice your size takes a poke at you in a bar. Then, even if the brute connects, you know it will all be over in a few minutes and you can go on living your life, with or without a steak over your eye. But the fear I saw sweating out of Jake Diltz's pores was the kind that said 'don't go buy anything on time; tomorrow may never come.'

It was getting late. We had been in McCarthy's almost two hours and the bartender was rinsing out the last of the glasses telling everyone to drink up and go home. He also said something about bedbugs biting, but I didn't catch it. Jake Diltz and I rose and started for the door. The little man grabbed my arm halfway there.

"Here, Kovachs," he said, stuffing a fat envelope deep into the side pocket of my overcoat. "There's 205 sambolios left from what the screenwriter gave me. They're yours. You're takin' over the case."

"I'm what? I shouted.

Two old-timers at the door were fumbling around in a vain effort to locate a non-existent knob, turned back and looked at us. "Shhh," one of them slurred, putting a crooked pink finger to his lips, "you'll wake the baby." Both of them, stewed like a can of Del Monte's prunes, giggled playfully as they pushed through the door and staggered out to the sidewalk.

I reached into my pocket to withdraw the cabbage. Jake Diltz faked a left and darted right around me. He reached the door three paces ahead of me.

"Keep the dough, Kovachs. You'll need it for train fare to L.A. and Seattle. I'll give you a honk on the Don Ameche when the rooster coughs and give you the rest of the lowdown. See you, old buddy." He winked, tipped his hat and then burst through the door like a pellet of puffed rice from one of Quaker's guns.

There was nothing left for me to do but to go home and get some sleep. If I had tried to make any sense out of it I would have come down with a major league head-thumper. While I was walking to my car I tried to concentrate on the friendly patter of the rain, the flickering neon signs on Mission street, the clutch on my car that was 5,000 miles past repairing, the Berlin Airlift — anything to keep my mind from Jake Diltz and his 205-dollar story.

CHAPTER 2

In the morning, over a cup of twenty-four-hour-old murk and the last piece of what was at one time an apple pie from the Golden Crust Pie Shop, I tried to come to terms with Jake Diltz. His story was a pip. No getting around that. Even if I couldn't put it all in a tall glass and drink it down, it was one hell of a tale. Jake himself was another matter. Yet, once he had a couple drinks in him he did begin to make sense, even if it was in a farfetched way. On the other hand, he sounded an awful lot like a guy who had spent too much time in a forward trench at the front.

There was no figuring him or his story until I talked to him again and, though I had an itchy feeling that further contact with the strange little homunculus would bring me trouble in large wicker baskets, I had an adolescent curiosity to hear the rest of the dope he promised to "stuff in my wig." Also, there was a matter of 205 dead presidents that I wanted to press in his sweaty palm.

I peered out the window to see if it looked like rain, but caught myself before making any foolish wardrobe decisions. In Frisco, looking at the sky only tells you what's happening at the moment and then only over your own head. Thirty minutes later the fog might come rolling in or go rolling out and the temperature drop or shoot up by ten degrees or more. Then there was the wind to consider. Sometimes it just doesn't pay to wear a hat in this town. Furthermore, it's the places you are going rather than what's going on in the blue yonder that should tip you off whether to wear a top coat or short sleeves; wool or cotton. I employ the "layer method". If I'm going to a couple different places in different parts of town, I put on sweaters, flannels, gaberdines, top coats and the like. Then I peel them off as the temperature and climate dictate. It makes for a lot of extra bulk, that's true, and sometimes the front seat of my Nash looks like I've been out collecting for the Salvation Army. But I never get caught short in a bone-chilling cold at the beach or a steamy wet fog in the Richmond. Never.

Figuring in the rain factor was the same thing. It depended more on the time of day and the part of the city you were in than hunting out dark clouds or checking the newspapers. It didn't matter all that much to me anyway. I don't like rain slickers, have been known to hurt myself with umbrellas and have a childhood dislike of galoshes. Rain, to me, means the wearing of the older of my two hats as far as my wardrobe is concerned. Besides, I like the stuff.

I put on the older of my two skimmers and walked out the door of my Bernal Heights flat into a pouty February morning that nipped slightly at the extremities.

The Nash took me downtown to a Howard Street garage where I paid a guy named Russell thirty cents. That kept the city from lining its treasury at my expense and south of Market hooligans from selling my tires.

I stopped and bought a **Chronicle** from Satch, the newsie who runs the stand outside the Palace Hotel. I took the stairs to my office on the seventh floor. The elevator in the Monadnock Building was on the blink again. It was less reliable than one of Fibber McGee's inventions.

I huffed down the hall to my office trying to catch my breath. I caught it just before reaching the door. I stood in front of the door and clasped my hands over my head to open up the lungs. It helped. I could see enough through the fish-eye glass to know that I was going to have to wait to read Herb Caen. But it wasn't all good news. Two brown blobs moved slightly. I opened the door and they became two men in identical brown suits. One was sitting behind my desk. I would have been offended, but then I did have only two chairs in my small ten by ten. The man sitting in my chair bounded out of it the moment I entered.

"Please excuse us," he said, scooting around the desk and extending his hand for me to shake. "Your door was unlocked and we thought you wouldn't mind too terribly if we came in and waited for you. You are Mr. Kovachs, are you not?"

I shook his hand as a matter of western courtesy and nodded my head confirming my identity. The man in the brown suit, that is, the taller and younger of the worsted twins, continued.

"Please forgive us if we have stepped out of bounds. Allow me to make the introductions. I am Dr. Smythe and my colleague is Dr. Jonas."

"Smith and Jones," I said, shooting small arrows with my eyes. "How convenient it must be for you."

"That is Smythe and Jonas," Dr. Smythe corrected while wagging a scolding finger at me, "not Smith and Jones."

"Perhaps we should come directly to the point, Dr. Smythe," said the other man speaking for the first time. Both his eyes and his tone were impatient.

"Yes, I believe you are right, Dr. Jonas," said his colleague. Dr. Smythe nervously rubbed his long white hands together and began pacing the floor. I threw my hat on the clothes nail on the wall next to my desk, parked the goods in my detective's chair, leaned back and lit a fresh Chesterfield. I had an idea Dr. Smythe's story was going to be at least two smokes long.

"You see, Mr. Kovachs," he began, running a long smooth hand lightly over the top of a freshly cropped and lotioned head of waxy blond hair, "Dr. Jonas and I are resident physicians at Crescentview Hospital in Santa Monica. We are also both graduates of the Stanford Medical School — the same class actually — and after years of successful private practice, we decided to . . ."

"Dr. Smythe!" Dr. Jonas barked.

"Yes, yes, quite so, Dr. Jonas. To make a long story short, Mr. Kovachs, Dr. Jonas and I are psychiatric physicians, the co-directors of the Experimental Chronic Psychosis Unit at Crescentview."

"That's fine, doc," I said, staring off into the eyes of the eight-by-ten glossy of Rita Hayworth I kept framed and handy on my desk. She always suggested wonderful faraway things. "But I'm a little low on psychosis just now. How about if I promise to give you a ring the next time the bogey man starts sending me hate mail?"

"I am afraid you don't understand, Mr. Kovachs," said Dr. Smythe. "You see, much of our work in the ECPU is of a highly sensitive and experimental nature. Why, both Dr. Jonas and I have staked our reputations on more than one patient's treatment program."

"You're right, Dr. Smythe," I said, "but unless

you're auditioning for the Nobel Prize, I don't understand. And if you are, you have the wrong Riley Kovachs. I haven't had anything to do with the Nobel Prize for years."

"Look, mister, this is serious," growled Dr. Jonas. His patience, like a weak sedative, was wearing thin. His colleague glided over to where Jonas was standing and put a hand on his shoulder.

"Please, Frederick," he said, "we agreed I would handle this. I am sure Mr. Kovachs meant no disrespect, did you, Mr. Kovachs?" He looked at me hopefully.

"I don't know, it's still too early to tell."

"Quite so." Dr. Smythe coughed nervously. "We will take only a few more moments of your time. In short, Mr. Kovachs, one of our patients, a patient who is currently undergoing a totally new and experimental treatment program, has, uh, how shall I put it?"

"Broken out of stir?" I said, finishing Dr. Smythe's sentence. He wasn't amused.

"He walked away, Mr. Kovachs! He simply walked away. Ours is a minimum security hospital. We don't treat our patients like common criminals."

"My mistake." I don't think either of the two tongue-depressors thought me really repentant.

Dr. Jonas was becoming angrier by the minute. His face was stretched tight and his neck at the collar line had turned the color of beefsteak rare. He reached inside his brown suit coat and pulled out a cigarette. He lit it with a match and blew the first smoke through his nose like a freight train highballing out of the yard. He started to glom the things on my desk with his eyes. He didn't seem to care whether or not I noticed him. Dr. Smythe, however, did, and kicked his story into the fast lane.

"Our patient is a classic paranoid with a latent schizophrenic personality. While he is relatively harmless to others, he does present a threat to his own safety. He is a very disturbed man, Mr. Kovachs, and we must return him to Crescentview immediately."

"His name wouldn't happen to be Jake Diltz, would it?" I said, stating what was becoming as obvious as an eclipse of the sun.

"Why yes, yes it is," chirped Dr. Smythe, clasping his hands in joy. "Did you hear that, Frederick? Jake is using his own name this time. That is a terribly good sign."

Frederick just said "hmmm" as he stood in the middle of my office with his arms folded like tomorrow's laundry.

Dr. Smythe turned to me and continued speaking in quick, excited tones. "We hired a private investigator — Dr. Jonas and I — when Jake disappeared. Hired a man with our own money. We received a call yesterday evening that Jake had been seen in San Francisco. Dr. Jonas and I took the first available plane. We arrived less than two hours ago. Our investigator informed us that he followed Jake last night — shadowed is the word I believe you people use — and that he spent a good portion of the evening with you, Mr. Kovachs."

"Your man's good, doc, but why didn't you go to Jake Diltz's hotel. That would have made a lot more sense than coming here with your life story."

"We did, smart guy," said Dr. Jonas, crushing out his cigarette in my desk ashtray with his knuckles. What remained of his patience had just gone west. "We went to his hotel this morning, but he had checked out."

"Gave you the slip, eh?"

"Look, Kovachs, this is a very sick man we are dealing with here and he is in desperate need of immediate medical treatment. I should think a little civil cooperation from you is not asking too much."

Dr. Smythe spoke up, hoping to derail his partner who was just one small step away from becoming a hot head. "What Dr. Jonas is trying to say, Mr. Kovachs, is that we would be extremely grateful if you could provide us with information concerning the whereabouts of Jake Diltz. The longer he remains at large, I am afraid the more serious and potentially irreversible his condition becomes. We must locate him without delay. For his sake."

"And maybe just a bit for yours, too, eh, Dr. Smythe?" I said.

The Stanford grad blushed at the comment. The other Palo Alto alum cracked his knuckles like they were dry twigs. I don't know why I was so protective of the little man I had known less than twelve hours, a man who promised to get me in more hot water than a vat of Maine Lobsters. He wasn't even my client, though I had a big hunk of his cabbage choking my back pocket. Maybe it was just a simple case of professional instinct that made me play the nasty clam with the two pill bags from L.A. At least I'd like to think so.

"In a sense, Mr. Kovachs," said Dr. Smythe, choosing his words as carefully as a Napa Valley vintner selects grapes, "you are correct. Although what is crucial here is not our individual careers, but that of our profession. You see, Dr. Jonas and I have designed a treatment program for this patient that can only be described as revolutionary. If we are successful, we stand to advance the cause of psychiatric medicine at least a decade. A full decade! Do you realize what that will mean, Mr. Kovachs?"

Dr. Smythe's eyes grew larger and he began smacking his lips. Dr. Jonas looked out the window, generally ignoring his colleague's claim to medical history.

"That sounds fine, doc," I said, "and I wish you luck, but I don't know where Jake Diltz is."

Dr. Smythe' face sunk. He clasped his hands together and walked toward me taking quick, short steps. "Please, Mr. Kovachs, I entreat you to tell us where Jake Diltz is."

"And I repeat, I don't have a clue where he might be. We parted company last night at the door of McCarthy's bar as I'm sure you already know. I don't know where he went from there. I never expect to see him again."

Jonas turned away from the window and walked over to me. He bent over and jammed his face into mine. He spoke with an erect finger separating our two noses. "Look, wise guy, I've had just about all I can take from you. If you know what's good for you, you will tell us where we can find Jake Diltz!"

"Is that any way for a healer of the sick to talk?" I said, picking up a pencil from the green blotter on my desk and pushing away Jonas' finger. Dr. Smythe intervened, rapping the corner of my desk like a school teacher trying to get a student's attention.

"Gentlemen, please! Let us control our tempers. Dr. Jonas, if Mr. Kovachs says he doesn't know where Jake is, then we must take him at his word. Mr. Kovachs, I am sorry to have inconvenienced you in any way. If you hear from Jake I would be most appreciative if you would contact me at this address." He took out his billfold and withdrew a business card. He wrote something on the back before giving it to me. "Dr. Jonas and I can be reached at the Bedford Hotel. We will be there through tomorrow."

I took his card and gave it a quick once over before putting it in my shirt pocket. I gave the pocket a little tap for Dr. Smythe's benefit. He seemed reassured.

"Thank you, Mr. Kovachs. I hope with your help we will be able to locate Jake. He is so terribly disturbed. You see, he has an unnatural fear of doctors. He has this delusion that all physicians are diabolical and perform unnecessary surgery on people." Smythe chuckled uncomfortably. "Brain surgery, I believe is his latest delusion. Before that it was appendectomies. He is what the Freudians call a classic paranoid. He is convinced the staff at Crescentview is trying to do him bodily harm. That notion obviously contributed to his decision to leave us. You can see, can't you, Mr. Kovachs, why we must locate him and be as discreet and gentle with him as possible."

"Sure," I said, "but does Dr. Jonas?"

Jonas's face turned beefsteak rare again and he started for the door. "Dr. Smythe! Our business here is finished!" he said through a pair of unnaturally tight lips. He opened the door and stepped out into the hall.

"Just so," contributed Dr. Smythe, bowing slightly as he backed toward the open door. "Good day, Mr. Kovachs."

He closed the door behind him and returned to a formless blob on the other side of the fish-eye glass.

CHAPTER 3

I shook open the **Chronicle** and scanned the headlines. Thirty minutes later I had read everything but the old ladies sports pages and Herb Caen. The phone rang. It was Jake Diltz.

"Kovachs, I'm a gonner. They're ready to put the mitts on me. There's no time to lose. It's curtain-pullin' time. I'm in a bean wagon on 30th and Mission. Hal's Donut Shop. Get here pronto! I got some more dope to stuff in your wig. Hurry, man! And if you ain't carryin' a speaker, you better get one. These skibos mean business."

He hung up before I had a chance to ask him about doctors Smythe and Jonas. In fact, he didn't even allow me a hello.

I closed up the office and put my feet to working the stairs. I reached my car in five minutes. A minute later I was speeding up Mission Street. It was choked with traffic beginning at 16th. I swung over to Valencia and took it to where it angles into Mission a block past St. Luke's Hospital. I pulled into a meter space near the corner of 29th and Mission. Hal's was just two doors beyond the intersection on the same side of the street. I lit up a Chesterfield while standing on the corner waiting for the light to change.

I still had the match in my hand when I noticed the flashing lights on top of a red and white ambulance parked in front of Hal's. I forgot about the traffic light and dashed across the street. A small crowd of people were jammed in front of the diner. Most were pressed against the glass peering inside.

I shoved my way through a dozen people to reach the doorway in time to see a burly white-suited man kick open the door from the inside with a booted foot.

"Make a hole," he growled at the onlookers. Behind him was a blur of commotion. Two more white coats were locked in a furious struggle with a man sewed up in a strait jacket. The man was using his head to butt them and his feet to kick over tables and to wrap around counter stools in an effort to prevent being dragged to the street and into the wagon. The diner had been turned into a shambles of broken plates and cups and overturned furniture. The man doing the wrecking was Jake Diltz.

The two attendants punched him savagely in the face to slow him down so they could put a gag in his mouth. But from Jake Diltz's puffed and bloody lips still came cries of bloody murder.

"The Nazi shrinks got me! They'll get you too. Nobody's safe!" Through a pair of terrified eyes nearly swollen shut by repeated blows, he saw me. The attendants had him off his feet and were carrying him through the door of the diner. They had given up trying to stuff the gag in his mouth.

"Kovachs!" he screamed. "I'm a dead duck! They've nabbed me. Got to save Farmer . . . !"

One of the attendants, fat, bald and greasy as the burgers Hal dishes up, drove a fist into Jake Diltz's pulverized face. I spit out my cigarette and lunged at the pus-gutted attendant. I hit him with my head in his massive solar plexus. He gasped, making a sound like an old car experiencing four flat tires at the same time.

Jake yelled at the top of his lungs, "Too late to save me, Kovachs! I'm buzzard meat! Must see Trumbo! He'll know how to find the movie guy and Dr. . . . !"

Partly from another blow to Jake Diltz's face, a face that would never be the same again, and partly from a mule kick to my ribs by one of the other meat wagon maulers that sent me down and dark, Jake's words became a muffled blur.

When I came to, I found myself propped up against the store front next to Hal's. An old man held a glass of water to my lips.

"It's a damn shame," he said, "these lunatics have to come and destroy our neighborhood. I guess you just walked into the fan, huh, mister? Lucky they didn't take you for a gooney bird and haul you away too."

"Yeah," I said, breathing through a dozen very sore ribs. Even swallowing the water hurt. When my eyes got off the merry-go-round I focused on the empty stretch of curb in front of Hal's where an ambulance used to be. "Say, pop," I said to the old man, "do you know where the ambulance went?"

"Don't rightly know," he said, scratching a pink chin. "Plates say she was from out of town. Maybe down the Peninsula somewhere."

I took another sip of agua and rose to my feet using both the old man and the building as aids. I said thanks to both and stepped off tentatively in the direction of my car. I lit a Chesterfield. It helped ease the pain some. Something Dr. Smythe said about being discreet and gentle almost made me laugh.

CHAPTER 4

I drove out toward the Presidio to collect both mind and body. I had an unexplainable urge to be near some water. Some running water. San Francisco has an abundance of the blue-green wet as every school boy knows, but running water — creeks, streams and rivers — is another matter. Islais and Mission Creeks have long since dried up and are now man-made channels off the Bay. Only Lobos Creek remains, and that's where I headed.

I drove through the Park, exiting on 25th Avenue and continued north to El Camino Del Mar. I turned right and drove a few hundred yards. Del Mar turns into Lincoln Park Boulevard at Bowley. I pulled off the road and parked a hundred feet or so up Bowley.

I still had the presence of mind as I climbed out of the Nash to reach in the back seat for my copy of Armstrong's **Field Guide to Western Wildflowers**. I tucked it under my arm and crossed Bowley and walked down the cinder path past a carpet of sea fig that was just beginning to open up.

I reached the great gnarled trunk of the Monterey Cypress where I sometimes sit and read or identify flowers. I deposited my bones on a smooth, flat section of exposed root. The sky was low and steamy gray. The air was stiff as a starched shirt, but not cold enough to make the nose run. The hum of the water generator near the bridge that is Lincoln Park Boulevard and the lush green nasturtiumed hillside on the other side of the creek conspired to disengage my mind for a time. I thought only of the elements. Rather, I absorbed them — color, touch, smell and sound — through my open pores.

The creek environs were a walloping rich green. Rushes, big root, blackberry bushes still months away from bearing fruit, wild cucumber, majestic cala lillies poking through the brush, any number of nettles and flowering weeds and, of course, the floppy round pads of nasturtium gave the tiny trickler the look of a brook deep in the recess of a dense forest.

I got up momentarily to pick a small orange flower growing among the nasturtium. Its petals were cupped and its pistil sturdy and exterior. A pattern of blood-red veins through the four petals gave it an exotic quality. I hunted through Armstrong trying to put a make on the oriental smeller. But I'm the kind of guy that, if there isn't a color plate or at least a drawing, it might as well be a cement stump as a mountain penstemon for all I know. The scientific identification key at the beginning of the book made about as much sense to me as the rules to Bridge.

I walked the stream for a few feet looking for some easier flora to identify. Although the creek winds around the fences to some pretty chi-chi Sea Cliff back yards, ducks don't seem to mind. They think its a bona fide wildlife refuge. I've seen mallards and greenbills dive out of the sky to waddle around in the miniature waters.

I walked the stream bed until it became clogged with overhanging fuchsia and vines- green, thick and spreading- that reminded me of something I have seen in Tennessee called kudzu.

I hopped up from the shoe-top stream to the sandy

path that parallels it and pushed my way through the toyon, shrubs, and periwinkle, while Lobos nose-dived underground. A couple hundred feet later I emerged from the thicket and Lobos from the earth. The stream made its reappearance, flowing through a large, unfriendly cement block that held in place six-foot iron rods that looked like the bars to maximum stir. Despite the degradation of flowing through a sewer, Lobos Creek continues trickling thirty yards across Baker's Beach, barely scratching the sand on its way to the sea. Not much as streams go, but it's all we have and I never had much trouble making the most of it.

I stood in the loose blond sand and gazed across the frisky sea. From the Golden Gate Bridge and the eye-catching vertical outcropping of serpentine just below it on the south side, I let my eyes roll north and west toward the lighthouse at Fort Cronkhite. The coastal prairie of Marin was at its greenest in February. The hills were shaded by a light brown chapparal and outcroppings of red chert. Trees exist only on the three sides of the bowl whose base is Kirby Cove. They say on a clear day you can see all the way to Point Reyes.

The sky was soft with a shy touch of blue mixed with the low clouds that were nibbling away at Tamalpais' peak. Further west, a gray-white steam blurred the contours of the coastal landforms. The lighthouse at Fort Cronkhite could only be seen on nautical maps.

I smoked a Chesterfield as I watched the clouds moving subversively inland, preparing to sock in the coast. I could have stood there in the soft sand and waited for it to happen, but a couple of kids playing in the inches of water that are Lobos Creek were shrieking as they hopped across its five-foot girth, trying and failing to make the six-inch cut bank of sand. It brought me back to the city.

I turned to retrace my steps to the Nash. The ritzy Sea Cliff castles perched on top of the craggy coast a hundred feet above the ocean were there to remind everyone on the beach they were allowed there only at the cliff dwellers' largesse. I didn't like that kind of reminder. Among other reasons, it brought up recent and unpleasant incidents in my checkered past. Like Jake Diltz and the little cocktail party at a certain Mission district sinker factory.

I left the beach and returned to the Monterey Cypress tree to do my reminiscing. The sharp pain in my ribs as I sat down helped me to remember.

Two frisky labradors who could have passed for twins spotted me from the top of the hill across the way and came bounding down its steep path toward me. They crossed the stream and came to where I was sitting. Both took turns sniffing my pants leg and, satisfied that I was a kindred spirit, bounded away to search for a lower form of life to play with.

Poor Jake Diltz, I thought. Maybe he was a classic paranoid with a schizophrenic personality. Maybe his tale was pure celophane and maybe he was a refugee from a mental ward. Then again, maybe the brown tweed pair from Los Angeles were the ones feeding me the hole in the donut.

Those and other things tugged at me as I sat staring into the clear waters of Lobos Creek. If I had been somebody else I might have said to hell with it and gone down to the Orpheum to catch Benny Goodman. I had already paid for a ticket. But I was in a business that made it hard to do that. There were some principles involved. Integrity and things like that. But if you want the truth, in the detection business, a large part of what passes for integrity is just so much wall plaster. There was Jake Diltz's 205 clams to consider. Even a certified rat would have felt some sort of obligation to do something for the guy with his cash burning a very big hole in the pocket.

I didn't like what my alternatives were narrowing down to. I got up from the tree feeling the pain in each rib as I did and began down the stream again. By the time I reached the nasturtium I turned back. I had decided to make some inquiries on Jake Diltz's behalf. It was the least I could do.

It took only a few minutes to get to the Bedford Hotel on Post Street. It took only another minute to learn I could have saved myself the trip.

"Doctors Jonas and Smythe are no longer guests at this hotel," said a maroon-suited clerk with his nose pasted to the ceiling.

"Kind of sudden, wasn't it?" I said. "They just checked in this morning."

The clerk flipped a few pages in the guest register. He dropped his eyes, but his nose was still tilted north, which left him looking like a Pekinese watering a shrub.

"I beg your pardon, sir," he said through a pair of lips that would have looked better on a sea bass, "the gentlemen checked out shortly before noon today."

"Any forwarding address?"

"I should think not, sir. We don't provide that kind of service to temporary guests," he said, like I had asked to smell his socks instead.

"Okay, Ruggles," I said, "you've been a peach." The desk man said something about my being a droll fellow as I turned and pushed my way through a jungle of alligator and leather bags sitting patiently at the heels of customers waiting to pay thirty dollars a day to get a room with a view.

I drove back to my flat where I applied a cold wet towel to my kicked ribs. A pot of dark French that was strong enough to have liberated Paris all on its own did me more good than the towel. I called a person I knew slightly who was a coordinator for the local Hollywood Ten defense committee to get a line on Dalton Trumbo. The friend said Trumbo left for Los Angeles two hours after last night's meeting.

I made a few perfunctory calls to area hospitals in a hopeless effort to locate Jake Diltz. I knew before dialing the first number the chances of finding him were slim and none. I wasn't disappointed.

A second cup of the French left my eyelids fluttering to the beat of the "Marseillaise". I felt I might never sleep again. Jake Diltz had vanished. The Happiness Boys from the southland funny farm had taken a powder as well as liberties with my sensibilities, such as they might be. Benny Goodman and a third cup of Brazil water would have to wait. I had to find Trumbo. There was no other way out.

CHAPTER 5

The Coast Starlight hissed its way into L.A.'s Union Station. I made up my bed, which only required a flip of the handle under the seat springing it back to an upright position. All that was left was to see if my legs still worked, and assuming they did, grab my bag and step off the Pullman's contribution to insomnia and then to lower my nose into a cup of what keeps Rio de Janeiro awake at night.

I didn't bother to shave before I got off the train. I grabbed the morning edition of the Hearst fish-wrapper and made my way into the station ham 'n' egger. The smell of burning coffee drove imaginary toothpicks under my eyelids. Two cups later and the previous ten-hour symphony of bawling infants, the yakkers across the aisle two rows back and the farmer from Salinas who began snoring like an untuned radio two minutes after he deposited his overalled hulk into the seat next to me, were but fond memories. I was wide awake and ready to spring into action. The only detail to contend with was not having a clue as to the location of said action.

The newspaper provided little in the form of ideas. The Annual Pasadena Dog Show opened the day before, the Ferreri murder case was heating up and sounded like something straight out of James M. Cain and a nude woman was arrested reading passages from **Deuteronomy** on a downtown sidewalk.

Frisco and L.A. seemed to be in a dead heat in the Looney Tunes department. In a way, it relieved me a little. I'd spent so long in San Francisco I thought it was the 'Playland of the Touched'. All this made for a morning's entertainment, but I was only spinning my spokes as far as Jake Diltz was concerned. I figured with so little to go on I was going to have to play it from deep and straight away center field. Three rounds of station house coffee and instinct told me to point my nose in the direction of Hollywood and try to sniff out Dalton Trumbo.

I flagged down a cab outside the depot on Alameda. The driver turned onto Sunset and took it all the way to Hollywood. It was slow, but I didn't mind. In fact, I had him make the loop around Echo Park so I could take a gander at the Pepper trees and the Wisteria. I read somewhere once that Echo Park has a lot of Western Peony. It does, but I was a couple weeks early to catch the blossoms.

Despite what everyone writes and says about Los Angeles being a crummy place, a town with no style and even less class, a city where the rococo is grafted on to everything from tiled roof Spanish revival architecture to the embarrassing lawn furniture and swimming pool paraphernalia — no matter, even if it weren't true — you've got to love the flowers and trees.

If you can be on the lookout for a scarlet bougainvillaea trailing up the side of the house, you might not notice the swimming pool built to look like a Greek ruin with statues of armless women running amok. If you can drop your lamps on a silk-oak Grevillea or the lavender of a flowering Jacaranda you might be spared the sight of some of the awful all-night joints, the batallions of stucco San Simeons built by recent money and some of the down-on-their-luck people who haunt Bunker Hill.

Sure, it's a game, but maybe that's the point. It's got me through a lot of long and tough years in Frisco. If you can wiggle your eyes like they were those little steel marbles in the glass-covered clown puzzles the kids play with, and you can drop them into the slots that please you, then maybe you can live, or coexist as they say, with what is ugly, vile and obscene. Then again, maybe not.

Once you tire of the game of bouncing eyeballs, you've got to shake hands with the real world and hope there's no electric palm buzzer in its mitt.

That's about where I was as the cab wound its way past Silver Lake Boulevard and on toward Hollywood, USA.

"You know where the Writers United office is?" I asked the guy in the front seat doing the steering.

He jerked his shoulders up and practically stood up in his seat and turned around. "You said a bad word, mister. Red screenwriters are about as popular as a fire in a crowded theater in this town."

"So I have been told," I said trying not to give anything away before I had some dope on the hackie's persuasion.

"What is it you wanted to know? Where their office is? That's a rich one, that is. They folded their tents after the hearings in D.C. No more office, no more fronts, no forwarding address, no nothing."

"You don't seem too broken up about it," I said, changing my approach. The cabbie turned around in his seat once again, which made me a bit jumpy, especially when he sailed through the intersection at Sunset and Hollywood while looking at me. But the cab seemed to know what it was doing even if its driver didn't.

"Hey, mister, don't get me wrong," he said. "I think them movie writers got a raw deal, a real raw deal. What really put salt in my beer was when their buddies and those double-dome bigshots who sit in air-cooled offices turning out their box-office hits took French leaves when it came to helping out the guys on the hot seat. Took run-out powders, every last one of 'em. I'd of hated to had any of those rats in my platoon when we was crossing the Rhine. You get what I mean?"

I did and sat back on the tape-patched seat and fuelled up a Chesterfield. I had gained a certain confidence both in the driver and his driving, such as it was. L.A. is a town where it helps to make friends fast. But then what town bigger than a cheese ball isn't?

The cab driver spent the next few minutes telling me how divided, bitter and frightened the entire film community had become since Parnell Thomas' H.U.A.C. started nailing up the pelts of Hollywood scriptwriters in the fall of 1947. Since that time the studio execs fired the ten unfriendly witnesses and went on record saying they would give walking papers to any film employee who forgot Mothers Day and the principles of "Americanism".

"Yeah," the cabbie continued, "I don't know all the ins and outs of this thing the way some do, but I can tell a whole lot about what's going on with the movie crowd just by looking in the rearview mirror of this cab and hanging my ear on the arm strap. I can tell where they stand in this mess two minutes after they park their goods in my back seat. They don't have to say nothin' either. I can tell by the look in their eyes, the way they smoke their cigarettes, little things like that. You know, like making with the small talk, reading the papers and dropping me a tip. You get to know your rides pretty well, I'd say."

The cab driver took no small degree of satisfaction in styling himself a boulevard sociologist when it came to sizing up the inhabitants of the dream factory.

"Yeah, I've been pushing this crate since '33, with four years vacation in Europe, of course. There ain't no producer, actor or writer that yours truly hasn't hauled across town at least once. I can tell you the tippers from the deadbeats, who's workin' and who ain't, who's cheatin' and who's fallen for a new face without reading Hopper or Parsons. I can tell you who's red and who's red, white and blue and mostly I can tell you who's yellow. Plenty of yellow in my Yellow." The cab driver stopped to chuckle at his little joke. "But don't get me wrong, mister. I take money from all colors. As long as they got the long green anybody can ride in my hack. That's what democracy is all about, ain't it?" We both chuckled over that one.

"Don't pay me no mind," he continued. "I run off at the mouth too much. The missus says it's going to get me in hot water one of these days. But that's the way I am. Have been ever since I can remember. But, there I go again. Let's see. You wanted the Writers United office. Well, there ain't none. Period. Next question."

"I'm looking for Dalton Trumbo," I said. I felt the cab driver had demonstrated his trust and I would be safe in dropping the one name in Hollywood that was guaranteed to raise temperatures faster than the Kinsey Report.

"Trumbo!" the cab driver exclaimed, raising up and turning around in his seat again. I was getting used to it. "Whew!" he whistled through his front teeth. "You start right at the top, don't you? No beating around the bush with you, is there, mister? Yessir, where is Dalton Trumbo? That's a loaded one, that is. Maybe I shoulda buttoned my lip before I got carried away on this chinfest. Mister, either you're with the Feds or you're some kind of nougat from Van Nuys in town on a sightseeing tour. Whoever you are, I just run out of words."

"Hold the phone, pal," I said, taking advantage of the cabbie's self-imposed verbal drought to try and set the record straight. But he was having none of it. For no apparent reason he grabbed the gear-shift like it was trying to make a getaway, jammed it up into fourth and jerked the cab into the passing lane, middle-fingered a loafing Chrysler and sprinted two blocks to Columbia Square where a red light brought his metal bronco to a squealing halt.

I withdrew my chest from the back of the front seat and reached over and tapped the cabbie on the shoulder. I pointed to my snap brim on the floor of the passenger's side.

"Since you're the closest, how about you getting it."

He turned around and shot me a glare hard enough to dent a fender.

"Look, pal," I said, "you've got it all wrong. I've had nothing to do with the government since I filed my last tax return. And I only did that because of what they do to people who don't. I'm working on a caper out of Frisco. Trumbo may be able to help save the skin of someone who got a pretty raw deal from Uncle and his nephews here in movie town."

"Hummphh," snorted the cab driver through the nostrils of a ruddy nose. "A shamus! How do I know you're on the up and up? You might be a paperweight for some studio domo out to throw the nets on the rest of us who don't think pink lemonade is a communist conspiracy to poison America. The little woman was maybe right this time. Maybe I'm a lobster waiting to be boiled. What the hell! Everybody in this town is either a dues paying member of the Robert Taylor Flag-Fanning Society or a scared Wilbur just waiting to be turned over to the Boy Scouts or eighty-sixed from his job. I'm sick of it."

I tried to interrupt and reassure the cab driver that I wasn't J. Parnell Thomas wearing a wig and was on his side, more or less, as I could tell. But his imagination only made his gums bump at more r.p.m.s. The whir of words was broken when a string of cars behind the idling cab leaned on their horns to get him to go with the green light and get the hell across the intersection at El Centro.

The cabbie jabbed his head out the window and yelled something down Sunset at the impatient honkers that vigorously challenged the ancestry of most of the ethnic and economic groups west of Plymouth Rock.

It gave me an opportunity to restore some balance to the situation and perhaps save the both of us from a thrashing should the citizens of Sunset Boulevard take steps to organize against us.

I cupped my hands around my mouth and shouted, "Make a right, and step on it!"

Instinctively, the driver pushed the throttle of his tired old Plymouth to the floor. The cab leaped into the intersection and screeched around the corner, leaving most of the rubber of its two rear tires clinging to the pavement where the cab once was. Flying around the corner I sailed across the vinyl seat like a child hurtling down a sliding board. Lucky for me the door was closed to brake my acceleration. The handle nearly broke my arm.

"Pull over, will you, before you murder the both of us," I said the moment I was able to speak.

The cab pulled to the curb two blocks away where it idled spasmodically under a frightened palm. When I was reasonably sure the driver was not going to make another attempt at the land speed record, or my neck for that matter, I reached over the front seat with my good arm and turned the ignition key to the off position.

"Hey, whadidya do that for?" said the surprised cabbie. I didn't answer for obvious reasons.

"Look, pal," I said, "if you weren't always trying to kill me, I might learn to like you."

The cab driver started up again, which I reasoned might be a fatal mistake if I allowed him to continue. I dazzled him with my best basso-foghorn voice which I had been practicing in various bathtubs since my voice changed more years ago than I care to remember.

"Now hear this!" I crowed. "This is the real spiel coming at you!" It worked. I had lassoed his attention. To be sure, he must have thought me a registered lunatic. I continued, nevertheless.

"For your information, I am not with Thomas, Sam Wood, Roy Brewer or any other collection of what we might agree to call finks if we stopped to listen to each other. I'm with Kovachs, Riley Kovachs. **Soy solamente, amigo**. I'm connected with nobody but myself. Yesterday, a frightened little man tumbled down from the sky to tell me it was falling. I didn't know it would fall on him, but it did. He's gone now, probably for good and I feel kinda responsible.

"But before he left, he gave me a hunk of dough and pushed a case that had grown too big for him to handle into my lap. So, you might say I'm working for him if you're trying to figure out what's in it for me."

The cab driver was calmed. Whether it was what I told him or something completely different I'll never know. But he seemed ready to knock me his lobes a little while longer.

He pushed back his cap and rested his chin on an arm that he draped along the top of the front seat. "Yeah, maybe," he said with more than a hint of skepticism. "Go on with it. I'm listening." He reached out with his left hand and flipped off the meter.

I told him about meeting Jake Diltz after Trumbo's speech at the Hollywood Ten support meeting and just enough of the little man's story of conspiracies hatched in high places to make it interesting. I was brief because I wasn't sure how long I could command the cab driver's attention. That and blabbing too much to a man I had known for twenty minutes begged for the cropped version.

"To make a short story even shorter," I said, "the little man stuffed my pocket with a month's salary and told me to do a favor for a former movie star named Frances Farmer. He said Trumbo might be able to help out."

"Frances Farmer!" the driver hollered through my last sentence like it was a cheap screen door. He jerked his arm from the top of the seat and turned all the way around so he could look at me face-to-face and vice versa.

"You sure have a way striking it rich in the poison name department, ain't you, mister? Frances Farmer gave a lot of people in this town conniption fits, alright. About as popular as Walter Reuther is with the Ford family.

"I remember I gave her a ride once. A beautiful dame, a class A knockout. Picked her up in front of Paramount and took her to RCA. She was real friendly to me. Talked all the way about how she hated to be interviewed. I remember it because she was on her way to be interviewed. A real swell lady in my book. Too bad about her. They say she couldn't hold her booze. They say it drove her nuts. A damn shame. I'm sure those stogies sitting on their cans over on Marathon Street had a hand in driving her bananas. No sir, it wouldn't surprise me one bit if they did. Say, you said she was in a jam. What kind of jam? Last I heard she was stashed away in an attic somewhere."

I held up my hands. "I've said too much already. I've got to talk to Trumbo. That's what the little man said. Do you know where I can find him?"

The cab driver scratched his chin and fixed a stare in the direction of the overhead light. "That's a hard one, that one is. I heard he moved up to the mountains, but I don't know where. The left don't hang around in public so much anymore. You and me both know the reason why. Let's see. Last I heard some of the radical filmwriters used to whet their whistles at a place over on Cherokee. What was the name of that place? Clancy's! That's it, Clancy's. You might find him there."

"Well then," I said, experiencing a slight rush at the first sign of movement in this caper, "let's go to Clancy's."

The cabbie turned on the ignition and raced the engine. I put my hand on his shoulder. "Let's do it nice and easy, okay?"

The driver smiled an embarrassed smile, pulled his cap down on his forehead and eased the cab out into traffic with the steady reserve of a presidential limousine.

It was only a few blocks to Clancy's. It was also only nine o'clock in the morning and the bars don't open until ten. I convinced the cab driver I couldn't afford to have him wait even after he offered to shut off his meter. I didn't need a partner and though I had grown fond of the man behind the wheel, I think his chatter and his driving would have sent me straight up the proverbial wall, if not through an actual one. All this I told him in a way that spared his feelings.

CHAPTER 6

Down the street from Clancy's is deLongpre Park. I hung around there smoking cigarettes and looking at the clumps of bamboo someone potted a long time ago.

I strolled to the middle of the small park to look at a statue. It was a four-foot bronze nude standing on a sculpted glove in the middle of a lily pond. It was called "Inspiration." The inscription said the brown hunk is a memorial to Rudolph Valentino. I scratched my chin with the edge of a match book and wondered how many hundreds of statues dedicated to dead idols were currently desecrating the otherwise handsome parks of Los Angeles County.

I grew tired staring at Valentino's pectorals and took a short hike to the nearest drugstore for some smokes and a package of gum. I found a place that carried both plus a whole lot more.

I killed a little time thumbing my way through the book rack. Not much interested me until I saw a copy of a Raymond Chandler novel in a little wire hopper near the top of the rack next to a best seller on canasta. **The Little Sister** had just rolled off the presses.

I took it to the counter with a naive intention of making a simple every-day commercial transaction — my money for somebody else's goods. But the man on the other side of the counter, dressed in a starched smock the color of new dentures, had other ideas. A thin mustache the size of an eyelash and looking a lot like a French tickler told me he dealt in more than just paragoric and cough syrup. He took my money, alright, but then looked sideways, the way touts do at the race track, and from beneath the counter produced a bootleg copy of **Hecate County**. He said I couldn't live another minute without it.

I told him I was from San Francisco where we didn't burn books. About sex, anyway. Besides I had been tipped off by a fellow pervert where to look for the smutty parts so I wouldn't have to wade through all the dull stuff. In fact, I spent an hour at a bookstore last spring breathing like an out-of-breath greyhound as I read the story of the Ukranian girl who gets picked up at a dime-a-dance joint and seduced by the narrator who writes about it in details that could make you forget about the situation in Palestine for a while.

Nothing to lose your saliva over, but some pretty warm stuff. The story where the devil speaks in French about the Moscow purge trials was silly. More I never read.

I walked back to deLongpre Park, smoked a cigarette, chewed some gum and began reading **The Little Sister**.

A cockeyed little dame from Manhattan, Kansas, who spends too much time thinking about the New Testament, tumbles into Marlowe's office with a cockeyed tale about a missing brother. With a name like Orfamay Quest, how could it have been otherwise?

Marlowe takes her twenty skins — bird seed — more to assure her he will play bloodhound for a day, rather than as straight detective's fee. He insults her a half-dozen times just to let her know he's no sucker trout ready to snap at any old hook.

Marlowe then drives to Bay City to dig up the Tom Sawyer brother whose name is an improbable Orrin. Orrin Quest. He goes to the boy's rooming house, a place that has the gaiety of a World War I bunker and many of the same odors. Inside he pops a small time grifter who's mostly thumbs when it comes to guns and knives, tolerates the manager who is full of more alcohol than a hospital cart and trades words with a slimy bald guy named Hicks who is going through the brother's room.

Marlowe skims the grifter out of his hardware and sends him back to Peoria, or wherever he came from; makes Hicks look bad and finds an ice-pick in the neck of the manager on his way out.

Marlowe and Chandler never waste time getting down to the rough stuff. The interesting stuff. It's not like that in real life, I thought to myself, staring hard at the face of my watch trying to hypnotize the big hand to jump from the eleven to the twelve. In real life you spend a lot of time in parks waiting for joints to open or in cars waiting for them to close. Sometimes, if you're lucky, you have a good book to pass the time. Mostly though, it was staring at your watch crystal and sorting out your fingers.

It was exactly two minutes and fifteen seconds past ten when I crossed the street in front of Clancy's. After all, I didn't want to appear like I had been waiting all morning to tie a bag on.

Even though Clancy's had only been pouring fire water for less than three minutes, I wasn't the first customer. Two guys with noses like bicycle horns were at the bar sluicing their breakfast. From the pies in their eyes I could tell it hadn't been all that long since they glugged dinner. Another guy sat on the other end of the bar huddled over a racing sheet.

I ordered a bloody mary. It had plenty of blood and very little mary, but that suited me fine. I only ordered it in the first place so as not to violate custom.

It took me a few minutes to read the inscription on the bowling trophies arranged by year on the shelf over the bar. Aferwards, I eased into a conversation with the bartender.

"I'm looking for a friend of a friend of mine. Name of Trumbo. I heard he comes in here sometimes."

The bartender, whose name should have been Paddy, even if it wasn't, squinted an eye at me while the brow over the other did a bit of a hula. He stepped toward me and wiped the bar next to my glass with a sopping rag that held more water than the L.A. River after a winter rain.

"A person asks the wrong questions in a town like this, it might be he don't ever have a second chance to ask the right ones."

"Look, pal," I said with a trace of pain in my voice, "unless you're John Garfield trying to pick up a little extra dough tending bar and are trying out some lines to your new movie on the paying customers, you can put the corn back in the can and shut the lid on it. I'm not with the cops, the feds, the studios, the Send-Em-Back-To-Russia Committee, or Stalin's Politburo for that matter. I just want to find Dalton Trumbo and talk to him for a while. Simple as that."

The bartender dropped the tough guy routine like a handful of hot sand. "A person can't be too careful in this town anymore. Not the way things have been going. Sure Trumbo used to drink here. Maltz, Bessie and Lawson, too. They all did. But after the hearing in D.C. they had the kiss of death wrote all over them. I had to ask them not to come in anymore. Nothing personal, you understand. I got along with every mother's son of them. But things got ugly, you know. Punk phone calls every half hour and then there was the brick through my front window. Had a tag tied to it that said 'Get rid of the Russian scum or we'll get rid of you.' "

I nodded, taking an occasional swig of tomato juice. The bartender went on like it was a confession.

"Well, that did it for me. I'm not the hero type. I ask you, what would you have done if you were in my shoes? Huh? I got a business to run and a family to feed. Like I said I don't have nothing against those fellas, but you know how it is. What else could I do?"

He looked at me through eyes that begged forgiveness. But I couldn't do that. I came looking for Dalton Trumbo, not to pass out tickets to salvation. I asked him again about Trumbo. He tightened his lips and the blood rushed to an already red and ruddy nose.

"Look, mister, I told you. He don't come in here anymore. I don't know nothing about nobody." He paused a moment, cooled down a little and then glanced down the length of the bar to the man noodling the racing form. "Little Albert. He might know something," he said to me looking at the other man. "He knows a lot of things about a lot of people in this town. For the right price he'll tell you anything you want to know."

I gave the bartender four bits and told him to pour Little Albert some more of what he was drinking and then walked over and took the stool next to him.

"You look thirsty, sport," I said. "How about another of the same?"

"Rye," said Little Albert without taking his eyes

from the nag funnies. The bartender poured the drink into a shot glass and disappeared.

"Word has it you're quite the expert on a lot of things besides the ponies."

"Maybe."

A quiet morning light fought its way through the dark glass of the front window to the part of the bar where I was conducting the unsuccessful interview with Little Albert. The sunlight all but died before it reached us. The thick layer of tobacco smoke didn't help matters, but there was just enough of the shine to get a good look at the monosyllabic tout at my elbow.

He was small, even frail looking, with bones sticking out where flesh should be. He was wearing a sport jacket loud enough to pick its own fights, and probably win most of them. A new hat, with a small feather some bird was glad to get rid of stuck in the band, sat on his head at a cocky angle. The hat was too big for his head, but the way he wore it made a statement. His eyes were dark and sunken and looked like an unused wall socket. He had a pair of thin lips that looked custom made for calling people names and he smelled like a woman's vanity dresser.

"Yeah," I said, "old mister grapevine says if a guy is looking for another guy and doesn't know where to find this guy, the guy to ask about the other guy is a guy called Little Albert."

"You're cracked!"

"So, here I am, a guy looking for another guy and you're Little Albert. Small world isn't it?"

"Go peddle your papers," said Little Albert flipping the page of his racing sheet and still paying me about as much attention as the floor.

"I'm looking for a mug named Trumbo. Does that

horse chronicle you got stuck up your nose have a line on him?"

Little Albert carefully folded up his racing sheet and threw back the shot of rye I had invested in him like he had just taken a short jab to the head from Joe Louis. He turned to me for the first time and gave me a grin. It wasn't much of a grin as grins go. Kind of like the grins landlords get when they raise the rent on you.

"I might not look it," he said, "but I'm a historian. You know what my specialty is, mister guy-looking-for-another-guy?"

"It's just a wild guess, but you look like the kind of historian that is real fond of presidents."

"Why, how'd ya guess? You got any presidents with ya, mister guy-looking-for-another-guy? I collect pictures of 'em. Sort of a hobby of mine."

I reached in my pocket and pulled out my wallet which contained my limited presidential portrait collection. I laid the wallet on the bar. "Before I go showing you the family album," I said, "I've got to know if you can deliver. Do you know where I can find Dalton Trumbo? Do you even know who he is?"

"Sure, I know where you can find him. Like you said, I know a lot of things besides the ponies. Now you going to give me a history lesson or do I go back to my paper?"

I opened my billfold and took out three singles and laid them on the bar.

"I don't want you to think I ain't patriotic," said Little Albert, squeezing the words through his tight and colorless lips, "but George Washington here ain't my favorite president. Too old. Ya got something more recent?"

I took out a five and laid it across the ones. Little

Albert was warming up.

"That's better. I like old Abe, don't you? Freed the slaves and everything, but old Abe still ain't my favorite. Like the guy on the Jack Benny show says, what else ya got, Jackson?"

I got the hint and produced a twenty dollar bill. Little Albert was cooing.

"Now there was a truly great man. Won the Battle of New Orleans, ya know. Yessir, I'm real fond of ol' Hickory. Got anymore like him?"

I closed my wallet and scooped up all but the twenty. I stuck my face real close to his. "Look, junior, school's over. If you don't like ol' Hickory here and give me what I want to know we just might have ourselves the Battle of Clancy's Bar right here and now."

Little Albert backed off and smiled his landlord smile again. "Hey, paly, don't get sore. I was just havin' a little fun with ya. A little fun, that's all."

"Where's Dalton Trumbo?" I said, picking up the twenty from the bar and stuffing it in the breast pocket of his hideous sport coat. "I can't stay here and flirt with you all day."

"Okay, okay! Trumbo lives up in the Tehachapis. There ain't no address, ya just got to know how to get there. I don't know exactly where his ranch is at, but there's a guy who works on the swing shift over at Columbia Square who is tight with him. Goes by the name of Len Fugate. He would know how to get there for sure."

I took the twenty from Little Albert's pocket. "That's more like ol' Abe information than ol' Hickory, wouldn't you say, Little Albert?" I stuffed the five dollar bill down the same pocket just to show him there were no hard feelings.

"Sure, sure. I was just havin' a little fun, that's all."

"You should take life more seriously, Little Albert. Too much fun's not good for a man in your condition." I tossed the last of the bloody mary down my hatch and gave Little Albert a good natured, but firm, slap on the back, the way pals do. "Goodbye, buckaroo, it's been real educational. Next time we'll have to talk about F.D.R. Collecting little silver plates with his picture on them, I think, suits your style more."

"Sure, sure. I was just havin' a good time. No hard feelings?"

I pushed my way through Clancy's front door and stepped out onto the sidewalk. The morning sun burst into my eyes without pity. My pupils wanted to foreclose on my irises and move to the interior. My stunned head lamps were helped by a cupped hand awning applied to my forehead and readjustment of my hat brim. In a moment I could see again.

I headed for the bus stop on the corner. Across the street in deLongpre Park a man was standing near the statue of Valentino. He was too far away for me to see his face, but the tom toms were sending signals to the brain that he was neither a student of sculpture nor a fan of the late screen lover. I stopped in the middle of the block and propelled an obvious stare right at him. He turned on his heels and walked away from the bronze shrine. Maybe it meant something. Maybe he thought I was a wacko from Sunset Boulevard.

I caught the bus to Culver City. That's where M.G.M. is. It wasn't that I felt I hadn't got my money's worth of tips from Little Albert, but there was no sense being a fanatic about it. Trumbo had been Metro's highest salaried screenwriter until a year ago and I figured somebody there must have the courage to remember him.

CHAPTER 7

It's hard to tell if M.G.M. is part of Culver City or the other way around. It covers more than a hundred acres so all the books say. And if anyone doesn't think the movies are an industry like General Motors, with factories like Southgate G.M., they should hop on over to M.G.M., or Warner's or Fox for that matter, and take a peek at central casting with its hundreds of extras standing around on one foot looking like they're waiting for a shape-up. Or a citizen could take a hike over to what Metro calls the Main Lot with its three dozen sound stages that are run like a strange combination of a cottage industry, the production line and indentured servitude.

But then M.G.M. and most of her snooty sisters don't allow the citizenry on their shop floors. Maybe they don't want folks to know that the movies have workers too — painters, secretaries, carpenters, mechanics — just like they do in the factories of Akron, Toledo and Chicago. The main difference is that the former produces dreams while the latter only durable goods.

The bus stopped on Washington Boulevard near M.G.M.'s side gate. The only sign you could see from across the street next to the Metro monicker, that is, was one that read NO VISITORS. It looked like it was carved out of a hard lump of bad manners.

I reached into my wallet for my press pass, a little number I had made for me by a reformed counterfeiter on Harrison Street in Frisco a few years back. That little card gets me into more places than a showgirl with good legs.

I walked up to the security gate and showed my pass to a guard who looked like he'd been protecting other people's property since he was old enough to drool.

"Kovachs," I said. "From the **Examiner** in Frisco. Here for a follow-up story." I started through the thick metal turnstyle that could have prevented the Allies from landing at Omaha Beach.

"Just a minute, pal," the bull croaked. "You're here for what follow-up story?"

Before I could scratch the gray for an answer a small posse of loud-talking men came up behind me. Some had cameras strapped around their necks and some others were toting tripods on their shoulders.

"What's the holdup, Groomis?" said one of their number. "We're already late for the press conference. Shake a leg, will you?"

I turned to the dozen or more men and picked out a face in the crowd and rushed over to it and began pumping its hand like it were an oil rig on Signal Hill. "Hiya, old man! Gee, I bet I haven't seen you since we were working London together. The screw here doesn't like Frisco boys and is trying to give me the bum's rush."

The man reclaimed his hand and just said, "huh", trying in vain to remember where he knew me from. I took a chance he was one of the hundreds of American journalists who spent some time in London between '39 and '45. It was a pretty safe bet. Like putting a tenner on Citation's nose.

"You with I.N.S. in '44?" he said, giving me my alibi.

"That's right. Say, it's been a long time since those days hanging around Whitehall waiting for our daily bread, eh?"

The others in the press party weren't in the mood to listen to reminiscences, real or imagined. They began shoving their way through the turnstyle. Groomis, a bit bewildered by it all, stood his ground, but I could tell it was only his previous training.

"Look, Groomis," said the man who spoke before, "if we miss the opening, my editor will be down here in person and chew you into little bitty pieces." The rest of the men grumbled their agreement.

"But what about this guy?" Groomis said, pointing at me.

"For chrissake, you big dummy," the first man answered, "didn't you hear? He's with us. Now, are you going to let us through or do we throw a flying wedge at you?"

Groomis backed off and we scrambled through the gate and toward the Publicity Department as we half-walked, half-ran, the fellow from London trotted alongside me.

"Say, you remember Claire McKay? She worked for the **Washington Post**. Was in London the same time we were."

"Sorry, pal," I said, trying to discourage him, "everything about those days is getting pretty dim to me."

"Sure, you remember Claire. Everyone would remember Claire. She wasn't the kind of gal you could forget that easily. Not with that front porch she had. Remember, she had a little flat in Bayswater. Used to treat the press real well." He nudged me in the ribs as we trotted. "I remember when it came my turn. Wow, could that dame . . ."

I broke away from him. He had grabbed my elbow and was beginning to breathe like he was on the verge of making a dirty phone call. But, after all, I did bring it up.

"You know where I can reach Claire?" he shouted after me. I didn't look back.

I caught up with the ringleader of the news hounds, the one who had given the slope-headed guard such a run for his money. "Say," I uttered weakly on the tail end of an expelled breath, "what's all the ruckus about? Who's holding the press conference?"

The man didn't break his stride. Instead he squeezed off a glance at me that suggested I had inquired who was buried in Grant's Tomb.

"This is the biggie, Johnny. All the studio domos are making their first major statement since Waldorf. Promises to be a real pip. Say, who you with, anyway? The **Cucamonga Yearly**?"

He smiled at me. I smiled back. "Yeah. This is just a sidebar to go along with our lead on V.J. Day."

"Well, better shake a leg or you won't make deadline." He smiled again. But like the last one it was hollow. Neither good-natured nor malicious, just hollow. He broke into a trot and disappeared through the front door of the Publicity Department building. I just stayed back and followed the flow.

Moments later I found myself in the executive dining room next to the commissary with a hundred other people and enough artificial light to make night obsolete. Men with cameras snapped off flash bulbs like they were small bore firearms. Others were setting up their tripods and those that were left were snaking black cords and cables through the competitive assembly to a box on the middle of a cherry-stained oak table big enough to permit half the residents of Pacoima to sit down to dinner at one time.

On one side of the table sat seven men backed by a like number standing at parade rest. They were either studio gunsels or lawyers, I couldn't tell which. The other side of the table, my side, was the working press. The working, shoving, bulb-snapping, cord-snaking press. With the flashbulbs going off as regularly as German buzz bombs during the Blitz and the din created by the press as they frantically tried to set up their equipment, I was left with two unenviable things to do. Go blind or lose my hearing. But before I could make my preference known, one of the seven seated men stood up and walked to the box of microphones. A silence obtained almost instantaneously.

The man introduced himself as Eric Johnston, President of the Motion Picture Association of America and thanked the press for coming. He said something about the motion picture industry being under heavy attack from all quarters and the studio leaders were assembled to set the record straight and unveil their plans for film production that would, as he said, "celebrate America and the principles of Americanism." Then he introduced Louis B. Mayer, head of M.G.M., who was to read a prepared statement from the Producers Association.

There was a scattering of applause as the mogul's mogul walked up to the lecturn. He is a little man and he had to have the mikes lowered from his eyebrows. He tapped the big silver microphone several times, which produced an awful thud.

"Is this thing on?" he yelled. "Can everyone out

there hear okay? Yeah? Okay." Louis Mayer cleared his throat, adjusted the moon disk eyeglasses on his moon disk face and began reading from some papers he held in his hand.

"Following the Congressional hearings held in Washington D.C. on October 25 to 27th, 1947 in which members of the motion picture community, including Jack L. Warner and Louis B. Mayer, gave testimony under oath, the executive membership of the Association of Motion Picture Producers, realizing both the international and domestic peril Soviet-style communism presents to America, the American way of life and the American movie, met at New York's Waldorf-Astoria Hotel on November 24 and 25th, 1947 to draft a policy statement that would serve as the motion picture's response to the threat of subversion in our industry.

"In that statement, which has been referred to as 'The Waldorf Statement', the motion picture producers publicly deplored the behavior of the ten Hollywood men who were cited for contempt by the House Committee on Un-American Activities, then holding hearings on communist subversion in the motion picture industry in Hollywood, California.

"The producers decided unanimously to discharge and suspend those ten witnesses and stated they would stay fired and suspended until such time as they were acquitted or purged themselves of contempt and declared under oath they are not communists.

"Further, in the statement, the Producers Association declared that they will never knowingly employ a communist or a member of any party or group that stands against the United States of America.

"And finally, wishing to nip a potential climate of

fear in the bud, the Producers Association called on all Hollywood talent guilds to, and I quote directly from the statement, 'work with us to eliminate any subversives, to protect the innocent, and to safeguard free speech and a free screen wherever threatened,' end of quote."

Louis Mayer paused and reached down to the table for a pitcher of water sitting on a tray with several glasses. He poured the water into one of them. "Pardon me, boys," he said, "I've got to whet my whistle." Some newsmen smiled. Some were still scribbling furiously on thin note pads and used the pause to catch up with what had been said. It was after all very bad policy to fail to quote Louis B. Mayer or Jack L. Warner or their highly placed associates often and in full. It was considered a sin worse than misquoting. A few flash bulbs crackled while Louis Mayer was dousing his thirst. The rest of us tried to come up with new ways to fight suffocation. And we weren't entirely successful. But Louis Mayer was doing okay. His only concern was his whistle and once the little critter was whet he was ready to plow on.

"Okay, boys, I still got a little more to go before you start throwing questions at us. Where was I?" He ran his finger down a typed page looking for his place. "Oh, yes. In the fourteen months since the Waldorf Statement, the signers of that document have been attacked unfairly, accused through innuendo and scandalized in the press and other places for being too soft on communist subversion on the one hand and for being undemocratic, neo-Nazi ogres on the other. You gentlemen of the press have been invited here today so that we may set the record straight and once and for all put an end to the irresponsible and cowardly charges that have fouled the air in Hollywood during recent months.

"The Producers Association wants to go on the record as categorically denying that the motion picture screen has become a "fifth column" for Moscow and that the executive leadership in the industry are "Russian stooges" who have instituted a boycott against anti-communist writers and actors.

"These wild and totally unfounded accusations only serve to weaken and divide the film community from the real enemy- the communist menace!

At that point, Louis B. Mayer paused and looked up from his text. He jerked off his glasses the way people do who want to use their specs to make a point. Up to then he had merely been reading words. Now he was ready to speak from the heart. Or so he led me to believe.

"You fellas know what I'm talking about," he said, starting up again. There were several nodding heads and a couple grunts acknowledging the sentiment. "This group that calls itself the Hollywood Ten, these ten hostile witnesses who shamed our motion picture family with their outrageous behavior at the Congressional hearings in Washington in 1947, have in recent months been going around Hollywood lying about the Producers Association, about the film community.

"I know I should stick to what's written here in this statement, but I feel too strongly about this just to read some words."

Louis Mayer turned and glanced over to his colleagues sitting at the table. "I'm sure you boys won't mind if I talk a bit off the cuff. I think I can say that I speak for all of us on this subject."

The Schenck brothers nodded silently. The Warners, Jack and Harry, smiled while Dore Schary and Eric Johnston looked down and fingered their water glasses. In a way, the Hollywood way, Louis B. Mayer had received another unanimous vote. He and the Warners weren't familiar with any other kind.

"Okay," said Louis Mayer. "These guys we canned have been hollering bloody murder for more than a year now. They scream about violations of constitutional rights, the First Amendment, anything that they think will get sympathy.

"Well, let me tell you something. We will never give in to the charges they make against us. We at Metro, as I'm sure the other boys do at their studios, maintain a continuous vigilance against un-American subversives and subversion. I told the Committee in Washington to pass a law regulating the employment of communists. It was my belief then and it is my belief today that the communists should be denied the sanctuary of the freedom they seek to destroy.

"Why do I still talk about the so-called Hollywood Ten today, more than a year after they were all suspended? I'll tell you why. It's because they have duped some honest people into thinking the producers did them an injustice and that we ran roughshod over the First Amendment and so on. But that isn't the half of it. These expelled men are making a movie about themselves. Can you beat that? It is a classic piece of communist propaganda designed to scare the pants off anyone who sees it. It hasn't been released yet, and I haven't personally seen it, but they tell me this film shamelessly drags the Congress, the Justice Department and the United States military through the mud, making slanderous and obviously untrue statements.

"These communists and their fellow travelers

spare no trick or gimmick in making themselves out to be lily pure martyrs while painting true Americans to be ignorant, cruel slobs. 'Government by stoolpigeon', they tell me one of them says in the film. Honestly! I ask you how anyone in his right mind could find fault with the Producers Association for giving these ten men their notices.

"I just want to say, in conclusion, to be on the lookout for their slick propaganda tricks. They can lull even smart people into believing almost anything. Those of us who make motion pictures for the American people want you gentlemen of the press to know the truth about the matter when this communistic film about the so-called Hollywood Ten comes out and tries to convince everybody that day is night and red is blue — red, white and blue. Know it for what it is. Know these men for what they are. We of the Producers Association are committed to making fine quality Americanistic films the best way we know how. We told the press and the American people in our Waldorf Statement that we would not be suckered, intimidated or otherwise strong-armed by communists or anyone else. Today, we say the same thing. We won't knuckle under to anybody who tries to stop us from bringing good, wholesome American films to the people of this great country of ours."

Louis B. Mayer ended with a patriotic fist banging the lecturn and beads of good, wholesome American sweat popping up like warts on his forehead. The working press became the clapping press when the M.G.M. maestro concluded his speech. Some even the standing and clapping press. The others, the serum of "Americanism" from Louis Mayer's two-fisted hypo not having entered their bloodstreams, remained seated, finishing up their notes.

Louis Mayer held up his hands in a half-hearted attempt to restore order. It was as plain as a cake donut that he was enjoying every second of the spontaneous tribute. A moment later, when relative quiet obtained, Louis Mayer spoke again.

"Thanks for the vote of confidence, boys. I'm sure it means as much to my colleagues here as it does to me. Thanks, again. One more thing before we open up for questions. The executive leadership of the movie industry has been criticized in Washington and ever since for not making enough films that are anti the communist way of life and pro the American way of life. Well, without haggling over this film or that, the Producers Association is here today to unveil our current production plans that won't leave one iota of doubt in anyone's minds as to just where we stand.

"But you've heard enough from me for one day. I'm going to turn that part of the program over to my good friend, Mr. Jack L. Warner. Jack."

Louis Mayer began clapping and pointing in the direction of Jack Warner who was rising from his chair. Mayer urged the newsmen to applaud as if he were introducing the keynoter for a Friar's Club soiree. Warner, the vasoline-haired helmsman of the studio that bore his name, took the lectern from the retiring Mayer.

"Thanks, Louis," he said. "I just want to say before I get going on our new lineup of films that I agree one hundred and ten percent with everything Mr. Louis B. Mayer said. I think I speak for my brother and the Schencks and Dore and Eric over there when I say what Mr. Mayer said represents us all."

I couldn't take it to the five dollar window at Santa

Anita, but it seemed like an awful lot of people in high Hollywood places were speaking for each other and agreeing one hundred and ten percent with any and everything. The stumbling display of unity was as transparent as an agent's promise.

"I'm really delighted to have this opportunity," Warner continued, "to present to you gentlemen our new and exciting lineup of coming motion picture attractions. They are guaranteed to make Joe Stalin's hair stand on end. Currently in production, or soon to be in production, are the following films: **The Red Menace**, **Guilty of Treason**, **I Married A Communist**, **The Red Danube** and **The Comrade And The Corpse**. These and other films that will put the cold jaws of truth on the neck of Soviet communism and subversion in this country will be ready for distribution within the next twelve months. We have printed material on each and every film for you boys to pick up on your way out. You will all be invited to special screenings of these films and I'm sure you'll agree when you see them that Hollywood has turned over a new leaf. No more will there ever be a question of subversives trying to sneak stuff into films in their own subtle ways. No more of their message films. From now on Hollywood is battle ready to go after the Russian bear and all her little cubs running loose in this country with the greatest weapon of the twentieth century. And I don't mean the atom bomb. I mean the motion picture film!"

Once more the press broke into applause. Flash bulbs snapped off, reminding me a lot of the heat lightning storms we used to have in Ohio. Before the clapping stopped, reporters began barking their questions at Jack L. Warner and his fellow producers. The louder the bark the more chance of obtaining a scrap.

"Is it true communists are still writing films?"

"Are you going to sue the Hollywood Ten for slander?"

"Is Congress planning more hearings?"

"Is Lester Cole still working under an M.G.M. contract?"

One thoughtful scribe asked, "Mr. Warner, just what are the principles of Americanism we hear so much about?"

Warner, who had returned to his chair, stood up and asked the reporter, "Do you want me to answer that as a motion picture executive or an American citizen?" The reporter shrugged his shoulders and said either would be satisfactory.

"Americanism," said Jack Warner, his fingers clutching the big silver microphone, "and you can quote me on this — Americanism is anything that promotes the American way of life. The American way of doing things." When pressed for specifics by another reporter, the brother Warner was only too glad to explain. "Home, family, standing up for your country and for what's right. Speaking your mind and having the right to get things off your chest without having to fear being shipped off to a concentration camp. In a word — everything they don't have in Russia!"

I figured I had received a good thirty years supply of Americanism in the past forty-five minutes and concluded there was no need to be a glutton about it. So I left before learning whether Warner's comments were made as a motion picture executive or an American.

I stepped out into the hall where the air was a hundred pounds lighter. I shook out a Chesterfield. The first pull tasted a lot like all outdoors, but after that it was like it always is — burning leaves at the end of my nose. But if they were good enough for DiMaggio I guess I could stand it.

I strolled to the other end of the long, narrow hallway, looking for a bathroom to wash up. I found one on the other side of a thick stained oak door with an ornamental brass-colored handle. It was bigger than most people's living rooms. Throw in my kitchen and it had more floor space than two of my three rooms. It was a lot tidier, too. It had an oriental inlaid floor that, as the saying goes, you could eat off of.

I took off my coat and began applying wet paper towels to the back of my neck and forehead. It

I took off my coat and began applying wet paper towels to the back of my neck and forehead. It
afforded me a chance to stare at the old frying pan in the mirror and survey the latest signs of wreckage and decay. It was native curiosity more than any philosophical lament over youth slipping into the shadows. I stopped trying to fight the wrinkle- and baggy-eye man when I was thirty-five. But, the way I figure it, I have plenty of gas left in the tank and there's still a lot of time to tie myself up in emotional knots waiting for the big five-o.

Then again, maybe I was being too optimistic. My contemplation on youth and age was brought to an involuntary conclusion when I couldn't help but notice mine wasn't the only face staring back from the mirror. Another face, an older, uglier, more powerful face was behind mine and it was tightening up and growing flush. The face grinned, but I couldn't find anything funny. A sharp pain to my kidneys reinforced my feeling. My breath had escaped with the blow and I turned around slowly while going down under a wobbly leg. I swung at the face with the strength that remained. I think I connected, but the face just continued grinning. Next I dove at it, slamming both the face and its body through the door of an unoccupied stall. A blow to the base of my skull had a way of telling me that my tackling days were over. Things began growing dark and it wasn't from anyone fooling with the lights. The last thing I saw before the shades were pulled was the brass toilet roll holder and the vision of a guy standing in front of Rudolph Valentino in deLongpre Park.

CHAPTER 8

I woke up to a dozen baggy gabardine knees and a wet compress on my head. The knees were absolute strangers, but the faces above them were vaguely familiar. One bent over me.

"Hey, there, London buddy. You okay? We came in here and found you stretched out under the toilet bowl."

I tried to get up, but specific pains in my back and head urged me otherwise. I asked for a glass of water and help off the floor. Three of them propped me up against the toilet bowl. Another brought me some water from a sip-and-a-half paper cup. I mumbled something about the guy who worked over my kidneys, giving the closest thing to a description I could come up with.

"Didn't see anyone like that, buddy," said the man who spoke before. He looked and sounded quite familiar. I had only to wait a moment before ringing up a sale.

"Look," he said, "we'll call security and get them

on this. After that you and me are going out and talk about the old days in London over a couple of stiff ones. I got stories about Claire that will make you forget all about taking a leap into this porcelain toilet here. Say, you sure you don't know where Claire is? I'd give a week's pay just for an address."

I feigned recovery and sprung to my feet. After a fashion, that is. The other reporters, anxious to file their stories on the press conference, had already gone. All but my pal from the London bureau of I.N.S., class of '44.

I told him I would wait in the commissary while he phoned in his story. But before his nickel could chime I was making tracks in the opposite direction. I wanted to lose him almost as much as I wanted to find the guy who gave me the kidney treatment.

I picked my way through the Publicity Building, looking for a door behind which someone might have Trumbo's address or phone number on a piece of paper somewhere. I took my chances and walked through a door that said "Hiring-Records". That sounded too optimistic. The room was smaller than it should have been, but I suppose it was designed that way on purpose. A cold, rugless linoleum floor seemed almost friendly compared to the frigid steel and vinyl furniture. A dozen people were cramped into that space. If I hadn't read the sign on the door or forgot I was in California I could have been persuaded I was in line at a New York immigration terminal. But who could forget they were in California?

The people, too, were different from immigrants. In the way they dressed at least. The young woman wearing an expensive wool jacket over a rayon dress, who had been dressed to the nines some hours before, looked like she was coming a triffle unglued from the top of her lustre-cremed locks right down to her expensive Berkshire nylons, which she probably couldn't afford, and the British walkers on her feet. She was staring into a woman's magazine, but I don't think she had turned a page since last Thursday.

Some of the other tenants looked disturbed. One man, wearing a suit that could have been inducted into the tailor's Hall of Fame for most times worn in one century, paced up and down the length of the tiny waiting room. He divided his time between mauling a cigarette and looking at his watch. The expression on his face suggested he had just bet the house on a nag that finished out of the money and was trying to figure a way to tell his wife.

The other waiters were doing a host of things to pass the time. Smoking cigarettes and doing crossword puzzles seemed to lead the list. Nearly everyone looked like they had been sitting there since the first planeload of food took off for Berlin. They say, in Hollywood, that's the name of the game — waiting for your name to be called. Waiting for the right job to be offered. Waiting to get **the** script, **the** part, **the** break that will be your ticket to stardom, comeback or just three squares a day. But it's no secret that the studios have been on the bum since the war ended. Metro put a quarter of its people out to pasture less than two years ago. Columbia dumped even more. Things hadn't returned to normal. Everyone in that room knew that there were thousands more just like them waiting for the same thing. If the looks on their faces meant anything, hope was just something else to be crushed out along with the cigarette butts in the overflowing ashtrays on the lamp tables. Maybe they just didn't have any other place to go or anything else to do.

I walked over to the metal desk that was positioned strategically between the waiting room and a door that had a small plate which read "Mr. Traub". In front of Mr. Traub's name sat a woman who was as much a guard as she was a receptionist. She looked like someone Wagner must have had in mind when he was writing those tunes about Teutonic maidens.

She was fifty, but could have passed for younger if she would have taken off the facial girdle that made her look as severe as the first step off the north face of El Capitan. Her hair, rendered a stone fortress by a Mar-vo wave, could have withstood gale-force winds. It was piled vertically on her head and was the color and quite likely the consistency of native shale.

She wore glasses that were planted across her face like a picket fence. They meant business. Like a **No Trespassing** sign. This was a woman who would turn you in for taking an extra minute at the water cooler on a hot afternoon. A perfect sort to crush the remnants of idealism any of the poor saps sitting on the company sofas might still have. In that way she was well placed. Real fourteen carat cold.

But there were no empty chairs and I wasn't holding my breath waiting for a career to materialize so I had absolutely nothing to lose by trying to pass time with her. I stepped aside to let the guy with the heebie-jeebies and the rumpled suit make his rounds and marched up to the desk.

"Mrs. Sturgeon," I said, picking up and reading the words on the brass nameplate that stood like a sentry at the far edge of her desk.

"That's Mrs. Stargeon, if you please!" she said, spitting pointy icicle-like words at me like I had a reputation for looking up little girls' skirts.

"Oh, I am terribly sorry. Mrs. Stargeon! You have to admit, though, it does look like Sturgeon. I bet a lot of people make that mistake."

"You are the first and I trust the last. If you are looking for employment fill out this form and wait for your name to be called." Mrs. Stargeon shoved a long sheet of paper at me. "And we don't loan pencils, so don't ask." I took the paper by instinct. I felt like I was about to begin an induction physical for the army. I returned the application to Mrs. Stargeon.

"No, ma'am, I'm not here for a job, but I want to thank you for thinking of me, Mrs. Stargeon. If I ever do need work I'll know just where to come and who to see. Actually, all I want is some information. A trifle really."

Mrs. Stargeon had already returned to her receptionist tasks and was doing a good job of ignoring me. She was making entries in a large book with ruled paper.

She spoke to me without moving her head from the book. "We don't give out information **to** anybody or **about** anybody! If you want to talk with Mr. Traub leave your name and a number where you can be reached."

"Well, gee, Mrs. Stargeon, I thank you for your offer, but I just don't think I want to put you through all the trouble of scheduling an appointment."

"No trouble." Mrs. Stargeon interrupted. She was paying me even less attention than before, if that was possible. "There's really not much chance you getting to see Mr. Traub."

"Mrs. Stargeon," I said in a voice that was politely pleading, "I am sure there is another way. What I want will take only a brief minute."

Mrs. Stargeon closed an open desk drawer with a firm shove. Two pens and a fresh number two pencil on the green desk blotter jumped. She looked up into my face. "Look, buster, who do you think you are? Who gave you the right to come barging in here demanding favors? Can't you see there is a room full of people ahead of you? Now either you fill out this application or hit the road. Or must I call security?"

I looked over my shoulder in the direction of job-seekers and leaned over Mrs. Stargeon's desk. I ran my finger along the leather triangle corner of the blotter. I spoke in a voice just above a whisper.

"I was hoping I would not have to reveal my identity, Mrs. Stargeon. The passions in Hollywood being what they are at this particular time. I trust you know what I mean."

"Baloney!" said Mrs. Stargeon. She wasn't buying anything.

"That is why the Committee wishes to maintain a profile as low as is humanly possible. You can understand that, can't you, Mrs. Stargeon?"

"I can understand a phony when I hear one. I think I'm going to have you put out on your ear, boyfriend. You must think I was born on a chicken ranch." Mrs. Stargeon was warming up her temper. It might have been all that weight on top of her head.

"Please, Mrs. Stargeon," I continued with a con that had about as much chance as Truman inviting John L. Lewis to the White House for cake and coffee, "this is a very sensitive matter. The Congressman would have come himself, but you know what with the Hiss thing in Washington taking all his time. The Congressman worked very hard for the indictment. I'm sure you can appreciate that, Mrs. Stargeon. It was in all the papers. I am acting as his chief of staff while he is out of town. The Congressman wishes to interview a former employee here. A Mister Dalton Trumbo. I simply wish to know where I might find him." Sounded on the straight to me, but Mrs. Stargeon's resistance seemed to take more than I had to crack.

"I don't care who you are," she said in a voice that approached a roar and which caught the attention, such as it was, of the bench-sitters, "or what Committee you say you're with. Even if you were on the level, which you aren't, I told you we don't give out information! If you want to know Mr. Trumbo's whereabouts I suggest you contact the headquarters of the Communist Party. Now are you going to quit causing a disturbance or am I going to have you carried out?"

I knew when I was whipped. "As you wish, Mrs. Stargeon. Your New Deal sympathies have been duly recorded. No doubt you will be hearing from the Committee shortly. I wouldn't be surprised if the Congressman or Mr. Stripling himself calls on you. And I was so hoping for your cooperation. Perhaps if you didn't treat people like they were out to cut your throat you wouldn't have the personality of a lukewarm beer. But that's just one man's opinion."

"Okay, buster, that does it. I'm calling the cops!" She was infuriated. Maybe nobody had ever levelled with her. Her finger dug into the holes of the telephone dial like a dame trying to scratch out the eyes of an unfaithful boyfriend and ripped off the number of studio security.

"I'm leaving, Mrs. Stargeon. No need to set the place on fire. One last thing. I'm having my driveway paved next week. You think the guy who does your hair would be interested in making some extra cash?"

Mrs. Stargeon picked up a dark, solid paperweight from her desk and chucked it at me. Good arm, but no control. I watched it as it sailed into the wall at the far end of the waiting room

"Get out!" she bellowed. Her face was a technicolor extravaganza. "Get out! Get out! Get out!"

I don't think it was so much what I said that worked her into a foaming Barbasol lather, but more the nature of her work. I mean, you can only draw pay to break people's spirits for just so long. No matter how much money they give you, no matter how much you hate people, it's bound to catch up sooner or later.

Mrs. Stargeon's unravelling brought the slumbering, smoking, staring, pacing job seekers to their collective and figurative feet. The faces they had worn a moment before, looking a lot like the freshman class at Zombie U., broke into sanguine, hearty smiles. Some laughed out loud. Hard out loud. Then they began clapping and stamping their feet. They were clapping for me for getting Mrs. Stargeon's goat; clapping at her to let her know how much they were enjoying her breakdown; but mostly, I think, clapping for themselves. The jobs may never come and Mrs. Stargeon's loss would only be temporary, but for one moment, one special moment, they had the opportunity to go right up and spit in the face of all that was humiliating them, making their lives miserable. It was a surge of power.

I made my exit out into the hall and lit a smoke. I hadn't even blown out the match when a man, one of the bench-warmers, came through the same door to join me. The laughing and clapping had died down some inside, but it was still being savored.

"Heard you tell that old prune you were looking for Trumbo," the man said. I nodded and flipped the match off the end of my forefinger in the direction of a knee-high ashtray potted with white sand standing next to the door. "Who you with?" he asked. "What's your angle?" His eyes were red and falling down over his cheeks. His face had seen healthier days. He looked like he'd been on a diet of cigarettes and air for a week.

"No angle, friend," I assured him. "I just want to talk to him some. We have a mutual friend. I didn't think asking around about him would start World War III."

The man smiled ever so slightly from lips that were puffy and pale. He extended his hand for me to shake. "Bert Glasser," he said. "I used to write scripts for a living. Now I wait in that office in there. I'd take anything, only there isn't anything to take. I liked the way you handled Stargeon. That old scarecrow has had it coming for a long time. Anyway, I know where you can find Trumbo."

I offered Bert Glasser a Chesterfield as a modest token of my gratitude and as we drew smoke he told me how he used to work with Trumbo before the business started. They attended the same meetings, signed the same petitions, sat on the left side of the aisle at the Screen Writers Guild meetings. He said he hadn't seen Trumbo or anyone else that was suspect for a long time. He said he was trying to hang on at Metro.

"At least they let me sit in their lousy office and take insults from Stargeon," he said. "Some of us partisans from the Anti-Nazi League and Progressive Citizens days aren't even allowed that. But that's the way it goes around here. You hang on to whatever little twig you can find. All you have to do is give up everything you ever believed in, turn your back on your friends and be willing to be humiliated each and every moment you are awake. Don't get me wrong. I'm no fink. Just a coward. Anyway, that's my problem. Trumbo has a ranch up in Ventura County. Los Padres Forest. It's way the hell away from anywhere. Twenty miles off the Grapevine on dirt and gravel. I could draw you a map, but it wouldn't do you any good. I heard there is going to be a gathering at his ranch tomorrow night. Some of the Ten and their lawyers and the support committee. What's left of it."

I was very interested in what Bert Glasser had to say. He had told me too much about himself not to be on the level.

"I was asked to go," he volunteered, "but, like I said, I've got to keep my nose clean. They might not let me sit in their waiting room anymore." Bert Glasser smiled again and winked a bloodshot eye. He was doing his best to make the most out of a bad situation. I asked him if I could get to that gathering.

"Yeah, I think so. There's a guy over at Columbia. He's a painter. A union militant. He's a buddy and I know he's driving up with some people tomorrow morning. Fugate is his name. Len Fugate. Tell him you know me. I'm not very high on anybody's list anymore, but it might help." Bert Glasser gave me the address where I could find Len Fugate. I jotted it down in my little notebook. It checked with what Little Albert sold me.

"Well, you'll excuse me," he said. "I've got to get back inside. It'd be my bum luck to get called while I'm out in the hall smoking a cigarette."

This time Bert Glasser didn't smile. He believed what he said and I believed he believed it. I shook his hand and sent him back to Mrs. Stargeon. Me, I had a bus to catch to Hollywood.

CHAPTER 9

The trip was slow, but it allowed me to catch up on my reading and thinking, such as it was. I pulled out my copy of **The Little Sister** from a crowded hip pocket to check up on Philip Marlowe. Seemed like he had his hands full, alright. The dame from Kansas, Orfamay Quest, kept blowing smoke in his eyes about the job she hired him to do. That and going limp into his arms and puffing up her lips like a trout. For smooching purposes.

Then there was that business at the hotel where the bald gnome called Hicks took an ice pick in the neck while the house dick, a low life looking for an angle, boosts the stiff's wallet. Marlowe catches him and sticks a finger up his nose. The dick tells him a woman was in the room moments before. Marlowe takes this dope and in a way that is inscrutable, as well as infallible — that's the way book detectives operate — parlays it into the name of a famous movie star.

He drives out to her digs on Doheny Drive and is met by a tall dark Mexican flamethrower named Dolores Gonzales who "smelled the way the Taj Mahal looks by moonlight." "The Gonzales," as Marlowe calls her, is as hot as a chile rileno and struts her stuff in front of the detective like she was selling encyclopedias. Giving away encyclopedias.

Something about a roll of film Hicks had that connected the movie star with a hood named Steelgrave who was known in Cleveland as Weepy Moyer. I'm sure it all made sense — impeccable, logical sense — but I could only think of "the Gonzales". And Dalton Trumbo.

The bus stopped abruptly and a lady's groceries tumbled off her seat a few rows in front of me. Nothing serious, just a bruised tomato or two from the spilled bag. I stopped staring at the girl in the Paquins Hand Cream ad across the aisle above the buzzer cord. Dolores Gonzales would have to wait.

I had to get a grip on things before reaching Columbia and Len Fugate. Sure, I thought to myself, Hollywood was like thin batter on a hot griddle. People ratting on each other, sometimes as a matter of course. People speaking in code, working under cover, everyone looking over their shoulder to see if anyone's gaining on them or standing under a tree taking notes. Bad blood everywhere. Bad blood between people who used to be friends, or at least could tolerate each other professionally. Too many scared, broken, frustrated, angry, bitter people. And Hollywood wore it around its neck like a lobster bib. That's the way it was in the town that brought us Shirley Temple and Judge Hardy's son.

Maybe that's why finding Dalton Trumbo was harder than beating the Cleveland Browns on their home field and was causing more hoopla than the Jane Russell bosom scene in **The Outlaw**. For all I knew — and it wasn't much — when I talked to Trumbo, if I talked to Trumbo, he would tell me nothing about Frances Farmer or Jake Diltz I didn't already know. Then where would I be? The leads in this case, if the whole thing wasn't just a trunk full of clouds to begin with, was thinner than a pair of 50 gauge nylons.

But then there was that kidney-hater in Louis Mayer's toilet to think about. Any quick physical movements on my part would remind me in case the memory began to fade. Maybe he was just an out-of-work lot hopper up on giggle juice and down on his luck. Maybe I was just convenient for him and busting my humps was his way of putting on the moan about his unfortunate circumstances. Baloney! Even if I did give that fish story any play, even for a weak moment, I still owed him one. And I like to think of myself as the kind of guy who pays off his debts quickly and in full.

I had a pocketful of cabbage from Jake Diltz, a growing curiosity to find Dalton Trumbo and a score to settle with a guy I didn't know too well. It wasn't much by most people's standards, but it was enough for me to push on. Marlowe would have to wait.

I stepped off the smelly diesel at Sunset where it meets Gower. I crossed the Garden Patio and through the main entrance to Columbia's five stories of glass and concrete. The girl at the switchboard, who had the face of a Woodbury Deb and the smile to go with it, directed me to Len Fugate without giving me any flak. Up to that point I had been persuaded to believe that stringing verbal barbed-wire fences was the way social intercourse was conducted in Hollywood.

I walked into the theater of the Columbia Square Playhouse. An episode of **Suspense** was on the air. I took a seat near the back. The gal at the switchboard said Fugate was working in the prop room and had a break after the show.

The story on the stage had my hair doing nipups. Three rum-soaked sailors who got along about as well as Stalin and Truman were holing-up in a lighthouse. That was okay until a million or more rats dived off a passing ghost ship and swam to the lighthouse for food and shelter. They gnawed their way up three levels of the lighthouse to the men in the tower. The rest, as they say, was history.

I left the theater before the next program, **Casey, Crime Photographer**, and Staats Cottsworth had a chance to sell any soap. Unconsciously, I kept an eye peeled for rats. And not just the kind that desert ships.

I circled around behind the playhouse to a door marked "Employees Entrance". It was open and I walked in surprised not to find a "pop backstage" guarding the door to prevent the kind of people Judy Garland plays from crashing through and annoying the talent. A guy leaning on a broom pointed me to the prop room. I walked in without knocking. A man was standing over a sink washing a pair of paint-stained hands. The room wasn't lit very well, but as far as I could tell he and I were the only people in the place. I walked up behind him, speaking as I went.

"I'm looking for Len Fugate," I said above the sound of the water rushing from the faucet.

The man's neck snapped around hard like he was just touched with a right from Ezzard Charles' glove. "So!" he said in a way that was even shorter than that two-letter word implies.

"So, are you Len Fugate?"

"Yeah. Who wants to know?"

"Friend of yours said I might find you here. Bert Glasser."

His face relaxed a little, but not much. His eyes were giving me a regimental inspection while he turned off the water and reached for a rag to dry his hands.

"That rat ain't no friend of mine," he said after a moment. "You got a bum steer, mister." He took a step toward me and looked me straight in the headlamps. Then he turned away. "Look, pal, I'm on my break so why don't you vamoose?"

"Bert said I might be able to cop a lift with you up to Trumbo's ranch in the morning."

Fugate, who had walked over to a wall locker next to the sink to get his lunch, stopped in his tracks before opening his black metal bucket. He returned to me and planted his toes opposite mine and drilled a high voltage stare into my hazel-colored orbs.

"Just who the hell are you, mister? You mind telling me that?"

"Kovachs's the name. Make a living, if you can call it that, getting other people out of jams. No cheap divorces, but not a whole lot that would interest you or anybody else. But, like I said, it's a living. I work at it and sometimes I even like it.

"A shamus!"

"For lack of a better word."

"You with the studios or the I.A.?"

"Neither. I'm with myself — Kovachs. Out of Frisco if you want a place."

"How do I know that? You got a card or a badge?"

"No. Don't carry cards because nobody believes them and my badge is in my desk on the seventh floor of the Monadnock Building. Next to a pint of Old Forester."

"You're goofy. You just might be some dingus from the I.A. checking up on me."

"Fugate, if ignorance helps my cause any, I don't even know what the I.A. is."

"You pulling my leg, or what? International Alliance of Theatrical Stage Employees. As if you didn't know. The goddamned company union we got around here. You can go tell your Boss Brewer that Len Fugate thinks he is a lousy sellout bum. But then he already knows what I think of him. That's the reason you're here checking up on me isn't it?"

"Whoa there, friend, and rest your jaw for a minute. You know, just about everywhere I go in this cheesy town, someone takes me for a sidewinder for some studio boss or a G-man. Now you tell me I'm a rock crusher for your union piecards. If I didn't have tree bark for skin, my feelings would be hurt. How about I put you on the right street."

"I'm listening."

"To repeat myself, I'm no thug for J. H. Blair or anyone else. I'm a private dick out of Frisco, just like I told you. I'm working on a cockeyed hugger-mugger I should have dropped like a boiling rock. But I didn't and I'm here in your palm-treed paradise for paranoids looking to have a few words with Dalton Trumbo so I can get a handle on the caper and get down to business. You could call Harry Bridges. If they'll let a phone into the court room he'll spring for me. I knew him some a long time ago. Period, end of report."

Len Fugate looked at me almost like an equal while scratching an ear. "Maybe you're who you say you are, I don't know. Things have been pretty crazy since the strikes in '45 and '46. And then with that H.U.A.C. thing the whole industry has gone stir bugs. I guess that includes me."

"Let me put it another way, Fugate. Trumbo's been fired, indicted for contempt of Congress and blacklisted, right?"

"Tell me something I don't know, willya?"

"Well then, what more can anyone do to him that

hasn't already been done?"

Len Fugate smiled for the first time since I had known him. It wasn't like I had made a joke or anything like that. But I did tickle something inside him, even if it was only dark and ironical. He took a smoke from a rumpled package in the breast pocket of his shirt. He held the pack toward me. I took one, though it wasn't my brand.

"Yeah, you got a good point there, mister. What did you say your name was?"

"Kovachs. Riley Kovachs. Hungarian and Irish, mostly."

"Yeah, what more can they do to Trumbo? Or any of them? Working on a case, eh?"

"I won't be if I can't get to Trumbo. He might not be able to help me much, but if I don't at least talk to him then I'm in a fast car with no wheels. And speaking of cars, I sure could use that ride up to his ranch tomorrow."

Fugate took a giant drag from his butt and crossed his arms in front of his chest. He gave me another thorough eyeballing.

"Oh, what the hell!" he said a moment later. "It's an open affair, more or less. I mean supporters of the Ten. No closed 'cell' meeting or anything like that. I guess if you really were a rat, you'd just find another way to get there. Yeah, what the hell. You got the kind of face I might be able to take a chance on. Gotta start trusting somebody sooner or later."

Len Fugate looked relieved. Maybe he trusted me and maybe he didn't. I think he had been in the shadows so long that it was finally getting to him. I was maybe just the right straw that happened to show up at the tent on the back of the right camel at the right time. Or maybe I really did have a face people could take a chance on. I'd like to think it was that. I know it would make my mother happy.

Len Fugate gave me an address and a time to show up. "Be on time, Kovachs, we won't wait," he said as I was backing for the door. I gave him a salute with a forefinger to assure him I understood.

I opened the door to the dark concrete hallway. It looked like the sewers of Vienna. Len Fugate called after me before I left the prop room. I turned to acknowledge.

"Oh, and Kovachs. Forget what I said about Bert Glasser. He's licking boots over at Metro, but he's no stool pigeon. It's the times we're in. A lot of us will live to hate what we did, but as the saying goes, you gotta eat in the meantime. Bert's a pathetic case, but there are a lot like Bert these days. You know what I mean?"

"Yeah, but there's still a couple of Len Fugates around town."

Fugate smiled. "You're okay, Kovachs."

I smiled back at him and gave him another salute before disappearing into the cold hallway.

CHAPTER 10

I walked out the back door of Columbia Playhouse through a lightless alley perfect for strong-arm bullies to sharpen their skills and then out onto a horn-honking, bulb-blinking, exhaust-choking, neon-blinding Hollywood Boulevard. My stomach was making noises like a large unhappy animal in a small cage. I hadn't tied on the feed bag since early a.m. and the old tripes were as empty as a blind man's cup in a bread line. I could have eaten a straw mattress with or without cream, but I decided on food instead and began sniffing out the beaneries in the vicinity. I was looking for an eatery where I could get a meal I could live to tell about and one that would cost me less than a lend-lease aircraft carrier.

I looked in the window of a joint near Cahuenga called Johnny's Perk O' Cup. I saw a lot of people gulping meat and potatoes and nobody heaving up on the floor, so I ventured in.

I ankled up to the counter and found a vacant vinyl-covered stool between a woman who looked like she came in there for the food and a beefy guy probably on a work break.

The joint was hopping. Food-wise that is. A pair of gals who had been pushing plates for longer than Johnny Mize had been poking baseballs over right field fences were working the entire place by themselves. Not that the dump was the size of a grand ballroom, but anytime you get more than twenty hungry people hollering for something to be shoved down their drains and insisting it be piping hot and on the table ten minutes ago, sister, you need help.

But these two ladies were pros from way back. They trundled their blue-veined legs around the floor with the precision of Elroy Hirsch slithering through the other team's line. Ballerinas half their age couldn't have begun to make the moves those two went through.

I planted my **avoirdupois** on the stool and waited for one of the waitresses to notice me. I was starved, alright, but I wasn't going to put either of those working gals through any paces. They were worth three times what they were taking home and I knew how it was.

A few minutes went by and one of them came over to the dame on my left. She had a pot of coffee in one hand, an order pad in the other and a pencil stuck in a head of hair the color of dried leaves. Her face was tired, but that went with the job. A little puffy under the chin and around the middle, she was on the bad side of forty. Her mouth was stern but not unfriendly. She was a business woman. She called out a grill order over her shoulder to a square open space above the milkshake machine.

"Ground cow in a barn! Pin a rose on it! Side of Saturday nights!"

She returned her head to the woman who was studying the menu like somebody was going to give a test on it and she wanted to be sure she made an "A". "What'll ya have tonight, honey?"

"Oh, I just can't decide, Myrt. What do you suggest?"

"Bromo Seltzer. Al's working the grill tonight. It ain't a fit night out for man or beast."

"Oh, I just don't know. I guess I'll try the meat loaf with gravy, mashed potatoes and bread. Is that a good choice, Myrt?"

"Sure, honey. Al! One-two-three and splash! Desert, honey?"

"I think I'd like the tapioca pudding."

"Bowl of fish eyes! Let'm swim for a while!"

Myrt moved over in front of me and began pouring coffee into a large thick cup.

"Murk?" she asked. It was only a rhetorical question no matter how you look at it.

"Sure," I said, just to keep the conversation flowing.

"How?"

"Blonde and sweet." She slid the sugar from in front of the woman who ordered the fish eggs and splash with the cool precision of a golfer sinking a championship putt.

"Okay, honey," she said, "what kind of damage you gonna do your stomach tonight?"

"Well, Myrt, since this hash foundry comes to me highly recommended I'll put my money on the special — ham, potatoes and cabbage and a slice of apple pie to top it off."

Myrt swivelled her head around toward the square hole. "Noah's boy with Murphy carrying a wreath! Then gimme Eve with a lid on!"

A man who hadn't shaved for a couple shifts appeared at the window with a cigarette pasted in the corner of his mouth. Nobody had to tell me it was Al. Had I seen him before I ordered I might have settled for a glass of water and a side order of wind pudding. He wore a scowl that implied I had greatly insulted him with my order. The window, however, permitted Al to be seen only from the collarbone up and I've always been one to count my blessings no matter how small they might be.

The man to my right growled from beneath his cap that he wanted some breakfast food — bacon and eggs, toast and jelly and he wanted it pronto. Myrt wasn't the kind of dame you could shove around. There was more than a hint of sarcasm as she hollered the order to Al.

"Cackleberries an' grunts! Blindfold 'em! Gimme one down with squish! Cowboy's in a hurry — throw it in a bag!"

The guy mumbled something. He sounded satisfied with the order if not the service. But you can't always tell everything from sneaking a sideways peek at a guy's ears. Before Myrt moved on down the line, the man ordered a steak, rare, as an afterthought.

"Slab of moo, let'm chew it!" Myrt barked, taking no notice of the man or Al for that matter.

The food tasted the way Myrt looked after an eight hour shift on her feet — exhausted and a bit salty. I passed the time between bites reading the front page of the evening paper. The woman on the stool next to me, the one who had made one of the biggest decisions in her life when she ordered the meatloaf, gave me dibs on the front section when she saw me staring over her shoulder. She probably figured she had to give up part of the paper or talk to me. She chose the former. Already too much excitement for one day, I guess.

The big blat, other than the Ferrari murder trial, was the hoopla stirred up over Mindzsenty. The papers had been lathering up over the treason conviction of the Hungarian bishop who wanted to return the country to the fascists and/or the Hapsburgs. The Pope was excommunicating everybody who thought Mindzsenty was a rat and CARE was pulling out of Budapest.

A story on Russian slave camps, DeGaulle warning a communist coup d'etat was imminent in France and a piece quoting Eisenhower on the grave dangers of dictatorship and centralized government made for a neat little package to scare the jehosephat out of Mr. and Mrs. John Q. Public. Raised some bumps on my dermis. Also took my mind away from supper.

The beanwagon was thinning out by the time I was challenging a second cup of Brazil beans that made me long for my own home-brewed battery acid.

My two saddlebags paid their freight and walked separately into the night to find something else to do. A man and his young son came in and sat nearby. After arguing over what movie to see the man told Myrt that he wanted a plate of hash and a side of baked beans for himself.

"Yesterday, today and forever and a thousand on a plate!" she barked.

He then ordered a waffle with peanut butter and syrup for junior.

"Gimme a collision mat with a scoopa glue! Douse it in oil!"

I tried to pry myself from their dad'n' lad banter and return to the paper. Some one slipped a nickel in the juke box and in a second Red Ingle and his Natural Seven came on like gangbusters and belting out their latest forgetable tune, something called "Moe's Zart's Turkey Trot". But it worked. I buried my nose in a story about the southern filibuster in the Senate to kill the Anti-Lynching Law.

I hardly noticed the two beefy gents in overcoats who parked their tonnage on the stools on either side of me. I did, however, notice that they sat down at the same time.

"How's the grub in here, mac?" said the man to my left. I turned my head to look at a face no one else would have wanted. Maybe forty, his skin was gray, the color of ashes after a fire and he had a pair of watery eyes that said absolutely nothing. The knife scar on his chin tipped me off that I could exclude him from the ranks of concert pianists if I had any doubts. I told him to lay off the ham, but I don't think he was sincere in his question.

"How's about we go for a walk?" he said in a way that left no doubt he wasn't asking me for a date.

"You're cute," I said, "but mother warned me not to go out with strange men." I felt something pressing against my right side. Like somebody was trying to goose me with a spoon. I looked over and saw a man who had the same tailor as the clown to my left. He was older, fatter and meaner looking. When I recognized him from the bathroom mirror at M.G.M. I knew the object in my side was no spoon.

"But then I never did listen to mother," I said.

"Pay your check, Kovachs. We got some business."

I reached into my pocket and pulled out a couple singletons and some loose change. Myrt saw me get up from the stool and came over. She tore the check from her pad.

"That's $1.32, honey."

I pushed the money toward her. "Keep the change, Myrt. My brothers and I got to be getting back to the farm."

"Gee, thanks, mister," Myrt said with genuine astonishment. Then thinking a minute she added, "These mugs are your brothers?"

"That's just what dad said the first time he saw them at the hospital." She threw back her head and laughed out loud. Myrt was the kind of girl who didn't know how to giggle.

The playmate on my right thrust his metal into my side and growled that the conversation was over and we must really be on our way.

"You boys don't look like farmers to me," Myrt called out as the three of us were marching toward the front door.

"Pigs! We keep pigs," I rasped, as the galoot with the gun scraped bone in a way I could never forgive him. I was virtually walked Spanish through the front door and down the sidewalk a few yards and then thrown down a brick alley darker than the inside of a bottle of India ink.

"You gonna get taught some manners, Kovachs," said the one without the gun. "Gonna teach you to keep your yap shut and your nose outta where it don't belong."

Before I could thank him for the lesson and be on my way so I could practice what I had learned, he indicated this crash course in thuggery etiquette was just commencing by driving a square fist packaged in brass deep into my middle. I went flying into the roughly masoned brick alley wall. As I bounced off I came at my teacher with the ham dinner which I lost all over him.

The slow-witted baboon with the pop gun drove a fat knee into my kidneys. The guy was a specialist. But I was a fighter. I turned on him and surrendered the potatoes and cabbage on his gun arm. But it wasn't enough. A closed fist came out of the dark and connected against my cheekbone. Speaking for the cheekbone, it didn't crack, at least I didn't hear it, but the impact sent a quiver of white hot arrows piercing into my orbs. I swung wildly, finding some face flesh and a couple knuckles worth of ivory. One of the monkeys yelled out when I planted a kick like it was the fourth down and I was punting from my own end zone.

But that, too, wasn't enough. One of them grabbed me from behind and pinned my arms while the other blaster rained his thick maulies into what was left of my guts. I let him have it with the apple pie.

"Let's croak him right here," said one of them. "Nobody'd be the wiser."

"Can't do it. Not after he went flirtin' and funny

with the waitress back there. She could put the make on us for sure."

I didn't know who was saying what, it was too dark, but I did support the second speaker. Kovachs was in a jam, but he did have the noodle power to see what was coming back in the diner. His patter with Myrt was his insurance policy and though the premiums were more reasonable than Mutual of Omaha's, sometimes he is given to wonder about the depth of the coverage.

"Okay," said the first voice. "But lemme finish him off. Just one more good chop to the kidneys."

That was the last thing I remembered for a while. I can't say everything went blank, because that's the way it was when I was conscious. But, whereas before I was just in the darkness, the last shot to the old filters made me a part of it.

I woke up sometime later to a three-legged alley cat licking what was left of my dinner from my chin. It was still dark, but it was the kind of alley that would be near pitch at high noon. I lit a match and looked at my watch. The crystal was cracked, but it ticked a few minutes shy of midnight.

I felt my head. It was dented some and was pounding like the percussion section of a jazz band. A sticky goo was clogging up my nose making it difficult to breathe. It didn't take a second match to tell me it wasn't marmalade.

I ached worse than an octagenarian with arthritis. If I could have stood up right away I'm sure I would have stood just as bent. I dragged my hulk along the ground to the alley wall where I struggled to sit up. I groped for my smokes. Only two left, but I needed just one. I struck a match to get the tobacco on fire. The phosphorous glow of the match threw a dim light that extended just beyond my feet. My eyes glimmed something a few yards away. It lay in a sprawling heap like a pile of dirty rags or maybe a hobo's bindle. Most likely it was a bag of leftovers from the hash palace around the corner.

The match burned down to my finger prints and went out. I was prepared to pass off the pile as just that — stuff you find in a dark, dead-end alley — but curiosity made me strike another match.

I crawled a few feet to the pile and poked at it cautiously, half expecting Norwegian rats the size of Mickey Rooney to jump out and show me their teeth. I lit a third match. The pile wasn't rags or a bindle or even bagged garbage. A fourth match showed me a face. Or what was left of a face. It was more like a couple pounds of red hamburger recently ground. A fifth match told me it was Jake Diltz.

I jumped back from the sight. It didn't take a fellowship to the Institute of Advanced Study to point out the connections between Jake Diltz and his tale about Frances Farmer and the two palookas who had just robbed me of my supper. The stock in what he had told me had just gone up a hundred points. The bottom, however, had fallen out of his future.

I felt sorry for Jake Diltz lying there in the filth of a back alley, just a short whistle from the tinsel and glitter place where all dreams come true. I was mad, too, that there are bums in this world who take certain pleasure in killing the Jake Diltz's. But I was too sore and busted up to remain there and get nostalgic. Jake Diltz knew what he had gotten himself into when he first came to me. And didn't he tell me over the phone just before he got carried out of Hal's Diner that he was a dead man? That knowledge, such as it was, helped not at all. I liked the little guy and in a way I had let him down.

I crawled away from Jake Diltz's body and slowly got to my feet. I took out my handkerchief and tried to wipe as much of the blood and ham special from my face as I could. I looked around for my hat. I found it among a couple rusty tin cans a few yards away, dusted it off and placed it on a head as sore as a bad carpenter's thumb. But I was alive and that counted for something. I walked away from the alley and back to Hollywood Boulevard. A few blocks later, somewhere on La Brea, I found a flophouse I could afford. It wouldn't have mattered. The pain in my back and head informed me in its own special way that I couldn't have gone another hundred yards.

I paid the man at the desk of the Bright Angel Hotel an extra two bucks to give me a wake-up rap on the pipes at 6:30 so I could make that ride to Trumbo's ranch.

Two minutes inside my room and I was out like a twenty-five watt porch light. The last two things that were going through my mind before the sandman came was the overwhelming musty smell coming from the ancient pink bedspread and how the joint impressed me as being neither bright nor angelic.

CHAPTER 11

The banging on my door kicked me conscious. I felt lousy. Like a troupe of circus elephants had been doing knee stands on my body during the night. But I was a little renewed knowing that my two dollars to the night man had actually bought what it had paid for.

I thanked the knocker, told him I was traveling on the American plan and like my bacon flat and crisp. He had no sense of humor and said something entirely too nasty for that early in the morning. I told him to get lost. He didn't put up a fight.

I still had some major league groaning to do. The hardest part was bending over to put on my socks. The next hardest part was straightening up. By comparison, the rest of my dressing was a lead pipe cinch. I was feeling rather proud of myself, actually. A look in the mirror put things back into perspective. The face was a little puffy and purple in spots and the nose was twisted in such a way that it appeared to be trying to sneak off my face. I could't really blame it if it was. With that face as scenery, were I a nose, I guess I would always be looking for a chance to make a getaway.

My morning toilet consisted of cold compressing the puffy parts, trying to realign the smeller and sponging off the places where the blood had caked. That was done while waiting for the shirt and jacket to dry. They smelled like a room full of sick animals. I doused the rough parts under the faucet almost before getting out of bed. In a half hour I was down on the street getting into a cab and heading for an address on Cashio Street.

I got to the house, which was a few blocks from La Cienega and Pico Boulevard, fifteen minutes before Len Fugate said he was leaving. I walked to the upper flat of the Spanish stucco, stopping just briefly to regard the bougainvillaea trailing up the side of the house next to the driveway.

Len Fugate answered my knock on the door. "Kovachs!" he said with a start as he ushered me inside. "What the hell happened to you?"

"Oh, that," I said pointing to my face casually. "A couple of your friendly Angelinos decided they needed my money more than I did. We argued about it and I lost."

"You were rolled? Did they clean you out?"

"Well, I lost the argument, but they didn't get my goods." I tapped my rear pocket where I kept my wallet in a demonstration of put up bravado.

Fugate shook his head. "Damn, man. You should have let them have the money. Couldn't have been worth a beating."

"Gee, I didn't think the old map looked exactly like Death Valley."

"Sorry, old man. Just a little surprised, that's all. Oh, Kovachs, these are the other people going up to Dalton's ranch. Solly. Helen. Arthur. This is the guy I was telling you about. Riley Kovachs."

The three were already standing when Len Fugate made the brief introductions. Helen and Arthur shook my hand perfunctorily. They weren't exactly happy to make my acquaintance. Solly nodded at me and grunted. All of them, including Len Fugate, viewed me through suspicious eyes, but that was to be expected. I just hoped they wouldn't become fanatical about it.

"Well, everybody's here," said Len Fugate after an uneasy interval of silence. "No sense wasting any more time around here. We've got five mean hours on the Grapevine waiting for us." Helen, Arthur and Solly nodded in agreement.

I couldn't say my four travelling companions looked particularly displeased that I was a last minute tag-along, but they weren't glowing with affection either. In fact, they didn't seem to be too terribly paly toward each other. It was like four people starting out on a business trip, I thought. Just initial impressions. Impressions of four total strangers through a pair of puffy cheeks, a beezer the color of a Polish sausage and influenced by a back that hurt worse than Tom Dewey must have felt the day after the election. And thus, impressions not entirely to be trusted.

The five of us emptied out of the house to the curb where Solly's shiny new blue DeSoto was parked. Solly and Len took the front seat while Arthur and I made a sandwich out of Helen in the back.

The DeSoto purred north on La Cienega to Santa Monica Boulevard and then onto Sunset. From there we took Laurel Canyon Drive past the million dollar mansions, palaces, rancheros and the stucco temples erected to the dubious taste of Beverly Hills.

The lawns were manicured by the blade and professionally tailored rhododendron and hydrangeas looked like they had just come back from a beauty parlor for shrubbery. The groomed palms and pepper trees were placed just so along the spotless streets. It was a splendid sight and I was prepared to cough up two bits to a guy in a uniform patrolling a gate at the other end of the drive just for the privilege. There was no gate and no toll collector, although Beverly Hills certainly had the heart to have both. There is something about the place that I'm sure even the highbrow residents notice. Impermanence and a transparent brittleness were as much a trade mark of Beverly Hills as its million dollar houses. And that was something no landscaper could change.

By the time our little party reached Highway 99 just south of San Fernando, the previous night's punch-out in the alley was catching up with me and my eyelids came clanking down over my lookers like hatch covers to a couple of Sherman tanks.

I might have slept the whole way to Trumbo's Ranch, but I was brought back to 1949 by a DeSoto full of voices several ranges above conversational tones. I wiped the nap from my 20-20s, lit a Chesterfield and tried to get a make on what all the commotion was about.

Solly was still driving, but he was looking across the front seat at Len Fugate and waving a menacing finger at him.

"Why do you always have to attack the Party?" he asked angrily. "Every time you're in a conversation that goes beyond first base, you always turn to baiting the Party. A right-wing Republican couldn't do a better job than you, Len. How come?"

Fugate was red around the neck and ears and I could tell there was a lot of steam being held under pressure inside him. He was holding it back, but not very well. He chewed hard on the end of a cigarette.

"Come on down off that pedestal, will ya, Solly?" he said sarcastically. "You know it is impossible to talk to you guys sometimes. If a person don't fall down on his knees before the shrine of Joseph Stalin and take the vow that Mother Russia has never, will never and can never do anything wrong, he might as well apply for a job with the F.B.I. You know what you sound like? A damn Catholic priest waving Christ on his cross in everyone's face who don't agree with you right on down the line. It's all or nothing with you."

"Bullshit!" rejoined Solly. "You know that's just goddamned red-baiting. You should be ashamed. Here we're trying to forge a unified front against the right-wing witch hunters and you come up with crap like that."

"United front!" Len Fugate smashed his cigarette butt into the ashtray just below the radio. Sparks flew onto the carpeted floor drawing a reprimand from Solly. "You want to talk about unity? Let's talk about the strike."

"What strike?" Solly demanded to know.

"You know damn well what strike. The C.S.U. strike in '45."

"Well, what about it?"

"The Communist Party didn't support it, that's what about it!"

Helen spoke without raising her voice. "That's not an accurate statement, Len." Her intervention seemed to instantly cool the rhubarb between Solly and Len Fugate. She leaned forward and draped her arms over the top of the front seat. "You must look at the strike dialectically, Len. You must take into account the situation the Party was facing at the time as well as the general situation of the country in order to make an objective assessment."

"Those are just excuses, Helen," said Len Fugate. "Look, you know me. I'm not against the Party. Hell, when we had that strike against Disney, the Party was there on the line with us. And it played an important role in getting the C.S.U. off the ground. The Party helped us make the break from the I.A. And I always defend the Party and its people against the right-wing. But what happens when our bacon was on the line in '45, when we took on Brewer and his crooked I.A. Where was the Party? I'll tell you where it was — breaking the strike!"

"Len, you pulled out the painters and other unions at a very bad time," said Helen, trying to keep the conversation on the level of a debate rather than a political brawl. "You know very well the Party fought for the no-strike pledge during the war. Most progressive unionists agreed with that policy. Winning the war against the fascists was a bit more important than a jurisdictional struggle between the I.A. and the Conference of Studio Unions. Don't you agree, Len?"

"I don't see any connections. We were in a critical life and death battle with those I.A. bums. Brewer and the studios were out to crush us. The war in Europe and the Pacific wasn't going to be won or lost by our picketing Warner's."

"Just a minute, Len," said Arthur, fingering his bow tie. He leaned forward in his seat. "I don't agree with the policies of the Communist Party on very many issues."

"Say none," Solly quipped.

"Well, I wouldn't be in this car if it were none," Arthur replied frostily. "If I may continue. I don't agree with the Communist Party on most issues, but the Popular Front to win the war was one to which I lent my wholehearted support. The subordination of ideology to a common cause — the defense of democracy — was not only noble, but vital to the war effort. Many communistic labor leaders served their country and their members well by deferring their narrow self-interest economic demands during the war."

"Yeah," Len Fugate shot back sarcastically, "and look where that got them — the workers, that is. General Motors laid off 140,000 in '46 and forced a wage cut on the rest. The O.P.A. was killed off by the Republicans with Truman, 'labor's great friend', standing by with a wet finger to the wind. Remember how prices jumped over the moon after the war? And the Wage Stabilization Board had the damn nerve to rule against even a measly 10% wage hike for the auto workers. That's what national unity, no-strike pledges and patriotism got the working man for spilling his guts on the ground in Europe and the Pacific while starving the dog at home. Phooey!"

"Len!" said Helen in the way a parent might speak to a headstrong son. "You must try to realize that the Party was in the hands of the revisionist Browder clique during that period. His right-opportunism led the Party and the working class down a dangerous road, especially after the Tehran Conference in 1943. Browder had poisoned Party thinking to the point that comrades were believing that capitalism was entering an age of enlightenment led by men of vision who were leading the country into a period of peaceful industrial expansion. Browder lulled the Party into thinking the capitalist class would carry out an anti-fascist, democratic and progressive policy at home and overseas. And he applied this reactionary formula to both the war and the peace following it. Socialist revolution was removed from the Party's agenda. But, despite the dark days of Browderism, the no-strike policy was correct and fundamental to winning the war."

"Yeah," Solly piped up. "Look who opposed it. John L. Lewis. An America Firster and big supporter of Dewey. He was an isolationist first and a trade unionist second."

"Baloney!" said Len Fugate. "Pure baloney!"

"Nothing will convince you, will it? Always hostile to the Party," Solly said with sarcastic resignation.

"Don't play Mr. High and Mighty with me, Solly. You sit in that writer's building down at R.K.O. cranking out scripts at $500 per and consider you've struck a decisive blow for socialism if you can sneak the work 'democracy' past the censor. Then you insist it is a matter of highest political principle to cross the picket line of the real class battle in the industry. Brother, you been smoking reefers or what?"

"The Party **did** support the C.S.U. strike!" Solly yelled, slamming his fist into the steering wheel and inadvertently honking the horn.

"Only after the war and only after you guys received a scolding from France and gave Browder the bum's rush!" Len Fugate amended.

"But that's precisely when things turned ugly and you lost a lot of your support," offered Arthur, trying desperately to figure which side, if any, he was on. "I mean I supported the peaceful picketing from the first day of the strike in March right through the summer. It was that horrible riot at Warner Brothers that I had to draw the line."

"Hey," said Solly sarcastically, "who died and left you in charge of the class struggle?"

"Well, I . . ."

"Nothing personal, Arthur, old man, you are what you are, but the first time someone gets a bloody nose in a hot struggle like the C.S.U. strike, you liberals run up the white flag and join the other side."

Arthur was insulted. "I did no such thing, my friend. I have always supported labor and other progressive causes. Even in less than liberal times I have registered my opinion. But when the working man uses violence, or his leaders manipulate him to violent behavior to achieve his ends, then all rationality is abandoned and he becomes the twin of his adversary. Both sides must be held accountable for their behavior."

"Let's hear it for objectivity!" said Len Fugate, raising his hand in mock toast. "The liberals are always looking to be recognized as the self-crowned princes of determining right from wrong and telling us peasants where to draw the line. A toast to middle class moral arbitration!"

"I don't think that is at all funny," said Arthur. Everyone in the car, myself included, tended to disagree.

"Speaking of arbitration," said Solly, "why don't we call for a cooling-off period in this car? No sense letting our tempers get the best of us, especially when we're on the same side in this thing and have a common enemy. Even if some of us are red-baiters."

"Solly!" Helen scolded.

"I'm just kidding. Jeez! Let's live with each other, okay?"

Solly's plea for coexistence was followed by an unnaturally long and uneasy silence. I didn't get the feeling there was the kind of bitter hostility between the caravaners that could paper a dining room. No, I could tell all of them had been down the political road before and this wasn't the first nor probably the last time they would clash in an ideological chin-fest. But by the same barometer, they were not chronic yatterers with short fuses blowing air about the neighbor's dog or the lazy brother-in-law. Matters of real substance brought them together and it was those same matters of substance that kept their tongues vigilantly sharpened waiting for the moment to convert the errant, or if that were not possible, to deliver a dose of political assault and battery on the chronically recalcitrant.

I didn't butt in during the ten-rounder about the C.P.'s role in the C.S.U. strike. It wasn't because I didn't have an opinion on the subject, but I felt it would be wiser to test the water before running out and buying a new pair of trunks. After all, they didn't know me from a Downey Flake donut and from the way they took to me when Len Fugate introduced us, I don't think they were exactly in seventh heaven about my coming along to Trumbo's ranch in the first place. I didn't want to give any of them an excuse in the heat of a political artillery attack to deep-six my chances with Trumbo.

I've been in the workers movement, supported all the anti-fascist drives and marches for Negro rights and union recognition. Attended the meetings, too, and I know what some folks are capable of doing in the name of brotherhood and unity. Hell, that's what was going on in the H.U.A.C. hearings in Washington. Budenz and Bentley and now Whittaker Chambers. Former comrades turned shiv artists in wrecking the lives of some good people. Stalwarts within the movement, too. A lot of blood spilt during the Foster/Browder bare-knuckler. And look what Stalin did to Trotsky. And to Kamenev and Zinoviev and Bukharin and Radek. Then there were the Smith Act defendants of 1949, C.P. leaders, who refused to support the Smith Act defendants of 1940, leaders of the Socialist Workers Party.

So, I figured it to my advantage if I just stayed in the dressing room for the bout. In addition to everything else, the four seemed to have simply picked up their ideological struggling where they last left off. It was not a good place for an **auslander** who was along for the ride under what must have appeared to be questionable circumstances to jump in the middle of such a fray swinging a heavy glove. I sat in the corner of the back seat of the big blue DeSoto smoking cigarettes and taking mental notes.

Solly was a screenwriter at R.K.O. I knew that

much even before we reached Laurel Canyon back in Beverly Hills. A $500 a week screenwriter. I heard that on more than one occasion. In Hollywood, everybody in motion pictures knows to the penny what everybody else is making. Even the radicals play the game. According to the great scheme of things, five hundred dollars a week put Solly near the bottom of the totem pole. Trumbo, on the other hand, I read somewhere, was pulling down something in the neighborhood of $4,000 every week. Pretty nice neighborhood. Solly never said so directly, but he didn't hide the fact that he considered himself among the "exploited" and "lower class" of the script writing community and looked upon people like Trumbo as the purple aristocracy. He seemed to be both proud of his "proletarian" status and a bit jealous of Trumbo's.

He was big. Not just tall, but big and angular with a square jaw and a good-natured face until it came to political fisticuffs. Then it became red, angry and twisted, especially when the subject under discussion was the merits of the Communist Party. Solly was headstrong in its defense — on every issue I was to find out. The curious thing about it was that he wasn't a Party member and said so at least once. He announced he was "close to the Party," but had some personal things to work out which prevented him from making such a momentous committment.

I have met several like him in Frisco who were stalwarts for the C.P. or on the other side of the socialist fence for the Socialist Workers Party.

On the surface, their behavior, like Solly's, appears puzzling. After a while it becomes apparent that they remain outside the official parties of Stalinism or Trotskyism because the Party doesn't want them for one reason or another, or on the other hand, they agree with the Party's political line and are willing to fight for it and the Party, but aren't ready, or flat out refuse to subordinate their lives to the discipline of the "revolutionary instrument". I don't know where Solly fit into that equation since it was common knowledge that the discipline in the C.P. writers and actors branches was considerably looser than in the more traditional industrial branches.

Arthur was Ivy League in dress, thought and personality. The only thing he lacked was the ivy itself. But he did have a little bow tie, probably school colors, growing under his chin. His face was mushy and plain, except for a pair of lips that looked like they had once been tortured by a persimmon. And there was a look in his eyes that suggested he was in a perpetual state of "exegesis", to use one of his own words. He was a Liberal man with a capital "L". He explained at one point during the journey up Highway 99 that, although in full support of individual, human and civil liberties, he could "appreciate" Truman's Order 9835 calling for the registration of communists as a condition of employment with the Federal Government. He saw registration as a far better alternative to blacklisting or imprisonment. I think all of us in the car, maybe for different reasons, would have reluctantly agreed that Arthur's position expressed a general caliber of thinking among a great many Americans — both the man on the street and those in positions of influence and authority.

On foreign policy matters, Arthur's enlightenment shone even dimmer. He found himself in pleasant and full agreement with William O. Douglas that Stalin's speech in 1946 condemning Churchill's growling about the "iron curtain" at Fulton, Missouri, was "the opening shot of World War III" and as such must make ready for the defense of the homeland. Arthur seemed to enjoy prefacing his opinions by tossing out the handle of some well-known public pundit the way rich women wave diamond-studded fingers in your face when they are trying to get you to take them seriously.

At one point, expressing his disagreement with the majority, Arthur turned the color of a puppy's tongue and insisted that the containment of Soviet Russia was the most important thing the United States could be doing in the post-war period and not only did he support the Truman Doctrine, but joined the Hollywood chapter of the Americans for Democratic Action and became its recording secretary so as to be counted as a good soldier in the crusade.

It seemed odd to me at first that Arthur would even sign a petition of support for the Hollywood Ten let alone ride in a car full of radicals to Dalton Trumbo's ranch for a political gathering. But, as he said, even insisted, the issue was not communism but the Constitution, and he put himself on record defending a person's First Amendment rights no matter how disagreeable his politics.

Nobody in the car agreed with Arthur on anything more substantive than the time of day, but he was an important penman for the city's main tabloid and he was public in his defense of the Ten/First Amendment, so, as Len Fugate let slip, he was tolerated.

Len Fugate was a trade union militant from the University of Hard Knocks. His features were rugged and fortyish. His hands were hard and calloused and his speech that of a self-made man. He had been on many picket lines in his time and the scar just below his hairline indicated that he had his head opened up at least one time by a cop's night stick. He was also a graduate of the School of Short Fuses and was the kind of guy who wouldn't sit still and take guff from Walt Disney or William Foster. It didn't matter who was turning the crank, Len Fugate was his own man, almost obsessively so, and title, rank or position of an adversary didn't matter one iota to him.He would surely burn Truman's ears and tell him what he could do with Taft-Hartley and do it sideways, if only he had the chance. Too independent for the Communist Party and, no matter how chummy they might ever become on political matters, you could bet that Len Fugate would always be pouring his own drinks.

Helen was harder to figure. When she talked, which wasn't often, she was a hundred percent business. Textbook lessons on dialectics seemed to be her long suit and she tried, and not without success, to lasso the emotional broncos in the front seat and steer them into the corral of "political objectivity."

A natural blonde with features that would draw a second look, she was over-dressed in a way that made her look older than she really was, which was probably thirty-five. She had worked at R.K.O. as a story analyst since the end of the war. Probably hooked up with Solly there, but no one said anything so I was just guessing. But she had been to college and that was no guess. I could tell by the way she talked. Eastern and a bit too refined.

Helen seemed almost too studied about her politics. She reminded me a little of Elizabeth Gurley Flynn, but only a little. She knew her Marx by heart, but there was a tinny edge to it all. She lacked Flynn's fire and depth. I found that distracting. That and the way she kept her knee snuggling along my thigh in a manner that ruled out coincidence.

CHAPTER 13

During the following hour the subject turned to world affairs. With the exception of Arthur, everyone found something to agree on. We took a look into our crystal balls, trying to imagine a world where Russia had the bomb and China was red. We were of two differing, but not necessarily antagonistic schools of thought. It was largely felt that, should those two things happen they would a) start World War III or b) prevent it. It was a subject that could have lasted to the Canadian border and back, were we going that far. But we weren't. We were on the stretch of the Grapevine starting out from Castaic. It was the proverbial "forty miles of bad road" and getting through in one piece took a team effort. And that was something our little group would have to work at.

We stopped for gas in Castaic before striking out. Everyone used the opportunity to get out and powder their puffs. Solly bought us all bottles of Nehi grape soda pop. He didn't say if grape was the only flavor available or merely his own personal favorite. Anyway, no one complained. I bought a pack of butts and sat in the car with Solly waiting for the others. Arthur was changing his shirt in the john and Helen was putting a call through to her roomate in L.A.

The kid pumping gas told us that the Grapevine

was being widened to four lanes and was torn up so bad the Highway Department had closed it until the summer. That meant we would have to suck in some air and tackle the roller coaster they call the Old Ridge Route.

The road, and that's being kind to call it one, was as narrow as a ballerina's waist. The thin ribbon of cement and asphalt hugged the side of the Tehachapi Mountain grades like it was hanging on for dear life. It was and so were we. The DeSoto groaned stubbornly skyward like an asthmatic sprinting up the steep side of Mt. Whitney. The Ridge Route was a highway engineer's idea of a cheap thrill. It had more hairpins than a Spanish **duenna**. Arthur buried his face in the back of the mohair seat and the several shrill screams that disrupted the mountain silence weren't made only by Helen. Solly's eyeballs were pasted on the hood ornament of his car. The rest of us couldn't help but take notice that the several gaps in the white guardrail weren't made by termites.

We inched our way up toward Reservoir Summit doing ten miles an hour on the "straightaways" and when we entered the bobby pin turns we were lucky if we did half that. My bladder had gone into shock, but I painfully held my water until we reached Liebre Summit where Solly mercifully stopped the car to let out those who had to seek out their own private bush. On the way back to the car I could see the road behind us. It looked like the flight pattern of a very drunk butterfly.

From Liebre Summit the road dropped like a cast iron balloon and if any of us had missed out on roller coaster rides as kids we made up for it in spades. When we rejoined Highway 99 just east of Gorman we knew that the worst was over and during the next fifteen miles parched throats cracked in a non-stop babbling stream of relieved conversation. We talked about everything but politics.

Solly let drop he was raised in Euclid, a suburb of Cleveland. That was a cue for a gum-bumper on the '48 Series. Though neither of us had been back to Ohio in some time we relived the highlights of the six game series with the Boston Braves like a couple of old time Buckeyes. Both of us agreed that the first game was the best, even though the Indians got beat 1-0.

"Feller pitched his heart out in that one," said Solly. "A two-hitter. It's a damn shame they didn't score him some runs."

I agreed, adding if Feller's pickoff play with Boudreau had nailed Masi in the eighth, the game might have turned out differently. But I wasn't going to be the one to take anything away from Johnny Sain of the Braves. He pitched his heart out, too.

"Yeah," said Solly grudgingly. "He did okay, but it should've been Feller's game. Hell, with Beardon, Gromek and Lemon on the staff the Braves were beat before the whole thing started. I'll be the first to admit, however, that Lemon was damn lucky he got Sibi Sisti to hit into that double play in the ninth inning of the last game."

"It's going to be another great season," I mused. "You keep your eye on Doby and Rosen. Those kids are going places."

Solly looked at me through the rearview mirror and grinned broadly. We both knew without saying a word the irony in my statement. The world may have been going to hell in a handbasket with thick-headed reactionaries in the driver's seat, but the world champion Cleveland Indians were sure to be led by a couple of rookies — one a Negro and the other a Jew.

It seemed like we coasted all the way from Tejon Pass to Frazier Park. While batting the fat with Solly I remembered that the San Andreas and Garlock Faults come together near Frazier Park. "Transect," is the term I remember from the geology books. I strained my corneas looking for the physical evidence of what certainly was the elbow of the earthquake zone in California. No sign of the junction, but as we drove down the road through Cuddy Canyon I could see that the San Andreas had been there. A very low scarp visible at the base of the straight ridge of mountains on the south side of the valley and a series of sag ponds on the floor of Cuddy Valley were two of the more obvious signs.

Solly stopped at the Chuchupate Ranger Station a few miles west of Frazier Park to double check the directions to the Lazy T. I spent the time picking the brain of a ranger named Alexander about the flora of Los Padres Forest. Satisfied that I could tell a Jeffrey from a Pinyon Pine and Rabbit Brush from Flannel Bush, I climbed back into the DeSoto and a squinting impatience revealed through eight eyeballs.

The distance from the ranger station to Trumbo's ranch was less than ten miles as the crow flies. However, we were human beings in a DeSoto and it seemed closer to forty.

The Lazy T appeared out of the trees as we entered a broad meadow. It was a long, low ranch house next to a large hole in the ground. I recognized Dalton Trumbo as the man standing in the open front door waving at us as we pulled up behind one of the two late model cars parked near the house.

"Welcome, argonauts," he said, smiling as we

piled out of the car and stretched our limbs. "Coffee's on the stove and the booze is on ice." Trumbo took a sip from a large coffee mug as he spoke.

"Make mine a double anything," Solly yelled, cracking a wide grin. "My nerves are shot and I need something strong and quick."

"Dalton," Len Fugate said kiddingly, "How's the F.B.I. going to find you if you insist on living way up here in Outer Treetrunk?"

"That's the whole point, lad. Only **companeros** can find me. Come on in. Alvah, Jack and some of the wrecking crew from R.K.O. and M.G.M. are already here. Beat you by half an hour."

As we filed up the steps to the ranch house Trumbo shook everyone's hand and expressed his gratitude they could come. Len Fugate introduced me by name only. Trumbo grabbed my hand and gave it a solid squeeze.

"Glad to meet you, Riley," he said. "Always happy to welcome a new face to the struggle against the forces of darkness."

Once inside the house, Trumbo introduced us to Cleo, his wife. We were poured drinks and then treated to a mandatory twenty minute tour of the house. It was clear that the house, as much as anything, was his pride and joy. When we returned to the large, sprawling living room we were left on our own.

Trumbo excused himself into another room to play with his son. "If we don't arm wrestle at least once a day," he said before disappearing, "he won't go to bed at night."

Cleo served me a drink of something brown and very strong. I was too polite to inquire after its specific contents. I walked over to a place where three men sitting around a coffee table were discussing the Spanish Civil War. The screenwriter named Alvah was speaking. I wondered if he was the same man who had fought in the Abraham Lincoln Brigade and wrote **Men in Battle** before coming to Hollywood. I wanted to ask him, but I just pulled up a chair and listened to their conversation instead. When Trumbo returned to the living room, I got up and walked over to him.

"I have another reason for being here," I said in lowered tones.

"Oh," replied the screenwriter, pouring himself a drink without looking up at me.

"I'm a private detective from San Francisco. Two days ago a little guy named Jake Diltz came up to me after a Hollywood Ten meeting — the one you addressed — and told me a wild tale about some Nazi doctors planning to operate on the brain of Frances Farmer. The little guy was scared. He said the Feds were tailing him and he wanted me to take over the case. He said you might know something."

Trumbo finished pouring and looked me hard in the glimmers. He produced a cigarette from a pack in his shirt pocket and stuck it in the end of a long black plastic holder. He fumbled around patting his pockets trying to come up with a match. He found one and burned the end of the tobacco.

"Riley," he said, "let's you and I take a walk outside. I want to show you the lake I'm building for the kids." We exited through a side door of the house. We only walked a few dozen yards before Trumbo stopped and pointed to the big hole in the ground I saw on the way to the Lazy T. "Going to be a lake in there soon," he said. "For the children. So they can go swimming. Working like a damn fool, too, to pay for all this." He gestured toward the house and the untold acres of trees that were his. "Got to work fast, you know. We'll all be in jail before too long. The ten of us, at least. I want to turn out as much as I can before they take me away."

I nodded. There was much on Dalton Trumbo's mind. He took a drag from his cig and a sip from the martini he had brought along. Then, without coaxing, he began on the subject that had brought us outside.

"What did you say that little man's name was?"

"Jake Diltz."

"Jake Diltz? Did he send you up here to see me?"

"In a way. He dropped two hundred clamshells in my bucket at a bar after the meeting to take over the case from him. I didn't want to take it, but he turned up dead in an alley a block off Hollywood Boulevard before I had a chance to return it."

Trumbo bit down hard on his cigarette holder when I mentioned Jake Diltz's death. "I don't think I know this Jake Diltz."

"A little mug wearing a dirty tent for a trench coat."

Trumbo looked off into the woods. Somewhere a bird chirped. "There was this fellow, I remember," he said, returning his eyes to me. "An odd little chap. He came up to me following the meeting and furtively slipped me a note. Then he just took off. Wanted me to meet him about a matter of life and death. I remember the note because it was so damn melodramatic."

"That sounds like Jake Diltz."

"He told you I knew something about Frances Farmer?"

"He was more specific than that. He said you knew some people who have information about a lobotomy being planned for her."

Trumbo shook his head. "Jesus Christ! Poor Frances. Those bastards won't be satisfied until they put her underground, will they?"

"Who? What bastards?"

"What bastards? **The** bastards. The bastards who are running this goddamn nightmare. The studio bosses and their director stooges, Parsons, Fidler, Hopper and some of those loathsome crumbs who get paid hundreds of thousands of dollars to stand in front of a camera. They all did their part to set her up. I saw it coming. Then they pushed her over. You've got to realize just what a truly vicious business this is, Kovachs. Frances Farmer was a lethal mixture to the reactionary moguls and their flunkies. She was a political progressive and hated the phoneyness of Hollywood. Her mistake was being outspoken about it. That made her a liability to the bosses and an embarrassment to the Hollywoodophile community. So they got rid of her. Just like they're trying to get rid of us now. In a couple of years, Kovachs, Hollywood's going to be a cultural desert whose main, if not only, product will be Army training films. Poor Frances, she was the first among us to go."

"Do you know anything about an operation penciled in for her that is going to put her brain in a jar?"

Trumbo finished the last of his drink. It was chilly in the mid-afternoon sun. Dalton Trumbo shivered slightly, but not from the cold. "It seems to me," he said, "there was some talk going around a little while back about that. I thought it was all metaphor. She's been jailed in that mental prison for so long. You know, lobotomy, like being cut off from the thinking world."

"Who did you talk to? Who did you hear it from?"

"Let's see. It wasn't that long ago. I was down in L.A. At one of the studios. Oh, yeah, it was Larry Berger. He knew her before the war. Worked on a couple scripts for her. He told me about it. I remember the occasion. He was with a doctor I've met once or twice. Maybe he got it from him. I was hustling up some work and wasn't able to spend much time with them. Like I said, I took it metaphorically."

"Can I find Berger in Hollywood?"

"Last I heard he was packing off for England until this business blows over. I'm sure he's gone by now."

"The doctor, then. What is his name?"

"Lord, man, give me a chance! I don't have a photographic memory!"

"Try! You don't know what I've had to go through the last twenty four hours to get this far. I don't have anything else to go on. Not a thing!" I backed off before blowing a gasket. I was beginning to sound like Jake Diltz.

Trumbo was not a man to be pushed, but he did want to help. He rigged up another cigarette in his holder. He lit it and began tugging at his chin trying to come up with something.

"Christ!" he said. "A, B, C, D, Dawkins, Hawkins. It might have been Hawkins. He is a psychiatrist, I think."

"Hawkins. Or Dawkins. A psychiatrist. Maybe. That's thinner than W.P.A. soup."

"Sorry I can't be more help. Like I said I took it metaphorically. But it wouldn't surprise me. Those bastards are capable of anything. They're trying to ruin me and the others and for what? **A Guy Named Joe? Thirty Seconds Over Tokyo? Mission to Moscow?** We're progressives and loudmouths just like

Frances, and the ruling class has decided we must go. I hope someone can prevent those lousy fascists from carving up poor Frances." Trumbo's voice grew. He was angry. "But I'll tell you one thing right here and now. They may send every mother's son of us to prison, but they will never wipe us out! We won't let them. Some day these bastards will be sorry for what they're doing. Look, I've got to get back inside. Good luck, Kovachs." Trumbo took my hand and gave it a pump. "If you find out anything, let me know. I'll do what I can to help."

I watched Dalton Trumbo disappear into the house. I stayed behind staring at a nearby fir tree. I lit a smoke and took a long pull. Maybe this whole business about Nazi doctors making the Farmer woman into a vegetable garden was just a metaphor run amok. I wasn't even terribly sure that I knew what a metaphor was at that moment, but I did know that the torturous road that led me to Dalton Trumbo, and I don't just mean the Grapevine, had yielded information that I could have tucked into a corner of a gnat's navel and had room left over for a traveling circus to put up a tent.

I had to admit there was a slight nagging feeling that Jake Diltz was just a poor dope with a sprung sprocket and a persecution complex. But it was a feeling that had wings and flew away. The frigid reality of his body lying in a heap in a Hollywood alley pinched my cheek and told me that whatever Jake Diltz had it was no complex. That was the real lowdown. So was Frances Farmer locked away in mental stir in Tacoma and this blossoming inquisition in Hollywood that was becoming as conspicuous as Robert Taft at a Wallace rally. A witch hunt being carried out by the same celluloid clergy that just may have also sent Frances Farmer to the stake several years before such activity became fashionable.

I picked up a cone from a Pinyon Pine and tossed it as far into the woods as I could. I hiked up my pants, tucked that gnat's navel's-worth of information under my hat and headed back to the Trumbo House.

CHAPTER 14

I spent a lot of time near the onion dip munching crackers and sipping white wine while trying to noodle out my next move. It wasn't as difficult as it might sound, but if I couldn't find a Dr. Hawkins or Dawkins shrinking heads at an L.A. address then all the onion dip in the world couldn't help.

By mid-afternoon the Lazy T was filling up with people. Left-wing script writers, workers from the studio unions, a sprinkling of actors, of whom only Lionel Stander and Gayle Sondergaard I could definitely recognize. Movement lawyers, former Wallace supporters, progressive journalists, spokesmen from the Civil Rights Congress, the group called H.I.C.A.S.P. and some of the other groups supporting the Hollywood Ten and/or the First Amendment. I was certainly the only private gumshoe in the joint. And that left me tugging at my collar when someone would innocently ask what I did for a living. If I told the truth I was inviting trouble in the questions that would be sure to follow. Like what was I doing breaking crackers with a ranch house full of reds twenty miles from the nearest paved road. I could always say I'm working for the wife or husband of some movie star "too big to mention by name" on an adultery stakeout, but I didn't do that kind of work. Ever. And never would. And wouldn't even pretend I did no matter how bad I needed a screen. I just told people I was a friend of Len Fugate's and an unemployed longshoreman. It was almost half true.

It was still an hour and a half before the meeting part of the gathering was to begin. The Trumbo's had set a swell table of barbequed ribs, potato salad, baked beans, the works. I loaded up my plate with a bit more than it was designed to hold. I was careful to make sure I was getting all the starch I could possibly swallow.

I walked to one side of the living room and sat down in a folding chair. Before I could start shoveling down my food Helen came over carrying a much smaller plate and sat down in the chair beside me. She scolded me politely for ignoring her and taking up so much of our host's time. I smiled back just as politely and begged her forgiveness.

By the time I had reached the point of no return with the smoked, dripping ribs, I looked up to find we were flanked by three or four other rib-gnawers discussing the latest about Paul Robeson. Some were exchanging personal memories about the man and politely arguing which of his **Othello's** was the superior — the Schubert Theatre **Othello** or the road **Othello**. Then the conversation turned political.

"You know," said one man — a man who looked a lot like Arthur — wiping his fingers with a paper napkin. "Paul Robeson stirred up a hornet's nest with those remarks he made on his West Indies tour. All this pro-Russian talk is bound to lose him support. Not to mention what it will do to the Negro cause. Why I understand most of his scheduled tour engagements have already been cancelled as a result." His cronies shook their heads sadly in agreement. I ate my potato salad and listened.

Then Helen spoke up. "What did he say that you find so objectionable?" she asked.

"Well," said the man who spoke before, "it's not so much what he said, but rather his attitude and, of course, his bad timing. These are perilous times for progressives and for one to take such a defiantly pro-communist posture, especially for a Negro. Why, it is like waving a red flag in the bull's face. It is a very unwise thing to do. Very unwise."

I washed down a lump of potato salad with a gulp of wine and added my two cents. "Seems to me, if what the man said rings true, then both he and what he said should be defended. What do you think?" Two of the three laughed. Actually it was more an embarrassed titter. Like my fly was standing open or something.

Helen, however, didn't titter. "I don't see what's so funny," she said sternly. "What's wrong with what Paul Robeson said? What's wrong with the Soviet Union? With communism?" No one answered. One of them cleared his throat like maybe Helen's fly were open. She went on. "Robeson spoke about the absence of racial oppression in the Soviet Union. Well, it's true, there is none. Both Lenin and Stalin have denounced the kind of persecution Negroes live with under capitalism in America."

Before anyone could reply to Helen, I spoke up. "There's a good chance Robeson will be dragged before the H.U.A.C. Now that the election is over they don't have to treat him with kid gloves. What will you gents do if he gets indicted?" The only sound to obtain in our immediate environ was the smacking of lips licking fingers smeared with barbeque sauce.

A moment later Solly came over and whispered something in Helen's ear. She rose, excused herself and followed Solly out of the room. My plate was nearly empty. I pleaded a life and death craving for a second helping of potato salad that had to be filled as my excuse to beg off from the three former Robeson admirers.

I treated myself to a small mountain of potato salad from a large bowl on the buffet table. I also found myself on the edge of a discussion between two absolutely normal looking people who felt Ronald Reagan was not only a good actor, who was quite possibly just misunderstood, but could be won over to supporting the ten blacklisted men if only he were approached in the right way. A third person who was also standing on the edge of the conversation and looked to be as amused by their conversation as me suggested to the pair that the best way to approach old Dutch was from behind the wheel of a Mac truck at full throttle.

I laughed out loud. Since I had my mouth full of potato salad at the moment, it wasn't a pretty sight. In fact, all three of the people found somewhere else to go and left me standing alone next to the buffet table wiping spuds and mayonnaise from my chin.

Helen and Solly appeared from nowhere. Both looked worried.

"Kovachs, old man," said Solly hurriedly and with assumed familiarity, "something's come up. Helen's in a jam and has to get back to L.A. right away. Her roomate tried to kill herself this afternoon. The telegram just came. She's not dead, but she's in pretty bad shape at L.A. General." I didn't say anything.

"I know it's a lot to ask," said Helen meekly looking down at her shoes.

"See, Kovachs, Helen doesn't drive. Can you take her to L.A.? You can use my car. I'd drive her myself, but I have to make a report at the meeting later on. I figured you wouldn't mind missing the meeting. It would be a big favor, old man."

"Solly," said Helen still gazing at the floor, "don't pressure Mr. Kovachs. It's such a long drive."

I held up my hand. "Let me finish my potato salad and a cup of goodby coffee and I'll be ready to go. There's still a bit of light in the sky and the sooner we dust the pike the better." Solly and Helen heaved individual sighs of relief.

In fifteen minutes I had finished eating, swilled a cup of industrial strength scorch, got Solly's keys and all the dope on how to handle his big new DeSoto, received a sack of ribs from Cleo to eat along the way and paid my adioses to Trumbo and Len Fugate who saw Helen and me to the door.

Trumbo reminded me to call if I learned anything and gave me a slip of paper with a number in Hollywood and one in New York where he was going in a few days to launch a stage play he had written.

"Say hello to my friends and piss on my enemies," he said with a wink.

Len Fugate slapped me on the back. "I hope you got what you came for, Kovachs. You seem to be an okay joe so I'll give you a little friendly advice. Watch out for the curves. They can be a lot more dangerous than you think." I thought I saw Len Fugate wink his eye, but I couldn't be sure. It was a few minutes past four. Less than an hour of daylight remained in the winter sky.

CHAPTER 15

By the time we emerged from the forest and reached Highway 99 at the little wide spot in the road called Lebec, the chilly peaks of the nearby Tehachapis were little more than smoky silhouettes against a darkening blue and buttermilk sky.

I made Solly's big blue dolphin turn to the right at Lebec and settled into the seat for the long ride back. I looked forward to the road and miles ahead about as much as being locked in a theater and forced to watch Judy Canova movies. But I had felt the sand pouring out of the glass back at the Lazy T. I could drive Helen to L.A. General to see her roomate and begin looking for a head shrinker called Hawkins or Dawkins. That was a saving of at least eighteen hours since the original plan was for everyone to bunk overnight at Trumbo's. But as I fixed my stare into the unfriendly dark and the antagonistic pavement which seemed to be taunting me, an eighteen hour saving looked like an investment that would pay no dividends.

During the first hour on the highway Helen and I spoke very little. I was fooling around with the radio trying to come up with something musical to steady both nerve and stomach. I tuned in one of my favorite pieces, the **Sabre Dance**, but, whizzing down the side of a mountain on a road designed by Dagwood Bumstead in two tons of potential runaway chrome and rubber, it wasn't quite what I had in mind.

I pulled in KNX just in time to hear a Basil Rathbone-voiced announcer tell me I had the great good fortune to have a ringside pew for "The Inglewood Park Cemetery Association Concert", featuring a half hour of "Immortal Melodies". That didn't please me either and I turned off the squawk-box before hearing the first immortal selection.

I turned to Helen and asked her to light a cigarette for me. This was one road that paid penalties for not having both hands on the wheel. She reached inside my coat pocket and took out my Chesterfields. She put two in her mouth and lit them with the car's pushbutton lighter. She inhaled once to get them going and then took one from her freshly painted lips and passed it over to me.

"Thanks," I said. "You did that just like they do in the movies."

"I go to a lot of movies," she replied matter of factly. It was very dark inside the car and for a short moment I imagined her to be Lauren Bacall. But I had the nagging feeling she was a whole lot more the Claire Trevor type.

"With Solly?" I said, picking up the conversation.

"With myself, mostly. There's nothing between Solly and me other than politics."

I said "hmm," not really knowing if that bit of knowledge made me feel better or not. I could feel her inching a little closer to me on the seat. Again I said "hmm."

"Who is Riley Kovachs?" Helen said in the kind of voice some women use to get men to follow them home. I felt myself clearing a throat that really didn't need clearing.

"Just an everyday mug," I answered, "a sometimes self-employed bloke with card-carrying proletarian sympathies and a taste in some things that is scandalously aristocratic."

"You are playing with me."

"Not at all. Just don't like being on the hot seat. I'd much rather talk about you. Like what schools you attended and how a girl from a solid eastern family became a revolutionary."

"My, you are a detective, aren't you?" she said in a voice warm enough to bake a potato. "How do you know that about me?"

"I didn't until this moment. Not for sure. In my business you go with your hunches. You size people up and let them fill in the details. What did you study in college?"

"Art history. Wellesley '34."

"Know anything about Breughel?"

"I did my senior thesis on Flemish painting. What do you want to know?"

"How is it pronounced?"

"What?"

"Is it Broygel or Broogel?"

"I believe either is correct."

"That's what I thought, but some people can get real stiff if you don't pronounce it their way. Do you agree that Jan, the elder, represents a vision anticipating the reformation in his secular portrayal of village life or is he just nationalistic and anti-Hapsburg?"

"My, my," heaved Helen. I could almost feel her eyelashes batting. "He is cultured, too!"

"I know. I'm just too marvelous for words."

"Well, I am surprised."

"I guess my brows can go just as high as the next guy's when they have to. Spent some time in Vienna before the war. Hung around the Kunsthistorisches museum a lot. There, and the amusement park. It has the biggest ferris wheel in the world. The museum has the best collection of Breughels in the world, but I'm sure I don't have to tell you that."

"No. I know it very well myself."

"Me, I'm especially fond of those paintings of the seasons. You know the ones I mean? 'Returning from The Hunt', 'Driving The Cattle Home'. I remember those two. You know what I like about them?"

"I'm fascinated. Please tell."

"The deception."

"Oh."

"Yeah. If you remember, the scenes in both paintings depict everyday villagers doing everyday things. Right? But did you notice the landscape?"

"Yes."

"It's mountains! Rugged, beautiful, pointy-toothed mountains!"

"I'm not sure I . . ."

"Belgium is flatter than the deck of an aircraft carrier. A gopher mound is the highest landform they have."

"Very interesting."

"That's what I think, too. The joke is on the person looking at the painting because he doesn't get it right away.

"It's a great con and Breughel's still pulling it off four hundred years later. I'd say that was genius, wouldn't you?"

"My, my, Riley Kovachs, you are a perceptive person aren't you? I like a man with a head on his shoulders."

"Keep it up, blondie, flattery will get you most anywhere."

We were about five minutes into her life story, a two hankie affair as far as her childhood was concerned, when I noticed two yellow headlamps in the rearview mirror. Other than a couple brave freight-hauling semis, it was the first vehicle I had seen in nearly an hour. But that's not what bothered me. From the way the lights grew rapidly larger in the mirror I knew the car behind them was traveling at twice my speed. That's what bothered me. If a guy wanted to send himself through a guardrail and on to the promised land I figured that was his business. But if he were also planning to outfit me with a pair of gossamer wings and a trumpet, then I had to draw the line. After all, I hadn't seen **Treasure of The Sierra Madre**, not to mention Alan Ladd's latest giddy-apper and I promised myself I wouldn't think about checking out until at least then.

But the guy in the other car didn't seem to care about my goals in life. When he drew to within a quarter mile he threw on his high beams. The rear-view mirror ricocheted the yellow explosion through my unsuspecting orbs straight to the brain nearly causing it to short circuit. The blindness was only temporary, but it was long enough to cause me to swerve into the lane of a truck lumbering up the grade in the opposite direction. I responded to its loud blasting airhorn and jerked the car back into the lawful lane just in time to prevent both Helen's and my future from being an eternity of cumulus clouds and hosts of Jack Benny look-alike seraphim.

But I had the feeling it was only a temporary condition if the car behind was to have the last say. It closed the remaining gap of two hundred yards in less time than it takes a midget to put on his pants. It was so close I could see the two doughballs in the front seat looking as unfriendly as the night. Dark hats covered part of their faces, but I had the creepy feeling that underneath were a pair of donkey-browed blasters with whom I had had experiences both recent and unpleasant. My attention was jerked back to the twisting licorice they call a road before I could run and tell the principal about it.

"Don't look now, duchess," I said to Helen, "but those guys on our tail are trying to kill us." She snapped her head around. Then without a word she slid from her cozy roost at my elbow to the other end of the seat.

"That doesn't mean we can't be friends, does it?" I said, trying some graveyard whistling. Helen didn't say anything.

The car behind us accelerated abruptly and slammed into the DeSoto's rear bumper. Both Helen and I were jolted forward. My hat slid down over my nose, which made driving very close to impossible. I freed one hand from the wheel and pushed the hat back on my head. Then came the gunshots.

"Any suggestions, Jackson?" I said to Helen, who was sitting like a lump of poured cement in the corner. She didn't say anything. "We will only be able to play cowboys and Indians with them for so long before they catch us. We can't outrun them. Not on this road. We could try to make it to the nearest town and raise a racket. That might drive them off."

Helen didn't say anything. The car was too dark to see the expression on her face. I couldn't tell if she had a case of the "nine-day trembles" or what.

Castaic was less than ten miles away and the last few were pretty straight if I remembered correctly. So it might have been possible. But the boys in the back had some other thoughts on the subject. They rammed us hard again and pulled out and around the DeSoto. I stepped on the gas, but Solly's wreck was no match for the metal brute to my left. It spurted ahead like it was shot from a very large cannon and then sliced sharply back into the right lane cutting us off completely. I swerved to the right to avoid a certain collision. Solly's big blue chrome factory left the pavement. I slammed on the brakes. The tires smoked along the loose rock of the narrow shoulder. Nothing helped. The car was obeying Isaac Newton, not me. Helen screamed at the top of her lungs. The moment the car fishtailed into the guardrail and I saw the white lumber fence splinter on impact, I followed suit.

The only thing that prevented Solly's car from going to DeSoto heaven and Helen and I along with it was a boulder on the oblivion side of the guardrail which threw a low block into the car's right front fender. It brought the car to an abrupt halt the way mountains have been known to stop low-flying airplanes. Helen and I, however, obeyed the laws of motion, if not those on the road. We kept going forward until the windshield changed our minds.

I was still chasing the bats out of my badly rung belfry when I was interrupted by the barrel of a gangster's best friend against my cheek.

"Get outta the car, boyfriend," barked a voice that sounded like steel wool being pulled against a rusty surface. I recognized him without any trouble. It was Dr. Kidney. I think it was then I realized he looked a lot like Whittaker Chambers — large, puffy, with an unmistakably pathological look in his eyes. He pulled open the door of Solly's banged-up DeSoto and grabbed my arm. "Now, boyfriend!" he yapped, unhappy with my tardiness. "This time, you ain't got no witnesses." I looked over at Helen who had been coaxed out of the other side of the car by the second pistolero. "Don't worry about the dame. We got plans for her, too," said the palooka with the gun.

He frisked me with the barrel of his gat. Then he jabbed it into my side. The man had a one-track mind. The other blaster brought Helen around to my side of the car. He wanted a piece of me, too.

"I see our little lesson last night didn't have any effect on you, Kovachs," he said, cracking a very insincere smile.

"I'm a slow learner," I said. "You've get to give these things time."

The man laughed. "That's one thing you just ran out of, wiseguy," he said. "Start moving." He wiggled his gun in the direction of the guardrail.

"Say, you guys wouldn't mind telling me what this thing is all about, would you? Just for friendship's sake. If you're going to do what I think you're going to do, I won't be around to make things hot for anybody. How about it? Like a last request. I'll take it instead of a cigarette."

Doctor Kidney wasn't moved. "We ain't got time for that, bright boy. You're just tryin' to stall." He turned to his partner. "Lemme polish him off. Frank, willya? I'll do it with my hands."

His goombah, who also probably drew a second paycheck as his keeper, pushed him out of the way. "You big fool. We've got our orders. No messy stuff. Nice and clean."

"Like Jake Diltz," I clarified.

"Shut up, mug," said the keeper. "Yeah, nice and clean. Like your car skidding out of control and busting through the guardrail. You got any idea how long it takes to hit bottom around here, boyfriend?"

"No idea. Why don't I run down the road and make a phone call to Dr. I.Q.? I promise to come right back."

"Come on, Frank, lemme bust him up right here, willya?"

"Both of you, shut up and let's get on with it."

I could see the big lummox out of the corner of my eye sulking by the side of Solly's car, but I was too busy with my life flashing before my eyes to go over and console him. Then there was this gun in my back and I was marching down the road angling toward the guardrail. I tried with the questions again, but again only came up with a handful of feathers. But throwing questions at Frank allowed me to turn my head around and look over my shoulder. Helen and Dr. Kidney were standing next to the DeSoto staring forward at the man with the gun. He was twenty feet in front of the car and I was ten feet beyond him walking with my hands raised at the elbow.

There was only one thing I could do that might save the old dermis and it had about as much chance as Vishinsky being invited to an American Legion picnic. But then my options had been greatly reduced, so there was no debate concerning practicality.

I dug my toes into my shoe leather and from a standing walk began sprinting as fast as I could toward the guardrail. What might or, more accurately, what might not have been on its other side at that moment was of no overriding concern.

The railing was ten feet away and I reached it in less time than it takes to read a Hearst newspaper. I leaped into the air to hurdle the three foot fence. I heard a man shout, a gunshot and a woman scream in approximately that order. I would have been more specific about it, but like Dick Powell in **Murder, My Sweet**, who was in a similar jam thanks to the real Miss Trevor, a big black pool formed at my feet. I dove in. It had no bottom.

CHAPTER 16

It was still dark when I came to. My head and shoulder ached like Rockefeller Center had been torn down and rebuilt on my hat and I hadn't the good sense to take it off. I felt around for bullet holes and, finding none, realized my pain had been produced by a twenty foot fall from the guardrail rather than a dose of lead tablets. I was alive and, I hoped, alone. Any further information at that moment would have been sheer guesswork.

I sat up and shook out the cobwebs while trying to find my bearings. A small bright red and yellow fire ball burned a thousand feet below me. I knew without asking that it was Solly's DeSoto. What I didn't know was where Helen was. And there was no one around to ask. Maybe she was in the flaming DeSoto or lying nearby with a couple ounces of metal in her skull. But I had a feeling about her that made me think she was still drawing breath somewhere. I couldn't quite put my finger on it. Maybe it had something to do with faulty knowledge of Flemish art, or maybe she really was the Claire Trevor, a.k.a. Mrs. Grayle, type after all. From the starting gate I had her pegged as a survivor and would have been very surprised to find her scattered around the Grapevine. But I had to take a look for her, even if my better judgement told me she was on her way back to Los Angeles with the Tom and Jerry of homicide.

I climbed hand-over-fist up the rocky side of the hill to the guardrail and the road. Other than the break in the fence and some loose gravel scattered on the highway there was no trace of the mayhem that was played out only a short while ago. I searched the pitch darkness for twenty minutes looking for the blond Leninist from L.A. Nothing. I dusted off my coat and trousers, put a new crease in my hat and lit a Chesterfield. That was the easy part. The hard part was shagging a ride to L.A. I spit-polished my thumb, jerked it south and waited for my luck to improve.

Three cars and two hours later I was picked up by a couple of men in a Buick who were on their way to Los Angeles to look for work. They didn't ask too many questions, which was exactly the way I preferred it. I pulled my hat down over my orbs and put my consciousness on hold. Three hours later it was daylight and we were in Hollywood. The two samaritans dropped me at Main Street near the Baker Building. I put my nose into the breeze and followed it to the nearest cup of coffee.

Following a country quart of murk that tasted like it had been piped in directly from a rig out on Signal Hill and a couple sinkers that did just that, I got a handful of change and went to a phone booth. I looked through the directory and came up with four Hawkins and two Dawkins who carried pill bags. I called them all. It wasn't easy. Getting information from a doctor's receptionist is like eating pancakes without syrup. It can be done, but it's a very unpleasant experience. I finally found my man, sans receptionist, on Olive Street across from Pershing Square. His name was Dawkins and he sounded jittery. He told me to come over right away and to come alone.

I got to Pershing Square in fifteen minutes. Despite its theme, which could only be "Fifty Years of Imperialism", it was a pleasant place. A place with a sense of proportion. Amongst the Spanish War Memorial, an eighteenth century bronze cannon, the World War I statue of a doughboy on a twenty-foot granite base and an iron cannon from the **U.S.S. Constitution**, is a small plaque dedicated "in the memory of Benny, a squirrel," a little furry trooper who, according to the inscription, served his country and his park until one day in '34 when he fell under the tires of a moving car.

Dawkins' office was in an old brick building facing the square. I crossed Olive and hiked up the three flights to his office. The smell of medicinal alcohol and the dreary grayness of the stair reminded me of every dentist and doctor's appointment I had kept as a kid.

Over the phone Dr. Dawkins told me his office number was 310. If he hadn't I might not have found it because his name appeared nowhere on the opaque glass door. I thought that a bit strange. I tried the door, but it was locked, which I also thought peculiar. I rapped on the glass.

"Who's there?" came a voice from inside.

"It's Kovachs," I replied.

"What do you want?"

"I just called you on the phone. Remember?" I heard a chair scrape across the floor and footsteps coming in my direction. The door opened part way and a man stuck his head out.

"Can't be too careful. You will please step inside and take off your coat and empty your pockets."

"Hey, Doc, I didn't come here to get a physical. I want some information about . . ."

"Shhh!" Dr. Dawkins cut me off. He grabbed my arm and pulled me inside, locking the door behind me. "I know what you want," he said. "What I don't know is why you want it. You see there are several people who wish me dead for what I know. So you will please remove your coat and empty your pockets before we proceed further."

Dr. Dawkins was tall, forty and as angular as a geometry lesson. He looked more than a little frightened, but was in complete control of himself and the situation. I obliged him without further question. The small gun he was pointing at me made it no contest.

Satisfied I wasn't packing anything more lethal than Raymond Chandler's latest, he ushered me into his inner office. He locked the door behind us and went quickly over to the large black metal desk in the middle of the room and picked up a squashed pack of cigarettes. He nervously pecked at it until he forced one out. His hand shivered as he put the flame of a desk model Ronson to the tobacco. All of a sudden I felt as cold as he looked. The first drag off his straw seemed to relax him some. Anyway, he set the gun down on the desk.

"So, just who are you, mister? And what's your game?" he said.

"Name's Kovachs, Doc. And I gave up games when I lost the dice to my Parchesi set."

The Doctor squinted at me like I had just told him I

wasn't going to pay my bill. "Don't crack wise with me, mister, whoever you are. I must be nuts to let you in here in the first place. On the phone you said you were a friend of Larry Berger and Dalton Trumbo. What do you want from me?"

"Relax, Doc," I said. "We're not going to get anywhere with you sitting there waiting to go off like a bomb in the desert. I'm a private investigator from Frisco who has been dragged kicking and screaming into this mess. Hell, I have a ticket to see Goodman at the Orpheum tonight." I reached into my wallet and produced the ducat. "And that's where I'd much rather be. But I met this little guy who changed my mind. A little guy named Jake Diltz. He's the reason I'm here."

"Jake Diltz!" the doctor repeated breathlessly. "Jake Diltz is the only person beside myself who knows the full story of what's going on." Doctor Dawkins smiled slightly and took a big nosefull of air. He was as close to relaxed as I had known him. But it was only a passing thing.

"Then I'm afraid you're a minority of one, Doc," I said. "Jake Diltz was murdered night before last."

Dr. Dawkins didn't say anything right away. His eyes became glazed. He stared right through me. His cigarette burned unattended in the ashtray at his elbow. A thick yellow-gray rope of smoke rose from it directly into his eyes. He didn't seem to notice or care. From beyond the open window a dog with baritone tonsils barked without stopping. Doctor Dawkins' eyes were like lichee nuts pasted on the far wall. After a moment I tried to peel them off.

"Say, just what's going on here, pal?" I demanded to know. "A movie actress is going to have brain surgery. So they say. Bad as that may sound to you and me, it hardly seems reason to have a man killed. Not to mention yours truly who has been playing tag with a couple of gorillas who've been trying to cancel my stamp ever since I got to town. Now I've got a doctor who doesn't have his name on his door, keeps it locked and has just gone ga-ga on me."

Doctor Dawkins was still someplace else. I got up from my chair and walked over to him. I grabbed his shoulders and shook. "Snap out of it, man. I've got to get some answers from you. Like pronto. Or I'll be snipping out paper dolls before long."

Doctor Dawkins reeled in his eyeballs and focused them on me. He cleared his throat and reached for his cigarette in the ashtray, but found only a long gray ash instead.

"Sorry, Kovachs," he said. "I was just thinking about poor Jake. I'm next, you know. Maybe today, maybe tomorrow, maybe next week, but they'll get me. There's no doubt about it. No doubt at all!"

"Get a grip on yourself, man," I yelled into Dr. Dawkins' face. "You sound just like Jake Diltz did!"

"And for good reason. He knew they were going to kill him. And now they're going to kill me!"

"Who, man, who? Who's going to kill you? Who is it that's got you so jerked up?"

"Why, the C.I.A.! I thought it was obvious."

"Nothing is obvious to me. I come from the dumb side of town. Why don't you spell it out for me nice and slow in big capital letters."

Dr. Dawkins looked at me wistfully. "Yes, I guess that would be the best way. I don't want this secret to die with me. Yes, somebody has got to know the full story. And carry the knowledge forward."

With that bit of self-encouragement Dr. Dawkins snapped out of his trance and became all business.

Even the fear which he had worn around his neck like a cast iron stethescope disappeared. He pushed everything on his desk to one side and placed a small key into a locked drawer, pulling out several thick files which he laid in front of him. He motioned to me to pull my chair closer to the desk. I did.

"Okay, here goes," he said, taking a deep breath. "I worked with the O.S.S. during the war. I was one of "Wild Bill" Donovan's fair-haired boys lured from private practice to do intelligence work. It was the chance of a lifetime for a young man with ambition. I jumped at it. Adventure, intrigue, espionage. All that stuff. To a guy who had spent the previous ten years in L.A. listening to disturbed men vent their hatred for their fathers and guilt-ridden women talk about their jealousy of their children, who wouldn't?

"I was sent to China in late '44 to interrogate prisoners of war. Not the Japanese, mind you, but the Communist Chinese. Well, anyway, a lot of it was experimental. Drugs, psychological torture, punitive surgery, insulin shock. Things like that. After the war, the service encouraged a lot of us to stay on. Sort of twisted our arms in a way we couldn't resist. But most of us would probably have worked for nothing. It was all very exciting. They created the C.I.A. and we continued our work. Just like wartime, only no war. And we didn't use Chinese Communists for guinea pigs. We used people in this country. Prisoners, patients in mental hospitals, volunteers from the military.

"Well, I was working out of R and D at Langley. The Agency had this big project under wraps. The doctors and scientists were told to try and find if there was a way to condition and control a person's thought process. And his behavior too. You know, like could a human being be turned into a robot?"

I had to admit I was a bit skeptical. "Sounds like Buck Rogers to me, Doc," I said. "Why would the C.I.A. want to turn out human robots?"

"My dear Mr. Kovachs, you would be surprised what goes on in the C.I.A. Absolutely surprised."

"Oh, I don't know. I'm from the streets. Hillman and Murray standing up to Truman. That would surprise me! Not much else, I'm afraid."

"Maybe. Anyway, the Agency brass was spooked by the idea that the Russians could force top communist leaders to condemn themselves at the Moscow Trials. The RAND Corporation is at this moment putting together a major report on Soviet uses of hypnosis in their public trials. Then there are those purge trials shaping up in Hungary. The same thing. The Agency figured the Russians must have tampered with the defendants' minds to get them to do what they did. And if they could do it to their own, so the thinking went, what's to prevent them from capturing our agents and getting them to spill top secrets? Nothing! And worse, they could turn our agents against us without our knowing about it.

"This isn't just paranoid speculation, either. The Agency has knowledge that the Russians are conducting experiments with truth-producing drugs in the Crimea. This is making Agency top hats break out in a cold sweat. Now they've launched this project to find methods to control the mind. They're giving it top priority."

"I'll bet this business with the Mindzsenty trial in Hungary poured some gasoline on the fire," I interjected.

"Exactly! The Agency is convinced the Russians are winning the race to alter and control the mind. It is a race they are not prepared to lose. And that's where Jake Diltz and I fit in. Or don't fit in, looking at it from their point of view."

I lit a smoke and offered the pack to Dr. Dawkins. He refused and was irritated by my interruption.

"I left the C.I.A., Kovachs, when I learned the full implications of what they wanted us to do. Only problem is, you don't leave the C.I.A. You escape! If you're lucky, very lucky, maybe you can outrun them for a while. I've been running for almost six months.

"Look, it's one thing interrogating prisoners of war and conducting experiments to unlock the secrets of the mind. But it's something quite different to maim and torture a person's brain, not in the name of science, but ideology! Ours versus theirs. Democracy versus communism. I could see where it was heading and I didn't want any part of it. I got scared and left. I took some of their secrets with me."

"I think they frown on that sort of thing, don't they, Doc?"

"I'm no spy, Kovachs. I'm just a man who knows too much. Eleven months ago the Agency launched the project. It was so hush-hush it didn't even have a code name. Here, look at this memo. I'm not supposed to have it, but I made a copy of it. They want it back."

Dr. Dawkins pushed a small piece of paper toward me. It had no heading and no signature. Just a series of digits which were probably some kind of code. The memo read in part:

mission of the project:

1] evaluation and development of any method by which we can get information from a person

against his will and without his knowledge.

2] **how can we counter the above measures if the measures are used against us?**

3] **can we get control of an individual to the point where he will do our bidding against his will and even against such fundamental laws of nature such as self-preservation?**

I whistled through my teeth.

"Exactly!" said Dr. Dawkins. "And what are these methods that will turn a normal, everyday person into a wind-up doll for the Central Intelligence Agency? I'll tell you. Fatigue, hunger, drugs, hypnosis, toxic substances and endocrine and other ductless gland products, such as hormone injections. Then there's electro-shock and psychosurgery. I could go on, but I think you get the idea."

"And how," I said. "But where does Jake Diltz and Frances Farmer come into the picture? I'm getting less dumb, Doc, but how about giving me the crib sheet to all this."

"Diltz was a private investigator from Seattle. I didn't know him from a bump on the log until one day Larry Berger, a screenwriter friend of mine, told me he met a man who was all worked up over Frances Farmer and what had been done to her in that mental hospital in Washington. At first, Larry thought he was a little touched in the head. But then the man started to make more sense and, since Larry used to know Frances Farmer at Paramount before the war and had heard from sources near the family that a brain operation was being considered, he took a personal interest."

"Like maybe about three hundred dollars worth of interest?" I said.

"If you mean did Larry hire the man and pay him a retainer, I think the answer is yes, though I have no idea how much."

"It's not important."

"It was a couple days after Larry told me all this that something clicked in my mind. It took that long for me to make any associations. Mental hospital, drugs, psychosurgery. It started turning the wheels in my head and I recalled sitting in a cocktail bar in Georgetown with a couple C.I.A. project directors discussing our 'volunteer' subjects. I remembered one of them saying that it was unofficial Agency policy to concentrate on mental patients because they were crazy and nobody would listen to them if they started to complain. And if something went wrong during the experiment, well that could be explained away easy enough. It was a perfect setup, really. Inmates in mental hospitals have fewer rights than mass murderers on death row. And since they're certified insane, nobody, but nobody would ever take them seriously.

"So, anyway, this man says he especially likes to go after the 'famous whackos'. That's just how he put it — 'famous whackos'. I guess it was a feeling of power to experiment on some well-known personality or professional person who was locked away in an asylum. I don't remember. I thought pretty much as he did at the time."

Dr. Dawkins' eyes turned away from me. He wasn't embarrassed, exactly. Remorse maybe. Even regret.

He felt around his pockets for something to smoke. He came up with a crushed package of Camels. He peeled the cellophane and paper from one last remaining butt, put it to his lips and gave it heat. He took a hard pull on it. The burning tip crackled like a bowl of Rice Krispies. When he opened his mouth to speak both words and smoke came pouring out.

"So, I asked Larry to put me in touch with this man. Just to trade notes. I was curious and I wanted to talk to somebody, somebody who might know what I knew. I thought maybe this man's a fellow refugee from the Agency.

"To make a long story short, I met Jake Diltz and he told me about Frances Farmer and her imprisonment at Steilacoom and the things they were doing to her. He told me about a Congressman,too, and what the F.B.I. did to him."

"Sort of rang a bell, I bet."

"It rang a bell, alright, but there was nothing to tie Frances Farmer and lobotomy to the C.I.A. It was simply a curious coincidence at that point."

"You needed a smoking gun."

"Something like that."

"And?"

"And we found Dr. Walter J. Freeman."

"Freeman? Jake mentioned him."

"I'm sure he did. Freeman might not have anything to do with all of this. With the C.I.A. you can never be sure of anything, if you know what I mean. However, this man Freeman makes it hard not to draw some interesting conclusions. What do you know about him, Kovachs?"

"Only what you're about to tell me, Doc." The corners of Dr. Dawkins's mouth tugged a little suggesting a grin was there somewhere.

"Walter J. Freeman," he said, "is the head of Neurology at George Washington University in

D.C. He is better known as the father of American lobotomy and has, in recent years, perfected a new method of cutting the brain. He calls it 'transorbital lobotomy'. Others, even the psychosurgeons who use it, call it "the ice pick lobotomy".

"Whoa, Doc. I'm back on the dumb side of town. Transorbital lobotomy? Sounds Greek and gruesome to me."

Dr. Dawkins took a long drag on his Camel before squeezing the fire out of it between his thumb and the metal ashtray. Smoke poured from his nostrils as he shoved his chair back from the desk. He got up and went to the three-drawer metal filing cabinet that hugged the wall on the other side of the room. I leafed through his folder of C.I.A. memos and clippings. I stopped at a couple of names on a piece of paper. They meant nothing to me other than the fact they were C.I.A. psychiatrists and worked as a team and were attached to a nameless Southern California mental hospital. A bell began pealing in a far off valley of my mind.

"Here's the information on psychosurgery I've collected," said Dr. Dawkins returning to his desk. He pushed a thick brown folder at me. "I've been collecting everything written on the subject since 1946. That was my area of specialty as a researcher with the Agency, you know. I never did one, but they figured since I was a trained psychiatrist it should be my area. Psychosurgery, and shock therapy, both insulin and electro-convulsive. I'm a self-made expert. Go ahead and look through the file. I'll try to boil it down to layman's terms for you so you can get the gist of it.

In addition to some clippings from magazines and scientific journals, there were photstatic copies of medical treatises delivered at conferences of surgeons and psychiatrists. Walter J. Freeman seemed to be the author or subject of the lion's share of both the clippings and scholarly papers. One was titled simply "Transorbital Lobotomy". It was a paper read last year by Freeman at the American Psychiatric Association convention. I skimmed through it not really absorbing very much until I came to a picture of a living head with a long, thin needle sticking out of an eye socket. I whistled through my teeth. Dr. Dawkins knew what I had seen.

"That's the way a lot of people react when they see these pictures," he said. "Lobotomy is a fairly new technique in psychiatric medicine. The first was performed by two Portuguese doctors named Moniz and Almeda in 1936. It was a pre-frontal lobotomy. A surgical knife was inserted through burr holes drilled in the skull to cut and separate the frontal lobes of the brain."

Dr. Dawkins pointed to his forehead to show me where the frontal lobe area is located. I asked the obvious question — "What's so special about the frontal lobes that they need cutting?"

"Good question," said Dr. Dawkins. "Let's hear it straight from the horse's mouth." He leafed through the folder and pulled out several papers stapled together. "Here, Moniz himself says that after a period of personal meditation he concluded, ah, here it is and I quote — 'to cure these patients we must destroy the more or less fixed arrangements of cellular connections that exist in the brain and particularly those which are related to the frontal lobes'! End of quote. In other words, Kovachs, cut, destroy, annihilate the cell connections of the brain!"

"But why that particular part of the brain, Doc?"

"Yes, I'm coming to that. The dominant school of thought in the field of psychiatric medicine believes that each region of the brain is responsible for specific human physical, mental and emotional activity. The frontal lobes are said to be the seat of, among other things, emotion and motivation. It follows then that surgically interrupting the connections of that area will reduce unpleasant and disabling emotional responses among those psychotic patients."

"Is there any truth to that belief?"

"Some. Some of the theories are indeed based upon medical fact. A lot more, however, is pure voodoo. Science's knowledge of the brain and its functions is on about the same level of sophistication as internal medicine was in the thirteenth century. Then religion, superstition and politics were as important in making medical diagnoses and treating patients as any known scientific and medical fact. And like the medical practioners of the Middle Ages, many of today's psychiatric practitioners operate on the same premise. If a patient is afflicted, well, cut off or cut out that affliction. A leg, an arm, a brain. It's all the same.

"Kovachs, I've been in medicine all my adult life and it's not easy for me to say these things about my profession, my colleagues. But the truth is there. Too much of medical history is strewn with amputated limbs, burned torsos, mountains of mutilated flesh — a grim monument to man's scientific ignorance and prejudice. Now we are mutilating the mind with the same zeal we historically applied leeches to draw out a fever in the brain. Lobotomy is nothing but a ghoulish crusade to cure mental disturbance. And that's the best thing that can be said about it. Mutilating the mind for political purposes, i.e., the

Agency project I was part of, is the worst."

Dr. Dawkins stopped abruptly. He jerked his head and shot a glance out the window like he expected to see or hear something. "Don't mind me, Kovachs," he said, returning to me and the open folder on his desk. "I can get pretty worked up over this, sometimes. I guess it's because I've been a part of it for so long."

"Save your appologies, Doc," I said. "You should hear me when I get going on Flemish art or the Stalin school of literary criticism. But how about Freeman and this ice pick operation? Have any more dope on them?"

"You bet!" Dr. Dawkins returned to the thick brown folder. He pulled out several pages as he spoke. "The transorbital lobotomy was developed by an Italian named Fiambretti a few years before the war. Freeman and his associate, a Dr. Watts, brought it to this country, perfecting it along the way. Basically, Kovachs, it is a very simple procedure involving the insertion of a leucotome — the ice pick — under a patient's eyelid and driving it into the prefrontal area of the brain. Then, while lodged in the brain, the leucotome is swung in an arc that severs the prefrontal lobes. This type of operation has gained wide acceptance in psychiatric circles since the war ended. And there has been a literal explosion of transorbital lobotomies in the past year. Here, take a look at these articles."

Dr. Dawkins pointed to a small newsy article from **Science Newsletter** that hailed the transorbital lobotomy as "a safe, simple, ten minute operation that is really restoring mentally sick people to health and sanity." Another article quoted Dr. Freeman saying the beauty of his technique was that it could be performed by a psychiatrist in his office. No long, bloody surgery to upset the relatives. Just a table, an ice pick and of course a patient. In a third article Freeman suggested the patient be prepared to have his gray matter stabbed by strapping him down and shooting him a grownup dose of electricity to the brain.

Dr. Dawkins walked to the open window and stood there looking out while I went over the clippings and medical papers. Another item in **Science Newsletter** cheered the transorbital lobotomy as "helping to clear the back wards of our mental hospitals and relieving overcrowding in state mental hospitals." No vegetables here. The transorbitalized were put right back on the street.

It was getting a whole lot clearer. G.I.s returned from the front to wander around town, shell-shocked from the horror of war. This was an obvious embarrassment to the black tie and martini crowd who are always gathering at opera houses and civic auditoriums to raise money for their favorite charity. So they packed them away on troop trains to state mental farms. Only the farms weren't designed to hold all the war wounded. In short order the hospitals became collection houses for the scarred and socially misfit vets. The hospitals became sardine factories and this caused even more embarrassment and scandal for the genteel class. So, along comes Walter J. Freeman with his magic bullet and — presto, thrust, wiggle and 'on your way, son' — no more overcrowding.

Nice and tight, that. An operation that cures mental illness and the asylum housing shortage at the same time. A lot like the way General Motors is run, I'm sure. The only liability, according to Dr. Dawkins and the few who criticize Freeman and his retainers, was hundreds and maybe thousands of ice-picked victims who are wandering around the streets looking for their memories. But then, that was the point.

I looked over some more of the articles by Walter J. Freeman to find the D.C. headshrinker is a believer that the key to curing mental illness is in obliterating a portion of the patient's memory. One of his camp followers wrote in a paper delivered at a recent American Psychiatrical Association meeting:

> **Lobotomy frees the patient from the tyranny of his own past, from the anxious self-searching that has become too terrible to endure, and at the same time renders him largely indifferent to future problems and to the opinions of other people.**

I winced as I shook out a Chesterfield and set fire to the end furthest from my mouth. A person gets his brain cut up and he's left with no memory of the past, no concern for the future and without regard to the present and the people around him. Seems the only difference between that and death is the involuntary beating of the heart. But, by God, the patient has been treated and cured of his mental illness.

An article written by Freeman before the war tied a pretty yellow ribbon around the whole thing. He wrote:

> **It has been said that if we don't think correctly, it is because we haven't 'brains enough'. Maybe it will be shown that a mentally ill patient can think more clearly and more constructively with less brain in actual operation.**

In another article he turned political.

> **It is better for the patient to have a simplified**

intellect capable of elementary acts than an intellect where there reigns this disorder of subtle synthesis. Society can accomadate itself to the most humble laborer, but it justifiably distrusts the mad thinker.

Witch burning in white coats. More thorough than any rag tag select committee of Congressmen. I flipped to another article on case studies. One passage of Freeman's prose jumped off the page.

Women who've had lobotomies make better housekeepers. They make up the great majority of the case loads and the success of psychosurgeons. It is difficult for a man to support a family after lobotomy. But it is easier for a woman to do housework.

Take a woman, a thinking woman who is a lousy housekeeper and you've got Frances Farmer and Dr. Freeman's dream victim.

"Dr. Frankenstein has nothing on this bird," I said closing the folder and pushing it away from me. Dr. Dawkins still stood like a downtown mailbox staring out the window. He didn't say anything. "I said your boy Freeman sounds like more fun than a three-sided box of tarantulas."

"Kovachs, come here a minute," Dr. Dawkins said, ignoring my remark. I joined him at the window. "You see that man standing next to the brass cannon? The one reading the newspaper?"

"Looks like muscle for someone without a whole lot of money."

"Have you ever seen him before?"

I shook my head. "Only his type."

"Are you sure?"

"What are you driving at, Doc?"

Dr. Dawkins turned from the window. "Let's get out of the line of fire." I jumped sideways. "I'm sure that's the same man who was in the park yesterday. And the day before."

"So? City parks are full of creeps and cheap hoods betweeen jobs. He could be anybody."

"I don't think so. I think he's been watching me. What is he waiting for? He must know who I am. Why doesn't he just come up here and get it over with?" Dr. Dawkins voice, as well as his lip, trembled. He turned to me and grabbed the lapels of my coat and began shaking me hysterically. "Kovachs, you've got to believe me! You've got to take this information with you! It's got to live on! Nobody will listen to me! Nobody believes the American government could do such terrible things. Nobody . . ."

I broke Dr. Dawkins's grip on my lapels. "Take it easy, pal, willya? These things will break right off."

Dr. Dawkins took out a handkerchief from his rear pocket and mopped his dripping, flushed brow. "Forgive me, Kovachs," he said. "I'm at the brink. The very brink. I've taken my information to the press and the politicians and you know what they say?" He pointed his index finger at his temple and made a circular gesture. "They think I'm off my rocker. Nuts! I went to the people in the Progressive Party here in L.A. Hell, for all I know they may be a bunch of communists. I didn't care. They smiled and patted me on the head and said, 'very interesting'. And that is the most positive response I've gotten from anybody." Dr. Dawkins threw his hands up in the air to illustrate his frustration.

He walked around his desk and slumped his cargo into the stuffed leather chair behind it. His head dropped into his chest. He covered his eyes with one hand. His whole upper body began shaking ever so slightly. It lasted only a moment. Then he stiffened his back and slammed the desk hard with a closed fist.

"Damn it!" he barked. "This is no time to go to pieces. Got to face this thing like a man. Kovachs, did you read those articles by Freeman? His articles on lobotomy?" I nodded. "Well, then you know something about the man's work. But you don't know the man. You've got to know the man to understand just how utterly evil this whole business is. I'm not saying Freeman's a C.I.A. doctor or even working on the project we talked about. Like I said, in the Agency you can never be sure about some things, especially the people you work with. That's the way they structure it. Anyway, you're interested in the Farmer case and I happen to know about lobotomy and Dr. Walter J. Freeman."

"I am all ears, Doc," I said, offering him a Chesterfield. This time he took one. We both smoked while he talked.

"You see, Freeman and his leucotome — that's the medical name for the ice pick — have been traveling around the country visiting mental hospitals and performing transorbital lobotomies on hundreds of patients. Thousands. It's public knowledge. You can read about it in the newspapers. Freeman likes to keep a very high profile. The man is a publicity hound."

"Doesn't sound like the way a C.I.A. doctor would act, does it, Doc?" I interrupted.

"That's the point, Kovachs. It isn't. But maybe the splashy way he performs is itself a cover. I mean who would expect a grandstand player like Freeman to be tied up with a top secret Agency project? But then maybe Freeman is just a showboat and has nothing at all to do with the Agency or the project. It might be just a case of two separate entities sharing some common concerns. Like I said, who knows? But here's the point, Kovachs." Dr. Dawkins scooted his chair closer to the desk and spread his arms over the file folders. He spoke directly into my face. "Freeman is traveling to Washington at this very moment. He's due in Tacoma sometime tomorrow or the next day. He's scheduled to visit Western State Hospital at Steilacoom. And he's packing his tools. He's going to operate on a couple dozen poor souls. I guess I don't have to tell you the name of Steilacoom's star inmate."

"Frances Farmer," I said almost reflexively, stating what was as obvious as the law of gravity.

"See how it all fits into place, Kovachs?"

I nodded. I did.

"I want you to see the good doctor in action, Kovachs. I want you to know him like I do."

"Might be a good idea, but a bit difficult unless I were an inmate or a colleague, don't you think?"

"This is where I can help. Remember I told you what a publicity hound he is? Well, I've got a film of the esteemed professor of neurology at work!"

"Home movies? He has home movies? How tacky."

"It's only about ten minutes long, but it will show you everything you will want to know about Dr. Walter J. Freeman and the transorbital lobotomy."

"Great! Where's he playing? The Pantages or Grauman's?"

"Hardly. Right here in this office. Tonight. I have the film at home. I'd go get it and show you right now, but I've got a couple of patients coming in this afternoon. I guess this evening will be soon enough. Meet me back here at seven o'clock?"

"Might be a good idea if I stick with you when you go for the film. The man in the park and all."

Dr. Dawkins shook his head. "No, I don't want the man outside to connect you with me. Besides he can only follow one of us if we go separately."

I smiled. "You'd make a pretty good shamus, Doc. You know that?"

"Is that a compliment?"

"Could be. Say, while we're on the subject, ever hear of a couple mind readers named Smythe and Jonas? They claim to work out of a shrink joint near here called Crescentview.

Dr. Dawkins shook his head indifferently while reaching for my Chesterfields lying on the desk. I described the two brown tweed caballeros down to their hair lotion. Dr. Dawkins's face turned the color of someone who might have washed up on the beach following a storm. He tried to light his cigarette, but the muscles in his arm and hand wouldn't hold still.

"Seven o'clock, Kovachs," he said blankly after a long minute of silence. "Please be prompt."

I lit two cigarettes and passed one to Dr. Dawkins. He took it while staring right past me. I looked hard into his eyes. They told me nothing I didn't already know. I put on my hat and walked to the door. I turned around to say goodby, but stopped myself. Dr. Dawkins didn't seem to know I was in the room.

CHAPTER 17

It was a few ticks this side of noon when I left Dr. Dawkins and I was more tired than the muscles in a rich dowager's face. Although I had been unconscious on the side of a mountain for a good many hours, I couldn't bring myself to count it as sleep.

I walked into a hotel a couple blocks from Pershing Square where I found a desk man who tossed a key at me for a fin. After seeing the room I should have tossed it back at him, but my barking dogs and fat eyelids told me it was just as good as the presidential suite at the Ambassador. I took off my shoes, loosened my tie and hit the bed like a dropped bowling ball. In a moment I forgot everything I had ever known.

I came out of it several hours later. The room smelled stale. Rather, it still smelled stale. Like a small gymnasium after a double overtime basketball game. I opened the window. The air smelled a lot like a box of old books that has been kept in a damp place too long. It was still day, but the hard, dull orange winter sunlight that pushed its way through the dirt-streaked window was doing a fast fade.

I splashed some water on my face to wash away the sleep. I towelled off and pulled the room's only chair under the window and planted my goods therein. I had a couple hours to kill before catching the early show at Dr. Dawkins's office. I lit a factory-rolled ounce of the stuff that made Virginia famous and settled back to pick up Philip Marlowe where I had left him. It had been a while.

The last time I looked in on L.A.'s most famous peeper, a dark senorita with four gears forward was playing hard to get with him. Hard to get as a traffic ticket in a bus zone, that is. But Marlowe's on the case and there is no time for "the Gonzales", as he calls her.

No, Marlowe is more interested in doing a good turn for "the Gonzales's" friend, an actress named Mavis Weld. Seems she is in the brine up to her lovely hips. She was spotted by the house dick at the hotel where Dr. Hambleton/G.W. Hicks took an ice pick behind the ear. Given what I had just learned at Dr. Dawkins's knee about the other use for an ice pick, the murders in **The Little Sister** gave me an extra good dose of the heebie-jeebies.

To make a long and growingly complex story a bit shorter, Mavis Weld wasn't buying and tossed Marlowe out on his ear. He gets steamed hotter than a pismo clam and drives around L.A. for a long time pitching crabapples at everything until he cools off.

He loosens his collar and returns to his office to pick up some film that ties Dr. Hambleton/G.W. Hicks, Mavis Weld and the missing brother Orrin together. He opens his door to find a fat, greasy man in sky blue pants sitting in his chair. The man is accompanied by a runny-nose junkie who doesn't say much other than "in a pig's valise". The fat man is named Joseph P. Toad, if that's possible, and he is there to lay five C's on Marlowe. What for, Marlowe asks? For nothing, Toad tells him. Toad says he is just "a guy that wants to help out a guy that don't want to make trouble for a guy," and tells Marlowe all he has to do to earn the lettuce is "You ain't looking for nobody. You don't have time to work for nobody. You didn't hear a thing or see a thing."

Marlowe's feelings are hurt and he gets tough with Toad. The fat man backs down and tells Marlowe he is pitching his heft for Sheridan Ballou, big time movie agent and pain in the nose.

Toad and the junkie leave and there follows a little romp around the rosy with Orfamy Quest who just happens to pop in on Marlowe a minute after the Tweedle brothers split. She tells the private eye some more corn-fed fibs about her missing brother while trying to sit in Marlowe's lap. She is expecting him to wrinkle her dress in the way only he-men know how to do. Instead, Marlowe tells little Orfamy he thinks her sister is in the movies. Mavis, maybe? This sends the little ingenue from Kansas running out of his office screaming, "I hate you!"

Dames!

CHAPTER 18

I left Marlowe trading quips with Sheridan Ballou in the agent's office. Then I left my room and then the hotel. I walked toward Spring Street looking for supper. I ended up at the Clifton Cafeteria on South Olive. I polished off a chicken fried steak and a plopping of potatoes that looked real tired. But the price was right. So right, I didn't even complain about the plastic palm trees potted among the plastic boulders. And I paid little regard to the dark, amateur portraits of the Apostles that lined the walls, illuminated by small neon tubes. As I walked out a young lady dressed like a missionary home on leave shyly pushed a little newspaper into my hand. I took the copy of **Food 4 Thought** and walked out into the night. I dropped it in a can before crossing the street.

It was still an hour before show time so I walked into a gin mill on Fourth for a bracer. I had a couple that were wet, strong and straight up. I passed some of the time eavesdropping on a conversation the bartender was having with one of the customers. Actually I wasn't eavesdropping. The barkeep had a voice like a regimental cannon and anyone who was in the bar was an eavesdropper by definition. The man looked like he was born to tend bar and tell stories. He was more Irish than a bottle of stout — short, wide, hands as big as pillows with the texture of a blackberry bush and a face as ruddy and bumpy as a logging road in Oregon. He was lecturing the man on the other side of the bar on the I.R.A. and the Easter Rebellion. He was for it and I suspect in it from the way his face twisted up every time he mentioned the British.

The place was virtually deserted. A few fellows in workmen's clothes trying to take the sting out of the day's labor sat huddled around a table near the door. A couple more citizens sat languidly at the bar staring into glasses filled with different colored liquids searching for solutions to life's little problems. They appeared to be the kind that have been searching for a long time.

Words from Vaughn Monroe's throaty baritone pipes came rolling out of the big plastic and chrome upright juke box that was braced against the wall opposite the bar. An oldtimer at the end of the trough, who had been slumped over the wood with his head tucked into a bent arm, raised his head slowly as Monroe began his tale about the ghost riders. The old boy tried to light a cigarette, but couldn't keep the rolled tobacco in his mouth. His head dropped to the bar again and he was off on a rum holiday. It's doubtful he was even remotely aware of Monroe's cowpoke and the "herd of red-eye cows he saw a-plowin' through the ragged sky and up a cloudy draw."

At a quarter of seven I gathered up my change, snuffed the butt of my Chesterfield in a tin ashtray and walked out into the chilly night headed for Dr. Dawkins's movie house.

The building in which his office was located was empty and had a lot of that eerie creepiness all such places have after they close for the day. I don't know if it was just the night or the fact that it was empty, evacuated, like maybe a bomb was set to go off and nobody thought to tell me. But I knew I didn't like it.

I climbed the stairs to Dr. Dawkins's office. The hall was darker than a Kansas tornado. I felt my way along the wall to the office door. The door was unlocked so I didn't bother to knock. I called out the sawbone's name. A honking horn on the street below was the only reply. I called out again. Not even the horn answered back.

I walked through the waiting room to the inner office. A slight, sweet smell hung in the dark. The only light came from street lamps and a hissing neon sign outside the room's only window. I could see a film projector set up in the middle of the room and a white tripod screen in a corner. I groped for the overhead light switch and flipped it on.

A buzzing sound like a radio with a bum tube preceeded the flickering blue, then yellow-white overhanging tube light. Once my eyes adjusted to the brightness I saw Dr. Dawkins. He was sitting quietly at his desk with his head tilted slightly to one side. He might have been napping but for the bloody brown mess at his right temple. I walked over to him. A small calibre pistol clasped in the fingers at the end of an arm that dangled loosely down to the floor seemed to say it all. Dr. Dawkins had beat his tormentors to the punch.

Maybe that held some satisfaction for him, but it was still a terrible way to go. Even though I knew him to be a terrified man, a man who didn't want to end up dumped in an alley like Jake Diltz, I thought this an extreme and premature thing to do. I didn't figure Dr. Dawkins the type to cop the big plea.

I rolled my shoulders and sighed. I reached across the desk for the phone to call the cops. As I began dialing I glanced at the film projector and noticed a small reel of film threaded and ready to roll. I put the phone down. The cops could wait. If my guess was right the tiny celluloid reel was the attraction I had come to see.

I turned the projector on and the overhead light off. The projector made a droning, clicking sound as it cast the images on the screen. No credits, no music, no voices. Just pictures. A number of people were crowded into a room whose furniture had been shoved to one side. A couple of the people were wearing white surgical smocks. The others were in civilian dress. At least four people were toting large portrait cameras with flash attachments.

A tall man of about fifty appeared to be in charge. He had a large head with closely cropped hair. A pair of piercing eyes kept the peace over a severe face that was decorated with a gray and white mustache and goatee. His was the kind of face that didn't draw attention, it commanded it!

The man, who had to be Freeman from what Dr. Dawkins had told me earlier, clapped his hands.The others in the room responded instantly by retreating to the walls leaving the tall bearded man standing alone in the center of the room.

In the next moment a groggy, unshaven man clad only in a hospital gown was escorted by two attendants to the middle of the room to face Freeman. The man could not stand under his own power and had an unfocused and faraway look in his eyes. Freeman grabbed the man by the shoulders and shook him. Then he leaned over and appeared to be shouting something into his ear. But like the rum-soaked citizen I had just left in a neighborhood bar, the man was on holiday and not available to anyone.

Someone wheeled a metal hospital gurney to the center of the room and the two attendants placed the man on it. As he was made to lie down a mild look of terror swept his previously vacant face.

Freeman clapped his hands again and two assistants appeared carrying a large piece of outstretched cloth. The fabric was held up behind the man lying on the gurney. Then Freeman motioned with his hands and bright lamps, both floor and hand-held, were brought closer, making the area around the man on the gurney only slightly less brighter than the surface of the sun.

Another assistant came up to Freeman carrying a small box in two outstretched hands. The small ceremony implied that it might contain the Freeman family jewels and stock certificates. In a sense it did. Then, in a manner that can only be described as ritualistic, Freeman removed from the box a shiny metal object that looked like a letter opener that had been mated with an ice pick. He held it upright next to his face and pointed to it. Then he began moving his lips. He looked like he was trying to sell the thing to America's housewives. Freeman held various poses for the next few moments as the shutterbugs swarmed around him snapping off pictures.

I reached inside my coat for tobacco and matches. I shook out a Chesterfield and lit it without dropping my eyeballs from the screen. The powerful sweet smell of sulphur and phosphorous from a match held too close to my nose shot up my nostrils, stopping just this side of a sneeze.

Freeman bent over the man lying on the gurney, always stage front, and with one hand raised the drowsy man's eyelid. With the other hand he made a swinging movement brandishing his instrument. He swept it in a wide arc, finally bringing it down and inserting it under the man's eyelid. Water streamed involuntarily from my own unblinking eyes. Freeman jerked the ice pick while it was still lodged under the man's eyelid. Then he stepped back from his patient. The photographers moved in close to shoot pictures of the man with the ice pick two inches into his eye socket.

In a moment Freeman cleared them away and approached the man on the gurney again. Then with the moves and strength of a man driving steel, he plunged the instrument into the man's brain.

I jumped and jerked my head away from the screen. I tasted the chicken fried steak in my throat. It took everything I had to keep it down. I was away from the film only a second, but by the time I regained the courage to return my eyes to the screen, the "operation" was not only over, but the man on the gurney was on his feet and was being walked wobbly out of the camera range by the two attendants who had brought him in.

During the next five minutes three more patients were made movie stars. They were brought in individually on jello legs wearing pudding faces. Freeman repeated his moves on each one, the sole difference being the speed in which he conducted his operation. Following each performance, a slight grin came to his lips. Lips that were as hard and cold and thin as steel strapping.

But apparently the father of American lobotomy was not satisfied he was giving his audience their money's worth. He decided to make a real rodeo out of it. He had one more frightened soul brought in and placed on the gurney. This time he took two ice picks, one in each hand. The head of Neurology at George Washington University had the moves of a bullfighter. As the camera dollied in closer, Freeman raised his hands to his shoulder, hesitated an instant, and plunged the two gleaming spears into either eye socket of the comatose human bull. Again my head was jerked away from the screen. This time the chicken fried steak made its escape.

As I bent over the waste basket a sharp searing pain shot through my eyes. I thought I was experiencing a sympathetic lobotomy. But it was something quite different. Before I climbed aboard that imaginary elevator that would take me to a linoleum floor basement, I turned and saw an angry, sweaty face and a rubber sap the size of Texas.

I knew before the doors to the elevator closed that I hadn't been lobotomized and that Dr. Dawkins was no suicide.

CHAPTER 19

The choking sweet aroma of Tabu stiffened the hairs in my nose. It was the smelling salt that brought me around. First impressions told me I was in the back seat of a large automobile and it was moving. As the filaments in my lamps regained focus I saw the backs of two heads in the front seat that were as familiar as Grandma's homemade corn relish. It was the flotsam and jetsam boys.

I wasn't alone in the back seat either. On my left was the good Dr. Smythe looking as civil as an orange, while on my right was the Tabu. The Tabu had a name and the name was Helen.

Nobody spoke or even moved much. I looked out the window through the corner of my eye searching for a street sign. Chavez Ravine Road and Riverside Drive whizzed by. We were doing the whizzing on Riverside. That information didn't mean too terribly much to me, but I knew the Riverside referred to the Los Angeles River.

Nothing but the hum of rubber on pavement. Not even the sound of the H.U.A.C. stooge look-alike in the front seat scratching an itchy trigger finger. The quiet was almost as disturbing as the predicament, but only in an ironic sort of way. After all, everybody in the car was old friends.

I turned to the man on my left in an attempt to

break the ice. "Dr. Smythe," I said, "what a pleasant surprise. Still making medical history? At Crescentview, wasn't it? I can imagine the boys at the Agency will pin a medal on you for the way you handled Jake Diltz."

Dr. Smythe looked away and said nothing.

"Say," I said, just trying to be conversational, "will they be serving cake and ice cream at this shindig we're going to, or am I the only thing on the menu?"

The big, stupid gunsel who specialized in kidney disorders turned around abruptly from the passenger's side of the front seat. "Shut up, you crumbum!" he snorted. "You're turkey meat!"

"I love you, too," I said.

With that, the large, ugly arrangement of molecules pulled his sap from inside his coat and jabbed it under my chin.

"Stop it!" said an irritated Dr. Smythe. He leaned forward and spoke into the driver's ear. "Can't you control your associate? We can ill afford these displays. You've made too many mistakes already."

The driver shot his right arm across the front seat, grabbing Dr. Kidney's sap arm. "Cut it out, Nunzio! You're not freelancing this time."

"Aw, c'mon, Frank," said Nunzio, sounding like a child who had been told to stay in his room until dinner. "I wanna piece of this clown."

"Later," Frank assured him. "You'll get your chance when we get to the park. You've got to hold it in until then, you big maniac."

I didn't need an engraved invitation to know what was on tap for "later". As to the park, the four thousand acres of ravines and steep hillsides they call Griffith seemed to be the likely candidate. So much for predicting the future, I thought. It was my soon-to-expire present that worried me more. Much more.

Following Frank's admonition, Nunzio turned around, put away his hard rubber persuader and began chewing his thumb. I felt like celebrating, but I knew that would be premature.

I turned to Helen and tipped my hat. "Hello, duchess," I said. "Last time I saw you, I thought you were following me over the side of a very nasty cliff."

"Well, you were wrong," she snapped back.

"Yeah. I'm sorry about that, but not terribly surprised. I don't know if it was the cryptograms Len Fugate was sending me as we left Trumbo's ranch or your fibs about Flemish art that tipped me off. Just for the record, Miss Art Major, it's Pieter Breughel, not Jan. Jan was his less famous painter son. Maybe, in the back of my mind, I knew that tale about your roomate attempting suicide was pure meringue. Anyway, I pegged you as the Claire Trevor type almost from the beginning. As in Velma Valento. From that movie. And I'll bet six bits the only thing you really know about Marx is Harpo, Groucho and Chico."

Helen turned her face to the window. She fumbled in her handbag for a cigarette. She lit it herself and blew the smoke toward the floor.

"Hey, there's no reason to sulk," I continued. "Just because you wormed your way into an organization, won their confidence and I suspect their friendship so you could spy on them and send them to jail or worse is no reason to be an old stick in the mud. Let's see. Jake Diltz, Dr. Dawkins and me. You are the deadly type, aren't you, duchess? And that's not even counting Solly. Is he ever going to be sore when he finds out what your playmates did to his new car. No, toots, Elizabeth Bentley doesn't have a thing on you. Not a thing."

Helen turned her head toward me. "Please stop it!

Don't make this any more unpleasant than it is."

"Well, I'll be. The lady's got feelings, too. Pardon me, sister. You see I have this silly old prejudice against scabs and finks that sometimes gets out of hand. Bad ol' me."

"Please!" she insisted.

"Shut your face, Kovachs!" said Nunzio joining the conversation.

I ignored him. "Say, duchess, who do you report to when you're not on the job buffaloing the comrades. The C.I.A. or the F.B.I.? I'm confused."

"If you aren't quiet," Helen said through her teeth, "I'm afraid we won't be able to restrain Nunzio. He's such a brute, you know."

"Seems I've heard that somewhere. Who's your next candidate for a pine quilt after me? Frances Farmer? Or are there more like Jake Diltz and Dr. Dawkins?"

"If you don't shut up!" The lady was mad.

"I know, you'll dish me up to your Stone Age boyfriend. What's new? I'm going to rendezvous with him anyway. So, you'll forgive me if your threats sound a bit hollow."

Dr. Smythe giggled. "He's got a point, you know, Helen."

Helen nervously crushed her cigarette in the ashtray on the door armrest. "Frank, can't you drive any faster?"

"Keep y're bloomers on," he replied. "We're almost there."

"I hope so. This thing has dragged on long enough."

A drizzly sort of rain, the kind they get once in a while in L.A., had been falling for the last couple miles. The water streaks on the windshield and the wet whine of rubber on concrete indicated it might turn into a downpour at any moment. I listened to the rain while trying to figure a way to call off their ball game. The sweet atmospheric juice made it all possible. The big sedan was experiencing an electrical short circuit in its windshield wipers. We were already in the park, halfway up a winding road.

"Hell, I can't see a damn thing!" Frank cursed. He wiped the inside of the windshield with his hand, but that only smeared the window. The problem was outside with a pair of wipers that had suddenly dropped dead.

"Let's do it right here," said Nunzio. "Right now!" I could almost hear his heart pounding with anticipation. "We can just dump the body out the back. Nobody will see us in this rain."

"No!" Frank said sharply. "Let me think. We've got to find a place away from the road. I wish I could see."

"Frank," Dr. Smythe said softly. "I think you should pull over and go out and scout for a place."

"In this rain?" said Frank.

"Do you know of a better way?" Dr. Smythe answered.

"Yeah, I do," grunted Nunzio trying to be conversational.

"Shut up!" said his keeper. "I'm not going to tell you again. Come on, let's go look for a place to do it."

Nunzio belched a few single syllable anglo-saxonisms through the hole in his face they use to feed him, before turning up his collar and heading out into the wet dark with Frank. Dr. Smythe got into the front seat to keep an eye on the brake and to fiddle with the electrical system. That just left the three of us in the back seat — me, Helen and Helen's gun. It was a small calibre job, the gun, the kind desperate women in the movies carry. But I had no doubts it could do the job if called upon.

"That moll's jewelry doesn't become you, duchess," I said. "But then neither do Marx and Lenin."

She got superior with me. "If you didn't have such a smart mouth, you might not be in this jam. Did you ever think about that, Mr. private eye?"

I had. A hundred times. But I wasn't going to tell her that. "Dragon Lady," I said, "I wouldn't be in this jam if you weren't a snitch for the Feds. Did you ever think about that?"

Her lip trembled a little. It could have been the dampness. She leaned over the front seat and spoke to Dr. Smythe. "Do you think you could juggle a wire or something under the hood to get the wipers working?"

Dr. Smythe thought a moment. "Maybe it is just a loose connection. I'll take the flashlight and peek under the hood. Can you handle Mr. Kovachs?" Helen assured him that I would be no trouble.

The moment Smythe stepped out of the car Helen moved closer to me. She began speaking in a low rapid whisper. "Listen to me. We don't have much time. Shut up and don't say a word." I did and I didn't at the same time. "I don't care what you believe about me," she continued. "It's not important right now. Yes, I was recruited to be an informer by the F.B.I. It doesn't matter how. I've been playing along with them for almost two years. But what they don't know is that I'm giving away all **their** secrets to the Party."

"A counter spy?" I said.

"Something like that, yes. Anyway, I have kept my cover with the F.B.I. so that at the right time I can expose the network of government agents within the Party and other progressive organizations. I'm very close to doing that."

"How do I fit into your grand plan?"

"I don't know. You're a problem."

"What's the C.I.A. doing mixed up in this?"

"I don't know."

"Who gets the credit for killing Dr. Dawkins? C.I.A. or F.B.I.?"

"I don't know that either. I didn't know who he was until tonight."

"Lady, you don't know the answers to too many questions for it to wash. Just what is your game?"

"I don't have time to argue with you, Kovachs. Dr. Smythe will be back any second. Here, take my gun." She dropped the pistol in my lap. "Now sock me. It's got to look good. For my sake. I'll have to explain this to them."

"What?"

"You heard me. Knock me out." She reached over and grabbed my face and with both hands pulled my head toward her. Then she planted her wet lips on mine and gave me the kind of kiss that made me forget all about Rita Hayworth. "There," she said, breaking her grip. "I've wanted to do that for some time. It might mean something to you some day. Now hit me." She pointed to her jaw and shut her eyes tight.

I didn't take the time to figure out what it was all about. I drew back a closed left. I didn't pull the punch either. If I had thought about it I might have, but I connected with a blow to her jaw that might have made Jake LaMotta walk wobbly for a few minutes. Then I climbed over her limp body and out the door. Dr. Smythe saw me from under the hood and called out. Mutt and Jeff were returning to the car. They drew their cannons and began emptying them in my direction. I dove into the bushes and crawled a few yards before getting to my feet and flying through the bramble. I would have given Emil Zatopek all he could have handled in a middle distance race. The shots grew fainter as I raced deeper into the wet, muddy murkiness of Griffith Park.

CHAPTER 20

I fought my way past the barky fingers of the manzanita, through places only a rabbit could go, for twenty minutes and more. The city lights that popped into view when I reached a small clearing told me I had been fleeing in an easterly direction. I had a hunch the town below was Glendale, but that wasn't terribly significant. I had "escaped the reaper" once again! That's what counted. That and the lingering sensation on my lips from a kiss that packed the punch of one of Oppenheimer's bombs.

As I walked toward the lights — I felt it was safe to stop running — I thought about Helen. The mysterious Helen. I didn't know if it was dames or politics but I had the feeling, when it came to her, somebody had just bolted the door to the cloud chamber with me in it. It was a place I had been before. The old appearance versus essence game. Who was Helen? A bolshevik? An F.B.I. snitch? A double agent? Or just weak in the knees when it came to a pair of pants and a snap brim? Who knew? How could anyone tell? If the C.P. domos-the Fosters and the Dennises-couldn't tell which of the comrades wore snapshots of J. Edgar pinned to their shorts, how could I? If the "Blond Spy Queen", as they were calling Elizabeth Bentley and that paunch in a wrinkled suit who blew the whistle on Hiss, could have operated in the Communist Party for all those years, I guess anything is possible. It is certainly a problem these days. A deadly problem. A lot of people, including me, could swear to that.

I hopped down the steep hillside, at times sinking up to the laces of my shoes in the oozing mud. My clothes were wet and my face and hands scratched by the branches of the unfriendly bushes. I crossed the ankle-deep cement-bottomed Los Angeles River without incident.

On the other side of the river, I spotted a campfire in the distance. Cautiously, I made my way toward it. When I got within fifty yards I stopped to size up the situation. In a small clearing a fire was blazing from inside an old rusted trash barrel. The heavy smell of things other than burning wood reached even me. A length of thin corrugated metal had been jury-rigged with sticks to form a low canopy under which a number of men were sitting. Some were eating out of tin cans. It was a hobo jungle. I walked up on them.

"Welcome to the weeds, brother," said one of the men, a middle-aged Negro with a rich baritone voice. "Come on in and set with us for awhile."

"Much obliged," I said, accepting the invitation.

"You look like you could do with a little supper," the Negro continued. "Nothin' fancy here, but you're welcome to share our scoffins."

"I could use a cup of coffee," I said.

"Sure. Mojave, pour this brother some java." The man called Mojave got to his feet and walked over to the burning barrel. Next to it, lying on the ground, was a large can. The man picked it up with a hand wrapped in a red bandana and poured some of its contents into a smaller can. He picked up the smaller can by its attached lid and carried it over to me.

"Got to take it dark and straight, brother, we ain't got no cream and sugar."

I accepted the can and took a thirsty sip. Tears found their way out of the corners of my eyes. Mojave told me it was coffee, but it tasted like some of the stuff that was burning in the trash barrel. I winced as I sipped at it. It wasn't something you could drink outright. I thought I had found some grounds that were truly worse than my own.

"You looks a little outta sorts, friend," said the black man. "Ain't none a my business, but if you're on the lam, you're safe with us." I smiled and thanked him. He got up from the log he and most of the men were sitting on.

"Lemme introduce you to the boys," he said. He walked behind each man, stopping and offering a brief introduction as he went. "This here ol' coot is known as Big Rats. So called 'cause his daddy named him after B. Gratz Brown, a presidential candidate way back, if you remember history." The old man was in his seventies and, although teeth were just another memory for him, he was a hearty fellow.

The Negro stepped behind the next man and placed his hand on his shoulder. "This here ol' 'bo is A#2. He's been doin' the coast road since the days when California used to talk Mexican. They was a time when he was called A#1, but he don't hold his bowels so good anymore. So . . ." Everybody laughed, including A#2. He was at least as old as Big Rats. A spotted felt hat whose brim had given up the ghost years ago covered his head. He took off his hat, stood up and gave an exaggerated bow.

"Now this here 'bo," said my deep-voiced guide, "he be goin' by the moniker of Frisco Bill. They say he killed a scab during the hop strike in Wheatland in '13, but don' be askin' him about it, 'cause he won't say nothin' about it to nobody.

"Sweetwater Johnson here, is a colored brother from Chi. He's one 'bo that know everythin' they is 'bout the steel 'tween Chi and Philly. Frenchy "Bow-coo" here used to work in a bank in Montreal up in Canada. We like to think he used to own it 'fore he seen the light an' took up an honest way o' life." Frenchy said something in French I think was hello.

The brown-skinned hobo continued with the introductions. "Mojave here knows every yard bull and shack from Dago to Seattle an' how to beat 'em. He's a true profesh. If you rides the steel in the Valley, he's a mighty good pard to have.

"Kid Tobacco here can sail the juice thirty-five feet. Go ahead, show 'im." The Kid, a stocky middle-aged man with a brown mouth, puckered up and sent a stream of liquid cut plug that hit the trash barrel twenty feet away. "He be havin' dead aim, too," said the Harlem Kid, stating the obvious.

The Negro emcee next walked behind a small, powerfully built man wearing a bandana around his neck and a faded denim jacket. Like more than half of the 'jungle' denizens, he was better than sixty years old.

"This ol' 'bo," he said, "is the house radical. Wobbly Mike's his moniker an' he's been in more jails than L.A. has whorehouses."

"Been in some of them, too," Wobbly Mike guffawed, slapping his knee. All the hobos laughed with him.

My tour guide continued down the log. "Santa Monica Slim and the Jehosephat Kid here used to work the carneys. They knows everythin' about the sideshow from runnin' the Three Card Monte shill to trainin' wild hyenas.

"An' sittin' next to 'em is Steens Mountain Shel. He come from Oregon Desert country. Got some higher education in 'im, too. Been to college for a year. He's the stiff's expert on geodes, in case you got some questions to ask. Knows more about the Cascade Mountains than most us 'bos know 'bout the inside of a boxcar.

"Sittin' next to Steens Mountain is the last, but not the least of us. He's the baby of the bunch, but don' let that fool ya none. He's got more spunk than a coal tender full o' never-been-fed grizzly bears. Sailor Jack's his moniker. A road kid outta Oakland. Tells the best damn stories you ever heard."

The brown man then pointed to himself. "An' me. They calls me the Harlem Kid. Lennox Avenue an' One hundred an' twenty-fifth Streets to be more exact. Been trampin' since '37 'cept for three years at sea durin' the war. How 'bout you, brother. What's your handle?"

"Kovachs," I said. "Riley Kovachs."

"What's yer monica?" asked the hobo called Big Rats.

"Well, I guess I don't have one."

"Don't got one!" shouted Big Rats. "Every 'bo's gotta have a monica." All the boys on the log voiced their agreement.

"Brother junglers," said the Harlem Kid above the

voices. "Our guest is a pilgrim to the ways of the road and the weeds. It's up to us to give 'im his nom-de-rail an' hep 'im to our ways. Brother Riley, where is you from?"

"Originally from Ohio. Akron, Ohio."

"Akron!" piped the hobo introduced as Wobbly Mike. "I was there in '13. Us Wobs shut down Firestone, we did. Went back in '36 an' sat down with the tirebuilders at Goodyear. We showed ol' Pauly Litchfield an' his rats just who runs the tire shops. Damn good union town, Akron. Was you there in '36, son?"

I told Wobbly Mike and the boys I had been home visiting my folks in '36 when Goodyear blew. I had worked in the rubber shops in the late '20's, mostly at Firestone Plant #2 before coming to Frisco. Anyway, I did picket duty during the strike and helped pass out some of the strike bulletins for the union.

"I knew you was a rebel," beamed Wobbly Mike. "I just knew."

"I got it," said Frisco Bill, snapping his fingers. "Let's call him Ohio Red."

"No good," said Sweetwater Johnson. "They is a Ohio Red. Got him some hair the color of fire engines. He used to be ridin' the Rock Island.

"Akron is called the Rubber City, ain't it?" asked the Harlem Kid. I nodded affirmatively. "Well, how 'bout we calls 'im Rubber City Red?" The citizens of the Glendale weedpatch whistled and stomped their feet in loud approval.

"This calls fer a drink," said A#2, smacking his lips and reaching behind the log for his bottle. He took out the plug, wiped both his mouth and that of the bottle and raised it to his lips and took a big slug.

"Hey, pass that nanny goat sweat down this way," roared a thirsty Jehosophat Kid. When he got the bottle he held it skyward and toasted — "To our next freight and our last woman." By the time the bottle reached me everything had been toasted from Big Bill Haywood and Paul Robeson to the Valley of the Moon during apple harvest and a certain legendary kettle stew and its creator, a hobo called Chuck Wagon Larry. The only thing that can be said about A#2's sneaky pete was that it was worse than the coffee. In fact, it was probably worse than any liquid that can be consumed without killing you.

A couple innings of passing the poison and most of the revelers were rubbing their eyes with sleep. A#2 disappeared into the bushes and didn't come back for a long time. Several of the men tossed their bindles and stretched out for a night's snore. The Harlem Kid, Wobbly Mike and Steens Mountain Shel stayed up. They were waiting to catch a train north. I stayed up with them because that's where I was going too.

"Got some makin's here, if you want to pull one with us," said Wobbly Mike, passing over a little bag of Durham and some cigarette papers. I had a pack of Chesterfield's in my pocket, but I felt it was protocol to accept the offer, so I rolled one.

"Ain't none a my business, Red," said the Harlem Kid, "but you looks to me like you might be mixed up in some kinda beef. If you wants to talk about it, we's pretty good listeners."

I smiled. Steens Mountain Shel gave me a jump from the lit end of his cigarette. Nearly a quarter of the tobacco slid out the open end of the rolled paper and onto the ground as I leaned over to get the light. I took a big drag on what was left, toyed with the idea of taking another hit from the bottle of A#2's blink, decided against it, and began telling the whole story to the three strangers like I was giving a progress report to a client. I had no client, but they say no hobo is ever a stranger, so it wasn't as unusual as it might sound. Twenty minutes after I started, I finished with the details of my recent escape, such as it was, from Griffith Park.

"Dadblastit!" said Wobbly Mike, peering into the darkness in the direction of Griffith Park. "I'd like to see them monkeys bust in here, I would. We'd give 'em a case of the never-get-overs. I ain't had a good row with the class enemy since I was in Kentucky in '43 mixin' it up with John L.'s boys."

"Mmmm, mmm, mmm," said the Harlem Kid. "Sounds like you is in this thing pretty deep, brother 'bo. I knows what you're talkin' 'bout, though. The whole country's in big trouble the way I see it. Poor folks gettin' the boot nearly as bad as they was back in the Depression."

"That's a lot of malarkey, kid," said Steens Mountain Shel. "Nothing was as bad as that. Not in Eastern Oregon, leastways."

"Now, hold on a minute, you educated country 'bo," said the Kid. "Nobody got to tell a black man 'bout how bad things was or is. I'm talkin' politics. Back in the 30's a man could be busted, but they was all kinds of organizations, fightin' organizations, he could join up with to try an' set things right."

"Sure was," said Wobbly Mike. "I worked with the Unemployed League in Seattle. And there was the Tenants Council in Portland, the C.I.O. Organizing Committee in Frisco and Oakland, the..."

"That's my point," the Kid interrupted. "Today, the rulin' class tryin' to disallow that kind a organizin' from goin' on. Hell, us 'bos may spend all our time ridin' the steel and the onliest use we got for a newspaper is to make a blanket, but we knows what's what. We hears 'bout them fascists in Hollywood and Washington."

"Yeah! I don't give a spit for Harry Truman!" said Wobbly Mike angrily. "A labor-hatin' sonofabitch if ever one lived! The workers should send 'im back to his hat shop in Missouri!" He chuckled and spit in the dirt.

"That's right," added Steens Mountain Shel. "They should call it the Raw Deal instead of the Fair Deal. Last time I was in Mitchell, the only folks getting a fair deal was the big ranchers."

"Amen, brother," chimed the Kid. "The rulin' class got the workin' stiffs by the you-know-whats. Ain't been no Russian ever did me wrong. The fascists and the K.K.K. and the Jim Crowers — they do me wrong. But Truman's not worried 'bout them dog racists. No sir, he says we gotta fight the Russians. Maybe even blow up the whole world in the process, but we gotta stop 'em, he says. That's the onliest thing that counts for anything these days." He laughed ironically. "Looka here!" The Kid reached into the pocket of his coat and pulled out a wad of folded papers.

"I found this here **Life** magazine settin' on a bench near Spring Street. Nobody sittin' on the bench, so I kiped it." He unfolded the wad of papers. "They was this article. I tore it out. Just to keep a reminder what's goin' on since we won the war for democracy." Even in the dark, we couldn't miss the big wink in the Kid's eye. "It was written by the Chief of Staff of the United States Air Force. A stiff name of Spaatz."

Wobbly Mike laughed. "Go on with ya, Kid. Spats is somethin' they used to wear on their feet in old timey days."

"I know," continued the Kid, "but this drunk's got

the same name. He says, an' I'm readin' it straight like it was wrote:

It may smack of cynicism for a soldier, so soon after the war, to start laying out the strategy for the next. However, no one doubts that Russia has become the number one enemy of the United States and under its communist leadership is spoiling for a fight with the United States and Western Europe. A war is only a matter of time and timing. The first question is: is it possible to reach the vulnerable industrial heartland with the B-29?

"The B-29!" the Harlem Kid repeated. "Now, ain't that somethin'? I'll tell you who I'd fly them B-29's against. Them dogs who makin' life miserable for the colored people. I mean them segregationists in Washington D.C. just as much as them peckerwoods in the South who been stringin' black folks from trees."

"I know somethin' 'bout that," interrupted Wobbly Mike. "I was ridin' the Florida Atlantic between Atlanta an' Baltimore a couple a years ago. I was batterin' the privates for some grub in Greenville, South Carolina the day this mob of vigilantes and lowdown scabs broke into the jail an' took this poor Negro boy, a kid named Willie Earle — I ain't forgot his name — and beat him to a sorry purple pulp. Then they stabbed 'im an' blowed his head away with a shotgun."

"Happens all the time," said the Kid shaking his head from side to side. "Happens all the time."

"Then," continued Wobbly Mike, rolling a cigarette, "twenty-five of them stinkin' buzzards confessed to killin' the boy, but the jury found them not guilty. Not guilty!"

"What can you expect with a prejudiced dog for an Attorney General and segregationists in the White

House an' Congress?" said the Kid. "Last I heard, that bill to outlaw lynching is goin' to be talked into the waste basket. Ain't that somethin'? We needs a act of Congress to stop the hangin' of colored people! Do you hear what I'm sayin'? Justice, my brothers, is where you buy it in this country, an' poor folks is jus' plumb outta cash."

"Don't that jest beat the bugs a fightin'?" exclaimed Wobbly Mike. "We gotta have a revolution in this country. That's what we need. The class conscious proletarians got to rise up and sweep out all the capitalists an' their bootlickin' cooties with 'em."

"Amen, brother," said the Harlem Kid, slapping his knee.

Steen Mountain Shel nodded and added, " 'Bos and working stiffs could run the country a whole lot better than what we got now."

In the distance the low, breathless whistle of a train wrinkled the night air. "That's the Orange Crate Special," said Steens Mountain Shel. The freight, he told me, was coming from the Imperial Valley and was bound for Seattle. The schedule was acceptable and the fare was a bargain.

In another ten minutes the three hobos gathered up their bindles and together we began the overland journey of less than a mile to the Glendale train yard where the Orange Crate Special would stop for a few minutes. On the way I was given a crash course in freight hopping.

"Now, this ain't a bad road," explained Wobbly Mike, "but there's a shack what gets on at Modesto who'll bust open your coconut for you. But here'll be a breeze. Just watch us an' do what we do. If they's more'n one shack we might have to ride the blinds. No reason we can't hold'er down goin' outta the yard.

When that ol' peanut roaster starts red ballin' we can pick a spot to wiggle our trilbies an' toss our kip. But stay away from the reefers an' gonds unless you know what you're doin'. Side-car Pullman's your best bet."

The Harlem Kid acted as my translator. He said the ride should be smooth, but the brakeman who boards the train in Modesto is particularly ruthless when it comes to ditching hobos. To get on the train at Glendale, he said, we might have to jump a baggage car, one with sealed doors on the end, but only if there is more than one brakeman on the freight. The idea is, the Kid explained, that since the ends of the car are sealed the shacks can't easily get to it to toss off hobos. But, he said, turning Wobbly Mike's words into English, chances are that won't happen and we can hop aboard, lay low and out of sight on the top of one of the cars until the train reaches top speed. Then we can move around and look for a boxcar to bed down, or find an open gondola or refrigerator car, weather and other conditions permitting.

"Do what we do," repeated Wobbly Mike, "an' before you know it you'll be a tramp-royal, a blowed-in-the-glass 'bo."

"Yeah," added Steens Mountain Shel. "There's a lot of raw-heeled cheechackos out there who think they're too big for their own pants. They think they know it all their first time out. Think we're just a bunch of old weary willies. Some of them end up between the wheel and the steel." I didn't miss his point.

A half hour later the four of us were lurking in the bush waiting for the Orange Crate Special to pull out of the yard. When it lurched forward, we lurched with it, running in front of the engine. The train had only one brakeman so, as Wobbly Mike predicted, it was a breeze jumping the slow-moving freight and "holdin' 'er down". When the train reached maximum speed we repaired to the hobo's sleeping car and retired for the night.

CHAPTER 21

A wide path of morning sun came pouring through the open doors of our side-door Pullman, waking me from the snoring dead. I looked around the straw-strewn floor to find a veritable hobo hotel. There were two dozen other citizens of the rough besides our little party of four.

I wiped the night from my eyes and joined a traveler standing at the open door smoking a cigarette.

"Great day to be alive, ain't it?" said the man. "The hills are mighty pretty this time of year." I nodded, taking in the gentle rolling green hill country of the San Joaquin Valley.

"You can smell the earth," continued the man inhaling deeply. "It smells like life, don't it?" I nodded again while lighting a badly bent Chesterfield that had survived the previous day's workout.

"They call me Jerz," said the man. "Short for Jersey."

"What city are you from?" I asked.

"Me? I'm from Oklahoma. Ain't never been east of Tulsa. They call me Jerz because my last name is McDonald."

"I'm listening."

"Because my last name is McDonald and my brother's name is Angus. Angus. Jersey. I know it sounds pretty silly, but it just kinda stuck."

Jerz and I smoked our breakfast watching the Valley whiz by and talking about Alaska and the Klondike. Jerz was headed for a place above Whitehorse in the Yukon where he had a claim on a once famous creek.

"Train to Seattle, ferry to Skag, then overland to Bennet where I can grab the rods of the White Pass & Yukon and take 'er into Whitehorse. Sure, I know I can jump the train in Skag, but I like the hike. Besides, I don't have to be at my claim 'till the end of May. Plenty of time to enjoy the scenery. Could use a pard if you don't mind shinnying up a mile of sharp rock over the pass."

I told him I'd have to take a raincheck on his mouth-watering offer. Back in the days even before they built the Al-Can Highway I had been bitten by the great wild outdoors. I had myself taken a ferry to Skagway, the jumping off place to the gold fields of the Klondike, and climbed to the summit of the impossible Chilkoot Pass. I never went any further, but always wanted to return one day and retrace Jack London's trek of 1896-97 that took him into the Yukon. If there hadn't been the little matter before me I would have joined Jerz and the sourgonauts of the "hyporborean north", as London called it.

The freight clickety-clacked through the Valley morning. A persistent sun bulldozed its way through fat, fluffy clouds in an effort to suck the dew off the grass. Its warming rays splashed our faces. It tickled as it opened the pores. It soothed. It cured.

A half-dozen sun worshipers joined us and stuck

their maps skyward to get a taste of the solar refreshment. It was the closest thing to a hot bath most of them had known in a long time.

"Where the heck are we?" said one old hobo peering suspiciously out onto the oak woodland landscape.

"'Bout an hour from Modesto," said Wobbly Mike who had come to the open door to "take the cure" with us.

"Hell, that don't mean nothin' to me," piped the first man, a little fellow of about sixty with a Gabby Hayes beard. "I ain't been to this part of Californy since I had my own teeth."

"Where you normally ride, 'bo?" said another man.

"Santa Fe Road in the Plains and Southwest," said Gabby Hayes.

"The Atcheson, Topeka and Santa Fe," said a third man. "That's a good ol' road."

"The Dean Acheson-to-peek-at-Alice Faye, don'tya mean?" said Gabby Hayes, laughing loudly and slapping his knee. The other tramp-royals joined in the fun.

It was still morning when the Orange Crate pulled into Modesto. Steens Mountain Shel told me it would be in the yard for about ninety minutes to load produce. Wobbly Mike announced he was going out for some "scoffins".

"Say, Red," he said, "how 'bout you'n me teamin' up? I'll learn ya how to batter the privates for some grub. Maybe even get us a set-down. Ain't nobody can slam a gate better'n yours truly."

Wobbly Mike was the "profesh's profesh" when it came to getting a free meal. Inside a half hour we were sitting at the kitchen table of a working class home not far from the train yard. Wobbly Mike could charm the birds out of the trees. The housewife who invited us to the "set-down" of biscuits, jam, links and good strong coffee was paid handsomely with a story told by Mike about his experiences as a sailor on a whaling ship out of Nantucket. I didn't say anything, but his story sounded an awful lot like **Moby Dick**.

Following the meal the lady of the house gave each of us an apple and a couple biscuits to take with us. "I know how expensive the food on trains can be," she sympathized. I'm not sure she fully understood we weren't exactly traveling tourist class. We thanked her for her kindness and headed back for the steel.

"Nice lady," I said to Wobbly Mike along the way.

"You slobbered a bibful, there, Red. A real peach, that one. I always throw my hooks with the workin' people. They share what they got, no matter how poor they is. Them damned bourgeois give you a lecture on 'honest work' and 'self-respect' 'fore they give you a crust of bread. If they give you anything at all."

It was still morning when the Orange Crate pulled out of the yard. The bad shack was aboard and he was packing a crow bar. He ditched a half dozen would be gratis passengers before Mike and I even made a run for it. We had to hop a blind baggage to avoid the shack's eagle eye. It was almost an hour before we were secured and able to drop down into a boxcar. It had only a fraction of the hobo hostlers it had earlier that morning. Two of them, however, were Steens Mountain Shel and the Harlem Kid.

"Welcome aboard, brother 'bos," said the Kid, grinning. "Shack ditched most of us. We the survivors."

"Phooey!" spit Wobbly Mike. "Shack comes back

here, I'll break his thumbs. No good, lousy scum. Ain't nothin' worse'n shacks."

"'Lessen it be politicians," added the Harlem Kid. Everybody who heard the Kid's remark laughed and voiced their approval.

"Well, boys," said Wobbly Mike, "I'm plumb tuckered out. Reckon I'll pound my ear for a spell. Wake me if there's anything doin'." Mike gathered up some straw, which he called "donkey's breakfast" and took it to a corner of the car where he made up his mattress and went to sleep.

I stayed and talked politics with the Harlem Kid and Steens Mountain Shel for the next couple hours. Two 'bos named Popeye Pete and the Bituminous Kid joined us. If only government policy were forged in boxcars.

There was still an hour of good sunlight left so I propped myself up near the open door and pulled out my tattered copy of **The Little Sister**. I was curious to know if Marlowe was having any better luck than me.

I had left Marlowe pushing his act on the big time agent called Sheridan Ballou. Marlowe dropped a photograph in his lap and Ballou played "Who's on First" with him for twenty minutes trying to figure what Marlowe had on his client and how much it was going to cost him.

It was all clear as mud to me until Ballou poured two snifters of Armanac and Marlowe began spilling the real dirt. The photo showed the actress Mavis Weld with a guy named Steelgrave, who was really a Cleveland red-hot named Weepy Moyer, a mug who was dining on bread and water at the state's expense. Moe Stein was iced on Franklin Avenue the day the picture was taken. A newspaper in the photo gave it away.

So the snap shows Moyer was really out on a holiday and thus both he and Mavis are tied to the Stein snuffing. Clear? Marlowe surmises the pic was squeezed off by Orrin Quest, Orfamy's lost brother, and that Hicks/Dr. Hambleton took the icepick in the neck from someone close to Moyer or Mavis.

Marlowe thinks Mavis may have to take the rap for Moyer because of her association with him and wants to help her out. Ballou is convinced Marlowe is on the level and has his secretary write a retainer check for five hundred dollars and puts him on the payroll at a hundred dollars per.

That Marlowe! I should have some of his luck.

Both the light and my concentration were beginning to fade in the west. I could see the Sutter Buttes in the distance rising from the wide, flat floor of the Sacramento Valley. From the other side of the car the hazy Coast Range grew black before the orange setting sun. I thought about Fort Ross and Jenner-by-the-Sea on the other side of the modest range and what folks walking along their beaches were thinking about at that moment. I stared out the open door till the last speck of light was eaten by the hungry night.

I made a small hill of straw in a corner of the boxcar and stretched out. Before I flipped the off switch to my brain, I tried to interpret the past, assess the current and forge a strategy for the immediate future. Little things like that.

I figured I owed two dead guys something. I could have been religious about it and told myself I had an obligation to humanity and the future of decency or something high and mighty like that. But Jake Diltz and Dr. Dawkins were reason enough. And if they weren't, the political stink this whole thing had about it and the indelible image of a man jabbing an icepick into the brain of a living person were.

Whatever the reason or reasons I felt I had to see this thing through to the end. Whatever that might be. Wherever it might take me. Laying ahead both in time and miles was Steilacoom and Frances Farmer. And a reasonable assumption was that the lady was scheduled to fall under the knife of Walter J. Freeman, traveling missionary of trans-orbital lobotomy, sometime during the next seventy-two hours.

Those were the facts, sketchy as they were. Where that left Riley Kovachs was written in lemon juice. It was about as likely as Richard III getting a fair shake from that Tudor playwright that I could bluff my way into the mental hospital pretending to be family or a doctor and sneak Frances Farmer out the side door. No, that would be a tough trick even for Lamont Cranston. And he had the power to cloud men's minds. The only mind I have ever clouded was my own and I couldn't see where that would be to my advantage.

The way I boiled it down there was only one way to get into Western State Hospital at Steilacoom — in the back of a red and white truck.

CHAPTER 22

I spent part of the next fifteen hours "pounding my ear" on mule wheaties. Another part of it was spent dangling my feet out the open door stuffing my orbs with the spectacular beauty of the volcanic Cascades through an intermittently misty northwestern sky. And I spent some time thinking about Helen and her powerhouse kisses. That was the easy part. The hard part was trying to come up with a foolproof plan to break into that psychiatric warehouse they keep outside Tacoma.

I tried to recall the part of Jake Diltz's story that dealt with the particulars of Frances Farmer's commitment. I remembered one name that stood out from everything else. Rader. John Rader. The Honorable John Rader. The judge who personally sentenced her to that hatchery of human suffering at Steilacoom. It was the man's personal and longstanding involvement in the Farmer case that kept his name fresh in my mind. Jake Diltz told me that Rader was pure bedrock in the right-wing community in Seattle. He was a church deacon, an activist in the American Legion and a power in the State's Republican Party. Impeccable credentials.

And there was more. As far as I knew, Jake Diltz was no socialist, or even left-of-center for that matter. Just a man caught up in something that led him to draw some pretty big conclusions. So what he told me wasn't painted with a wide red brush. Just the facts as he knew them. Judge Rader, according to Jake Diltz, had been a labor and radical hater ever since he was old enough to spell the words "free enterprise". He fought against the Wobblies from his position as lawyer for the Union Pacific and as a patriotic breast-beater for the Legion. Diltz claimed that Rader was tied up with activities that led to the Everett and Centralia Wobbly massacres in the late teens. He didn't tell me just how the judge was connected, but he did say Rader was one of the leaders of a little sewing circle called the American Vigilantes of Washington.

Rader also was determined to remove the stain of

Frances Farmer from the crinkly white petit-fours of his native state. He had been denouncing the former movie star since the early thirties when she won that high school essay contest with her theme on atheism.

Only a Ponderosa Pine could have concluded that it was ironic coincidence that Judge John Rader had personally sent Frances Farmer to bedlam to spend the rest of her life. His hand must have trembled with excitement as he signed her commitment papers. In a way, I was looking forward to meeting him.

The Orange Crate Special pulled into the switching yard on the edge of downtown Seattle. I bid the Harlem Kid and Wobbly Mike a hobo farewell.

"Luck to you, Red," said the Kid. "They's ten thousand 'bos out there ready to lend a hand. Don' never forget that. I hopes you can lick them that's causin' all the pain."

"I'd give a month's worth of the best Durham they is to be a-goin' with you, Red," said Wobbly Mike. He was particularly fired up when I told him about Judge Rader. It was a name he knew. "They's a few things I'd like to discuss with hizzonor," he said, making a fist and pounding it into his other hand. "I owe it to my brother Wobs."

I held out my hand and clasped his. "Mike, I know you do. And I'd like to be there when you meet up with him. But not this time, old buddy. I work alone. And that's the way it's got to be on this one. But next time we'll be a team — Wobbly Mike and Rubber City Red."

"A damn good team, too," said Mike.

"The best," I added.

"You two ain't nothin' lessen the Harlem Kid is along," said the Kid.

"Of course. The three of us. We'll be a knockout."

"I'll be lookin' for you, Red," said Wobbly Mike. "Ill screeve my monica an' the date an' where I'm headin' everywhere I ride so's ya can find me."

I waved goodbye to the two tramp-royals and headed toward downtown Seattle, a meal, some fresh duds and the courthouse.

CHAPTER 23

I took a room at the YMCA to get the open road from my pores. I sent my togs next-door to the No-D-Lay Two-Hour Cleaners to get my serge shined and creased and the buttons chipped off my shirt. I took a long, hot soak in the bathtub and spent another twenty minutes with the local fishwrapper while waiting for my duds to return.

The **Post-Intelligencer** brought me up to date on witch burning as they practice it in the Northwest. Not to be outdone by Cal Berkeley, the University of Washington had put the necks of a half dozen of its professors on the chopping block for having been New Dealers and Popular Front communists a decade ago. Washington's Canwell Committee had teeth just as sharp as the Tenney posse which roamed the Bear Republic.

Four hours later my clothes came back. I got dressed, dragged a comb across my head and went downstairs. Then I hit the street. It was raining, but in Seattle, that is almost redundant. I stopped off at a stationery store and bought an envelope and a stamp. I put my driver's license and other identity cards in the envelope and mailed it to myself in Frisco.

I hopped a local to the County Courthouse. Twenty minutes later I was standing in the lobby checking the court directory to see where Judge Rader was warming the bench. I found he was pounding his gavel in a third-floor courtroom.

It was almost 4 p.m. when I walked into Rader's court. The man looked pooped. I guess he had put in another hard four-hour day sustaining and over-ruling motions. Ten minutes after I arrived court was adjourned and Judge Rader split for his chambers. I waited for the courtroom to clear before heading after him. I went through the unlocked door without waiting for an invitation. Judge Rader didn't appear pleased, but that only encouraged me.

"Mardonde!" I said crisply. "Lt. Colonel Roco G. Mardonde. Twenty-second Infantry Batallion, Omaha Beach all the way to the Bulge. Vice-commander, Legion Post 1209 Central and South-eastern Ohio." I saluted. Rader was surprised. A tiny smile came to his severe lips. I extended my hand. Rader's right arm involuntarily reached out to meet it. I grabbed it and shook it like I was trying to land a marlin.

"You don't know me," I continued, "but I've heard of you. Everybody in the national has heard about Jack Rader. Loved the profile on you in the **Legionnaire** a few years back. Anyway, what's Rocky Mardonde, third generation Italian-American, vet of both W.W.s, doing in the chambers of a famous man like yourself?" Rader motioned for me to sit down, although his eyes told me not to make myself too comfortable. I hastily pulled a plush oxblood leather chair with brass upholstery tacks to the edge of his large desk and sat down.

"Well, sir," I continued, "that's a good question. You see, I'm the loan officer at Ohio National in Coshocton and the bank ran a statewide competition in all its branches among the loan officers to see who could underwrite the most loans. Well, to make a long story short, yours truly signed away more of the bank's money than anyone in the whole state. First prize was a trip to the Rockies and the west coast. The missus and I just got in from two swell days at Mount Rainier. That's some beautiful hunk of rock you got there, Jack."

"I'm glad you liked it, Mr. uh, uh."

"Hey, I'm no mister. Call me Rocky. Everyone does. So, we hit Seattle this afternoon and I tell Angela, that's the missus, you go to the Pike Street Market, I want to look up an old Legion comrade."

"Well, I'm flattered, uh, Rocky, but I don't . . ."

"Don't mention it, Jack. In Coshocton, my front door is always open to Legionnaires. Wide open! That's what it's all about, isn't it?"

"Well, Rocky, I want to thank you for stopping by. Now, if you'll excuse me."

"Hey, Jack! I know you're a busy man and I'm not going to waste even a minute of your time. Hey! Down at the bank, I know busy." Rader smiled and got up from his chair to herd me toward the door. I held up my hand.

"Jack, this is only partly a courtesy call. The other part's dead serious business." Rader sat down. He pulled the sleeve of his robe past his wrist and glanced at his watch.

"Well, I am running behind schedule."

I held up my hands. "Boy, you don't have to tell me, Jack. With the crime rate going through the roof. No sir, you don't have to tell me. But what's on my mind is this." Rader reclined tentatively in his high-backed leather swivel chair. "I've just been elected president of the Eastern Ohio and West Virginia chapter of Americans Against Bolshevism." Rader smiled and leaned all the way back in his chair.

"You see, Jack, we've got two thousand red-blooded American men and women who've dedicated their lives to wiping out the red menace that's eating away at our country's sacred institutions. You know what I'm talking about. Most of us are Legionnaires and we know a little something about firearms. We've used them on a couple of occasions, too." I paused and flashed a grin I knew Rader would understand and appreciate.

"But it's these damn laws that are throwing one big monkey wrench into the works. I mean how are we supposed to stop communism if the laws and the Constitution are set up dead bang against us and for red spies and terrorists? Communist Russia didn't let any laws stand in their way when they plowed into Eastern Europe after the war, did they?"

Rader shook his head sympathetically. "It has not always been easy for patriotic-minded citizens to act on behalf of their country. New Deal legislation is a constant stumbling block to reconstituting the American Republic we remember so fondly. However, the Republican Congress has made great strides in putting the nation back on a sound footing. We must always be vigilant in the defense of freedom and liberty, but we must also be patient. I share your concerns. If there is anything I can do to assist your organization..."

"Well, doggone it, Jack, there is. We're holding a tri-state confab in Columbus this summer. 'Roll Back the Red Carpet'. That's the theme. If you could see your way clear to come out and speak about the law and how it's changing and how decent citizens can, you know, twist it in our favor to fight the reds. And, of course, we'd pay all your expenses."

"I'd be flattered, Rocky. You would just have to let me know far enough in advance."

"No problem at all, Jack. It will be such a great honor to have a man of your calibre, a fellow legionnaire to boot, to come and share with us, your rich experiences fighting bolshevism and atheism."

Rader's lined face cracked with a modest smile. He was at total ease with Roco G. Mardonde. Rocky continued. "Yes sir, we sure would like to hear how you and your vigilantes persecuted working men and Wobblies."

"What?" Rader said with disbelief.

"That's right. We would like to know how you took the law into your own hands in your crusade to save the rotten capitalist system from the rising tide of honest working people."

"What?" he said again, only louder. "Who the hell are you, mister?" He reached for the phone.

I jumped up and knocked his hand away. I circled the judge like a vulture staking out carrion. I waved my arms athletically as I went. "Who am I?" I shouted. "Roco G. Mardonde, first generation Italian-American. Victim of capitalist exploitation. Worker-communist-anarchist-avenging angel!"

Rader recoiled with horror. He made a desperate lunge for the phone. I spun his chair around and went for his throat. "I'm here in the name of Wesley Everest and the comrades your vigilante scum murdered on the docks at Centralia. Death to the capitalist parasite! Long live the proletarian revolution!"

I choked him only slightly as I yelled, but his face turned the color of a Santa Rosa plum. Mortal terror screamed from behind his eyes. I loosened my hold enough to permit him to break the grip. He pushed wildly at me. I fell away yelling "death to the capitalist parasite!" over and over at the top of my lungs.

Rader picked up the telephone to call for help, but two bailiffs came busting through the chamber door before he dialed the first digit. I turned and swung at the first one, connecting squarely with the side of his head. The second one, however, brought his drawn billy club crashing down on the back of my neck. I could hear Rader screaming hysterically.

"Kill him! Kill the filthy bastard!" I saw him as I sunk to my knees. He was in the far corner of his office with his big, high-back chair in front of him. He was holding on to it with both hands.

"Kill him! Kill the crazy lunatic communist!" He was hollering himself hoarse.

I got up only to be hit again by one of the bailiffs. The blow nearly took off my ear and my head began pounding like a bill collector at the front door. Then they got physical and were joined by several more armed and dangerous men. The last time I was able to stand on my feet the whole choir jumped me and wrestled me to the ground. While some of them were tenderizing my face with their fists, the others were busy strapping me in a canvas bag.

Through a pair of puffed and battered eyes I could see the room spinning around me. Everything looked wet and red and hysterical. One of the bailiffs dropped his knee from the chandelier into my chest. I saw flashbulbs of light going off everywhere. Then I saw nothing. I felt like I was drowning and tried to swim to the surface, but my arms wouldn't move. I tried to shout, but nothing came out. In the instant before I went under, I could hear Rader's raspy voice shrieking, "Take this wop maniac to Steilacoom! And do it now!"

I didn't have the time nor the inclination to congratulate my success.

CHAPTER 24

For the third time in forty-eight hours I woke up in a moving vehicle. This one, however, wasn't a boxcar. My eyes were nearly swollen shut, but I knew I was in the back of an ambulance. Blood was dried and caked in my nostrils, making it impossible to breathe through my nose. But I didn't think about that. The pain in my arms was central. I was trussed up in a strait jacket. The circulation in my arms was just a memory. They had been crisscrossed in front of me and nearly yanked out of their sockets. I could feel the pain from my shoulders all the way to the fingers. The straps cut into my flesh. I wondered if I was bleeding. It was unbearable. The worst thing, worse even than the pain, was the knowledge that I could not move my arms even a fraction of a twitch. That pain was a psychological one, but it hurt just the same. It was something like wearing shoes so tight you can't wiggle your toes. At first it feels irritating. Then a bit of desperation sets in if you find you still can't move them. In my case the desperation was followed by a feeling of suffocation. I gasped for breath and movement. I thought the nervous pounding of my heart alone might be sufficient to burst the restraining straps. But it wasn't. I gulped air and choked on my own blood and saliva while desperately trying to move my arms. Then I thought maybe if I were to free them I would discover them broken. My frenzy abated only when I slipped out of consciousness from the pain and fear of helplessness.

I was brought back by nearby voices. Two attendants were in the back of the ambulance with me. I hadn't noticed them before. One of them put his foot in my ribs to get leverage to tighten the straps on my canvas prison. It was hard not to notice that. I passed out again, but it was only momentary. The same voices brought me back.

"Hey, buddy! You in there!" said one of the voices loudly. The words came from the lips of a pasty-faced attendant who looked like he enjoyed his work. "Hey, paly, you're going for a ride. Know where?" When I didn't respond he looked as crestfallen as a dry pear, but that didn't stop him. "Steilacoom! That's where. I mean it's going to be your home for the next forty years. If you live that long."

A second attendant grabbed my head and turned it toward him. "That's right, sport. They just gonna forget all about you. Nobody socks old man Rader and lives to tell about it. You must really be crazy to do a thing like that. But don't worry none. You'll like Steilacoom. The rats do." He and his accomplice laughed so loud my head began to hurt worse than before. Fortunately, I slipped away before hearing another word from either of them.

Sometime later the ambulance stopped. The two attendants rolled me onto a stretcher and carried me out the back of the wagon. I knew without making inquiries I had arrived at Western State Hospital. Steilacoom! It was night and I could see only the dark outlines of several buildings. A biting, cold, wet fog stung my face and penetrated the canvas to my bones. As I shivered, the pain in my arms and chest grew even more intense.

I was taken inside one of the buildings and into a large gray room lit by bare lightbulbs stuck into the ceiling. I was then lifted from the stretcher and strapped to a large chair that was bolted to the floor. My ankles were strapped to its two front legs.

I looked around and saw that I wasn't the only armless mummy in the joint. Four others were strapped in duck harnesses. However, they weren't lashed to a chair. They were walking around the room looking like a pathetic bunch of bowling pins.

One of them, a middle-aged woman, was crying. She would alternate between a whimper and a bawl. Her eyes were red and her hair prematurely gray. She stopped crying at one point and began to shake violently and then slumped in the corner like a bag of laundry. She repeated the word "momma" without stopping. Two minutes later she was up pacing the floor again, crying hysterically as she went.

A jacketed man with the hair of a wet floor mop noticed me and came running over. He leaned into my face. The stench from his yellow teeth was equalled only by the stink of the vomit and urine which accompanied him.

His eyes were uncontrolled. They looked menacingly into mine. "Have you seen the Lord?" he yelled at the top of his voice. The sound rattled my bruised jaw. "Have you seen the Lord?" he yelled again. "I am the messenger of the Lord. I am come to spread

His good news. Have you been washed in the blood of the lamb, brother sinner?"

I was a captive audience for him. Words and insults would not drive him away. I tried repeatedly.

"I see Satan sitting on your shoulder, sinner." The man turned his body and fell into me. "Get off that shoulder, Satan! Get off, I say!" The man backed up and fell into me again. I swear I heard one of my ribs crack.

I could stand no more. I spit in his face with as much force as I could muster. The man recoiled and began screaming, "He's the anti-christ! He's the anti-christ!" Then he began kicking me savagely in the shins. On the third kick he toppled over backward and passed out.

A third person, a three hundred pound man with the face of a child came lumbering over to the passed out messenger of the Lord and without a word began jumping up and down on his face and chest. Blood flowed like a desert wash following a cloudburst. Two others, a young woman and an old man, began to shriek at the sight.

The crying woman was moaning loudly. It was bedlam. I sucked in all the air I could and screamed out for help. A slow moment later two white-coated orderlies, who looked like greased weasels, came bursting through the door.

I was still yelling at the top of my voice, "You bloody bastards! Do something!"

One of the weasels went straight for me, ignoring the mayhem at my feet. He swung a thick leather belt over his head like a lariat. "So we're bloody bastards, are we?" he spit through clenched teeth. Then he snapped the belt, which had a metal buckle for a tip, like Lash Larue cracks his bullwhip. The first shot caught me on the cheek under an eye. The second tore open the corner of my mouth. Both shots drew blood. I strained in the strait jacket to break the straps and go after him, but it was a hopeless gesture. People don't escape from a canvas prison. You have to be let out. And they let you out only after they're through with you. After they've broken your spirit and your mind. That's a lesson new admittees like me are immediately taught. Steilacoom was, itself, an enormous canvas prison and the same lessons applied. Only when broken in body and spirit are "rehabilitated" inmates turned loose. At that moment I wished for the cool comfort of some safe and far away place. A place like maybe the maximum stir at San Quentin.

Before I had a chance to black out from the latest assault, a large, burly nurse who had spun steel for hair and a walnut for a nose came in behind the orderlies carrying smelling salts and a sponge. The former was passed under my nose, while the latter was dragged across my face. It felt like a wet brick.

"Don't kill this one, for God's sake!" she reprimanded the cowboy with the brass whip. "This lunatic jumped Judge Rader up in Seattle today. They say he nearly choked him to death. The judge sent down word he's some kind of goddamn schizo red. The staff wants to examine him first thing in the morning. Throw him in the violent ward until then. We'll see how Mr. Mardonde will like his playmates out there."

Both the nurse and the orderlies made a point to laugh in my face. Then one of the white coats unbuckled the straps on my ankles while the other removed the strap around my chest that held me in the chair. The instant my legs were free, I kicked out with the tiny bit of strength I had left. I caught the cowboy in the place that sits closest to the saddle horn. He doubled over, howling like a coyote in a metal trap. His partner swung the back of his hand across my mouth, ringing my bell. It wasn't really necessary. I wasn't trying to make a break for it. I was only making a partial payment on a recently incurred debt. I had no other intentions.

I was next hustled out of the bloody room and marched through several doors and down a corridor, dark, dank, sweating with water seeping through wood-slatted walls. I was chilled by a frigid verbal wind swirling and humming up and down its length. One of the doors I was pushed through led outside. There were several smaller, drearier buildings behind Steilacoom's main administration wing. The cold winter air was no more severe outside than it was inside.

Finally, I was stopped at the door to a barracks-like shack. An orderly placed a large key into the lock and turned it. The metal door swung open and I was shoved inside. The door clanked shut behind me and I heard the key turning in the lock. Both sounds echoed loudly. Thoughts of Paul Muni and all the prison movies I had ever seen came rushing to my mind. I knew then why they called it **Twenty Thousand Years in Sing Sing**. I wasn't amused.

The ward was nearly dark. A couple small bulbs burned overhead, allowing me to peer dimly into the corners of the large rectangular hall. An angry wind from Puget Sound moaned and hissed as it penetrated the cardboard-thin walls and jabbed its icy fingers into my pores. I could hear people, the inmates, breathing irregularly and snoring and groaning. There was angry grunting and the grinding of teeth, too.

Some of the inmates, I could see, were strapped in their cots. Many others were curled up on blankets on the floor. To my advantage, my entrance went unnoticed. I leaned my back against the wall next to the door and eased my armless body slowly down to the floor. The odor of the ward was overpowering. I could smell and feel the human elimination around me. Some of it was my own. I might have been terrified by the sounds and smells of the violent ward, but a total, if not comfortable, sleep overcame me first.

CHAPTER 25

When I woke I felt like I had died in the night. Or, at least, that had been my wish. Every place in my body that was capable of feeling pain throbbed without relief. My eyes were caked with blood and saltwater. The inside of my mouth was filled with mucus and other foul tasting fluids. The floor felt like a polar ice cap and the smells and sounds were not only just as bad as the night before, but now eminently visible as well. I wriggled to a kneeling position. It was then I noticed the small crowd around me staring and pointing. Some giggled when I looked at them. Others seemed resentful and scowled or cursed. The rest simply looked like people on the street looking at the Christmas display in Macy's window. If anything could have surprised me at that point it was that the violent ward was co-ed. Probably too much bother to segregate the place but, since the protection of the inmates had a low priority, if any, I guess it wasn't that surprising after all. I think the surprise came in the fact that the institution's cruelty, in this instance, was to my advantage.

I saw a nurse among the crowd. She was not the one with the walnut nose, but someone stamped from the same mold. She was flanked by two orderlies sprung from the same litter as the two who whacked me around the previous night.

After a few moments of reciprocal staring, the nurse clapped her hands. "Attention, people! Attention! I want you all to welcome Mr. Roco Mardonde. He is going to be staying with us for a while."

"I don't like him," growled one of the inmates, who like myself was strapped in a strait jacket.

"What's he doing here?" said a young woman with a shrill voice.

The nurse held up her hand. "Now people, don't be that way. Mr. Mardonde has come here because he is not feeling well. He has a problem just like the rest of us. Now, let's leave Mr. Mardonde alone and get ready for breakfast."

People began drifting away and went to one of two long tables at the far end of the ward. Moments later the door to the ward opened and two trustees entered pushing a large metal can of oatmeal. The inmates who could feed themselves were given wooden spoons and a tin bowl full of the stuff. Those who were in restraint lapped up the gruel with their tongues.

Before the end of breakfast several people were vomiting wildly on the floor. Others messed their pants. Those that had pants. Some had no clothing at all. A couple inmates crawled on the floor licking up whatever lay there. The nurses yelled at the violators, which only ignited the whole ward. The yellers yelled. The criers cried. The hitters pounded the walls, the cots, the floors and each other. The ward was joined by three new orderlies who raced in carrying strait jackets and rubber clubs. In less than a minute bedlam reigned supreme. Steilacoom, among many other things, was a twentieth century version of a medieval pesthouse.

When order finally obtained some twenty minutes later, the day's activities got under way. They included, in no particular order of importance, being strapped in a cot, pacing the ward, being taken to the toilet, talking to and at each other, crying, screaming and mopping the floor.

I didn't get breakfast. I could have committed an anti-social act for a cup of grounds. Even the battery acid they serve in jails and asylums would have been welcome. That, and a cigarette. Dreams! But I still had my mind and my memories, Dr. Walter J. Freeman notwithstanding.

The straps on my strait jacket had been loosened by one of the orderlies on the nurse's orders. I guess my eyes were starting to bulge. The slight movement allowed my shoulders and elbows was welcome like a complete recovery from polio. In situations like these you learn to count your blessings by the millimeter.

It was an hour or so after I had been raised from the dead that I started to work. Work! The world's first shamus in a canvas bag. I remembered Frances Farmer as a sturdy blonde beauty in **Come and Get It** and **The Toast of New York**, but I knew I would find nothing like that on the violent ward where, from the report Jake Diltz made, she was still sure to be. Then there was the newspaper wire photo taken five years ago just after the courtroom brawl that landed her in the Western Washington charnel house the first time. Jake Diltz had shown it to me that night in McCarthy's. That was probably more like it. Thirtyish, near shoulder length dark blond hair falling in random shards. I remembered her face in the wire photo. It was rugged — hard, even — cynical and defiant. Yet it retained a beauty that was earthy and wholesome. And a pair of sizzling dark eyes that could knock planes out of the sky.

But that was a long time ago, too. I didn't think Steilacoom would allow her that. I was looking for a woman twenty years older than the wire photo, probably anemic and, I could believe, perpetually sick. What I found was quite different. A woman, a blonde-haired woman, sat at the far end of one of the tables, alone, smoking a cigarette. I approached her. She was the spitting likeness of that five year-old photo. Pastier in the face, harsher in the eye, but the same woman. Unbroken was the look etched on her face.

"Well, what the hell are you looking at?" she barked at me.

"Are you Frances Farmer?"

"So what if I am? Who are you? Bob Hope?"

"No. My name's Kovachs. Riley Kovachs."

"Never heard of you. Spin your wheels, buster. Can't you see the lady's busy?"

"I would like to talk to you, Miss Farmer."

"Miss Farmer! Ha! That's a good one. Look, boyfriend, why don't you just go over in the corner and spit up with the rest of the boys. You look like you could use the exercise."

"Look, Miss Farmer, I went to a whole lot of trouble to get into this dungeon to see you."

"Ha! You a comedian or something? You **tried** to

get in here? Brother! You really are crazy! Now haul your ass out of here! Go roll on the floor or something. Leave me alone!

I couldn't give in. "I'll try it again. Larry Berger. Jake Diltz? Those names mean anything to you? They sent me to bust you out of here. There is reason to believe . . ."

"There is reason to believe you are a certified looney. As well as an obnoxious jackass. What do you want from me, buster? A feel? You're a bit early, aren't you? The soldier boys aren't due for another run until tonight."

"What? Soldiers?"

"From Ft. Lewis. As if you didn't know?"

"I, I don't follow."

"Don't play dumb with me, you pervert! As if you didn't know that this is the biggest whorehouse in the state of Washington. Only the women here have no say in it. The soldier boys from Lewis are hungry. And some of the goddamn keepers here are their pimps. So, if you want any, you'll have to talk to them, take a number and get in line. Until then, bug off!"

There was a firey anger in Frances Farmer's eyes. Anger and rage. A rage that wasn't specifically directed at me. A rage that was kept under control because she was in a situation where she had no control. No control over her incarceration, her "treatment", the soldiers who took advantage of her. But her rage was the kind that kicked a hole through all this to let her tormentors know she wasn't beaten. A rage that warned them the moment she gained an ounce of position in the situation, they would be made to pay dearly. But I wasn't one of her tormentors and I had to meet tough with tough.

"Look, lady, we don't have time to talk about this filthy pit and what goes on here. You got a raw deal, sure, but I'm here to get you out. Let's talk about that."

She mocked me. "I have a better idea. Let us sit upon the ground and tell sad stories of the death of kings . . ."

"How some have been deposed; some slain in war; some haunted by the ghosts they have deposed," I said, interrupting her.

She was surprised. "Say, you know your Shakespeare, don't you?"

"Just the Henry's and the two Richard's. I fake the rest."

Her eyes softened. No longer were they harpoons to gaffe me. Her angry face softened some, too. Just a bit. It wasn't exactly a smile she was wearing, but it was close.

"Hey, bub," she said. "You're no looney."

"And neither are you."

"Ha ha ha! So we're both quite sane. That little bit of information and a nickel will get you a phone call. Except in here they don't have phones. So where does that leave us, Mr. Jailbreak?"

"Yeah, this place is full of irony, isn't it? Look, are we on the same wavelength? Are we going to be able to put our heads together and come up with a plan to push out of here?"

"You're cute. In a dumb sort of way. Here's a broad who's been stepping in her own dirt for more years than she can remember going to be rescued by Sir Galahad in a strait jacket. I could laugh."

I had to admit it did sound absurd. Ludicrous. But I had gained her attention if not yet her confidence. That gave me the opening to rattle off the long and twisted story that landed me in Steilacoom. The information about the suspected lobotomy gave even Steilacoom's most hardened mental p.o.w. a fright. I could see it in her eyes. She was skeptical about the ice pick job, but it tempered her sarcasm some. But who could blame her skepticism, given her situation and my tale, which even to me sounded like the raving of a mad man? Perhaps what kept Frances Farmer's ear tilted in my direction so long was that behind the rage and cynicism lay an unfertilized seed of hope.

"They can't keep me in this strait jacket forever," I said. "I talked my way into it and I can get myself out of it. And those boys in the good humor coats who pass out canvas bags and hard times can be had."

"You sound like something out of one of the lousy movies I made."

I couldn't really argue with her. "Yeah, but it's the only way out of here. I've been here less than twenty-four hours and I'm about to go stir bugs. How do you do it? You've been here four years, is it? I don't know, maybe you're used to it."

"You never get used to it!" she shot back. "Never! You live with it because you have no other choice if you want to go on living. But you never get used to it."

"Well, then. Are we a team?"

"Sure. A regular mutual admiration society." I knew she wasn't convinced either of me or the possibility of escape from the Devil's Island of Puget Sound, but I didn't have the time or strength to wage a campaign to win her over. I would carry her kicking and insulting all the way to Frisco if that's the way it had to be. I think she sensed that. She lit a cigarette and placed it in my mouth. I took it as a sign. Evidently, so did the nurse. She came over and ripped the tobacco from my face.

"No smoking for patients in restraint!" she said nastily. "You know that, Frances. Do you want to have your privileges revoked?"

The former movie star scowled at her. "In your hat, nursie baby! You can do whatever you goddamn want!"

"Frances! What have you been told about your abusive language? If you didn't have such a dirty mouth you might not be in here."

"Can you believe this broad?" Frances Farmer said, turning to me. "Like if I cleaned up my vocabulary I would be stamped sane and cut loose from this funny farm."

"Frances! That'll be enough! You have been doing so well lately. In fact, you have been scheduled for staff this afternoon. There are some visiting physicians who wish to talk to you."

Frances Farmer winced. Then she shot me a glance. We both knew what "visiting physicians" referred to.

"As for you, Mr. Mardonde," the nurse said, "you are scheduled for staff in thirty minutes. Your preliminary evaluation."

She called for two white jackets to escort me to a washroom and clean me up.

CHAPTER 26

After twenty minutes in a place that smelled a hundred times worse than the sewers of Vienna, I had most of the blood off my face. My eyes were still swollen and my vision a bit blurred, but they took off the canvas wrapper and gave me back my arms.

When the jacket was removed, my arms dangled in front of me like a couple of marionettes on a string. They ached, they wouldn't move when I wanted them to and they looked funny. But they were mine and they were back. I could feel the strength slowly returning with each passing moment.

I was led into a poorly lit room in the main building. There was a large, thick oak table in its center. Sitting on one side of it were six people looking terribly profound. I was dumped in a small chair opposite them. I would have studied their faces more carefully, but I was busy playing with my newly sprung fingers.

"Mr. Mardonde," said the man seated near the middle of the table. His face was partially obscurred by a large briarwood pipe that protruded from his mouth like a back porch. "You have been brought here so that we may become a little better acquainted." I laughed to myself. "I am Dr. Krimm. My associates and I will conduct the interview." He tapped the bowl of his pipe on the lip of a nearby ashtray. With a small penknife he produced from a pocket in his coat, he scraped the inside of the bowl.

"How about a smoke, Doc?" I said. "I got a nicotine fit something fierce."

"We are not here to grant you favors," scolded a baldheaded man sitting on Krimm's left. He had a voice that sounded like his tonsils had been marinated in a cranberry bog and a face full of red freckles that made him a ringer for Arthur Godfrey. "Just why do you think you are here, anyway?" he asked rhetorically.

"Forget it, Jackson. It was just a thought."

"Do you know why you are here?" said Krimm,

repeating the baldheaded man.

"I was a bad boy."

"A very bad boy, I would say," corrected another of the head shrinkers.

"Okay, have it your way. A very bad boy."

"Tell us something about yourself, Mr.Mardonde," said Dr. Krimm. "You had no identification when you were brought in here."

"Nothing much to tell, fellas."

"Oh, don't be so modest," Krimm prodded. "Where are you from? Let's start with that."

"I'm forty-two years old. I live in Long Beach, California where I am a biology teacher. I have a pet frog named MacDougal and in my spare time I play the cello. I'm divorced. No kids. For fun I go to the beach. On rainy days I stay in and work on my stamp collection."

A man at the far end of the table took off his glasses and pointed them at me. "Don't think we won't check this out. We're not fools, you know."

"Pardon me. My mistake."

"What?" shouted the doctor with the naked pate. "You're hostile, aren't you? Why are you hostile?"

"Me? Hostile? Don't know what you're talking about, friend. I'll be the first to admit the accomodations could be a little better, but on the whole everything's been real George."

"That will be quite enough, Mr. Mardonde," said Dr. Krimm, rapping a pencil on the table.

"He's hostile! Very hostile!" repeated the baldheaded man in his nasal twang.

"A classic case," said the only woman in the group. She adjusted her dark horn-rimmed glasses. She looked nervous.

"I'm afraid I must agree," said Dr. Krimm.

"It isn't normal for a person to be so antagonistic, is it, Mr. Mardonde?" said the woman.

I laughed through my nose. "It's not normal to be strapped in a strait jacket and tossed into the violent ward of a lunatic asylum. I guess I just took it the wrong way."

"Do you feel mentally ill?" Krimm asked in all seriousness.

This time I laughed out loud. "Sure! Why else would I be here?"

"I think he's being sarcastic again," said the bald-headed man.

"Do you know what you did that caused you to be brought here?" asked the woman, chewing on the end of her glasses.

"Let's see. Before I got the poo knocked out of me I remember having a disagreement with some mug."

The woman continued. "Do you remember with whom you had this disagreement?"

"Not really. Just some jerk."

"Some jerk!" twanged Arthur Godfrey's double. "That jerk was Judge Rader!" The man's head turned pink. It looked like it had been dipped into a pot of boiling water.

"You are a sick man, Mr. Mardonde," said Krimm. "Why would anyone attack one of the most respected members of the community? A Superior Court Judge!"

I shrugged my shoulders. "Dunno. Maybe it was something he said."

"Or maybe something you said," continued Dr. Krimm. He opened a folder at his elbow and began turning the pages. He stopped when he found the place he was looking for. "Judge Rader reports that after a short discussion on some matters of mutual concern you changed your tone and became violent. I quote, 'The subject lunged at me, grabbing me around the throat and commenced choking me. All the while he was screaming communist slogans such as: Stalin is my God and death to the capitalist parasite.' End quote." Dr. Krimm rapped his pencil on the table several times. Then he screwed his eyes into mine and asked, "Are you a communist, Mr. Mardonde?"

"What?" I said.

"Answer the question," said the baldheaded man. "Are you a communist?"

"Please, Mr. Mardonde, are you a communist or a communist sympathizer?" repeated the pyhsician turned inquisitor.

"Is that why I'm here?" I said, raising my voice for the first time. "Because you think I'm a communist?"

"You will please answer the question," said Kirmm sternly.

"Since when is a person's politics a mental disease?"

"Then you don't deny it?" said Krimm impatiently.

"Practically an open admission of guilt," chimed the man with no hair.

"I admit nothing. Nothing, that is, except my every right as a citizen and a human being has been revoked somewhere between Seattle and here."

"Aha!" proclaimed the baldheaded man rising halfway out of his chair. "That's the communist line if I ever heard it."

"You're right," agreed Krimm, "we've got us a live one here." He leaned forward and glanced down to the far end of the table. "What do you think, Dr. Freeman?"

First rule of sleuthing — when you make a mistake

or drop a clue, admit it. To yourself. There were any number of reasons why my tail didn't grow stiff and point toward Freeman the moment I walked into the room. Any number. But the simple truth is I didn't recognize the knife-thrower from D.C.

The instant I heard Freeman's name my head almost left my neck it jerked so sharply. Freeman, however, didn't seem to notice. He had a speech to make.

"Very interesting. Very interesting, indeed. I wish to first thank you, Dr. Krimm, ladies and gentlemen for allowing me the great privilege of attending your staff meeting. Now, as to Mr. uh, uh. . . ."

"Mardonde," said Dr. Krimm, helping his famous guest over a difficult hump.

"Yes. Mr. Mardonde. I think you will all agree that the patient is socially as well as mentally unbalanced and his particular psychosis is extremely dangerous. You see, he is a classic schizophrenic paranoid with latent hostilities. And his paranoia has been transferred into political terms. Politically pernicious terms, if I may be allowed. So, instead of the traditional hearing of voices or believing someone, a brother, a wife, even a pet is out to get him and do him harm, it is the free enterprise system that is his nemesis. His bogeyman."

"Ah, yes," said the baldheaded man. "Brilliant analysis, doctor."

Freeman continued. "I've seen it before. The communists especially like to prey on this type of individual. Twist and turn his mental illness against the democratic institutions of our land. In this particular case, the latent hostility is brought to the surface. The patient feels the pressing need to lash out at the symbols of the system. Judge Rader was such a symbol. That's why he attacked him. Mental illness and communist indoctrination — a lethal mixture, to be sure."

Dr. Krimm picked up the ball from there. "I think I speak for the entire staff," he said in an after-dinner voice, "when I say Dr. Freeman's reputation as the preeminent neurologist in America today is no exaggeration. I'm sure Dr. Freeman's penetrating analysis of this patient's illness is an inspiration to us all."

I felt like we were all obliged to stand up and applaud. I didn't, but at Krimm's signal, the others gave their visitor from D.C. a small ovation.

"Thank you, thank you," beamed the goateed Freeman. "You are much too kind. I would like to request your permission to consider this patient for tomorrow's demonstration. He is a remarkable specimen. It is my contention that we can harness his hostility by removing, as it were, a portion of his troubled thought process. I speak specifically of his troubled memories, those memories that plague him and are, in the main, responsible for both his social and mental illness. Remember, if you will, doctors, leucotomical surgery means fewer thoughts, and fewer tortured thoughts and memories mean a happier, saner individual."

Dr. Krimm tapped out the ashes in his pipe on the edge of the ashtray in front of him. He looked up and down the table. "Doctors, are we in agreement with Dr. Freeman's request to have this patient participate in tomorrow's demonstration?" No one said anything, but heads nodded reflexively and grunts of approval emitted from several mouths.

Krimm smiled broadly. "Fine, Dr. Freeman, you have your first subject." Krimm pressed a button located on the edge of the table and a nurse appeared through the door. "Miss Brawley," he said, "Mr. Mardonde is ready to return to the ward. Have him prepped for E.C.T. by nine tomorrow morning."

The nurse nodded blankly. "Do you want him returned to restraint, Doctor?"

Dr. Krimm hesitated, but the baldheaded man didn't. "Absolutely! This man is dangerous. It would be a serious mistake not to put him in a jacket."

Dr. Krimm asked for other opinions. All concurred. Dr. Freeman advised that, like with Judge Rader, I might take the nurses, attendants, patients and even the doctors for symbols to be attacked. Better safe than sorry, he counseled. It was unanimous. The nurse went to get some orderlies.

I had naively hoped when I was brought into the staff room I could convince them I was just a regular guy and didn't need to go around laced up like a boot. But one has a lot of naivety when it comes to mental asylums. Even the most cynical and hard-bitten of us. But then I learn fast.

Krimm looked at me. His eyes focused on my shoulder, not my eyes. "I hope you can understand this is for your own good. Everything we do here at the hospital is for the benefit of the patient. Tomorrow at this time you will thank us and I would add . . ."

I interrupted Krimm in mid sentence. "You Nazi butchers!" I shouted, leaping up from the chair. I dove over the table yelling. "You refugees from Hitler's bunker! You're not going to make a sliced salami out of my brain!"

With one hand I grabbed Krimm's throat and began choking. With the other hand I made a furious and frantic search of his coat pockets. Surprise was on my side, but I knew it would only last an instant.

Having been trained in the most modern techniques of picking pockets by some of the world's leading practitioners gave my assault a hint of a chance. I was looking for the pen knife Krimm carried to clean his pipe. It was a long shot, but it was also my only shot.

I got my hand inside Krimm's pockets in less time than it takes the DuPonts to make another million. And I struck paydirt almost as fast. I grabbed the small folded knife, pulled it out and stuffed it in my mouth. By that time everyone was screaming loudly, including, I suspected, Dr. Freeman and the baldheaded man. Then came the rain of blows to my head and neck. The orderlies had arrived. I rolled myself up into a ball to protect my face. I offered no resistance at all.

As the last strap of the canvas was yanked tight and I was being pushed through the staff room door, I heard Krimm say, "This man is to receive no supper tonight and I want him prepped for E.C.T. at seven! Sharp!"

"He's a lunatic. A homicidal lunatic!" hollered the baldheaded man in his Arthur Godfrey voice. He didn't know the half of it.

CHAPTER 27

I was given the bum's rush out of the staff room, through several doors and long corridors and out of the building to the violent ward where I was pushed through the door almost before the orderly opened it. Whether I fell on the floor and blacked out or just found a spot to lie down and began chopping wood at the same time, I don't know.

Sometime later the thick, rich smoke of a burning cigarette crept into my nostrils. I opened my eyes and saw Frances Farmer crouched over me.

"Well, boyfriend," she said, "did you get the Governor to give us a pardon?" She lowered the cigarette to my lips. I took a generous drag. She helped me to a sitting position. "I hope you've got some bright ideas about getting us out of here. This place is beginning to bore me."

I spit the pen knife from my mouth. Frances Farmer laughed. "Ha ha! Do you really think that'll hold them off?"

When words came to my mouth I said, "No, but it might get me out of this penguin's cocoon. Take it and hold it until I tell you."

"You'll pardon me if I don't applaud your ingenuity. They'll just put you right back in another one when they find out you've snipped the straps."

"Look, lady, I know I don't inspire much confidence, but you've got to meet me halfway. A slim chance to bust out of here is a whole lot better than none. We've got to work fast. We're going over the top tonight."

"Tonight!" she said loudly. Several nearby inmates turned around and looked at us. A couple of them drifted over to us. It made me uncomfortable, but Frances Farmer assured me it was alright.

"Yes, tonight," I repeated in a whisper. "Freeman's going to start throwing darts in the morning. Did you have a staff interview this afternoon?"

"Yes."

"And?"

"And what? Those clowns talked about some kind

of demonstration and asked me if I wanted to take part. I told Krimm to flush it. That baldheaded creep nearly swallowed his tie."

"Yeah, well, that demonstration is no march for the Smith Act Defendants. Freeman's going to operate on several of the inmates. I'm on the starting team and I'd bet a cup of North Beach expresso you're batting cleanup."

There came a look to Frances Farmer's eyes that was hard to describe. It wasn't exactly fright. After four years in a place like Steilacoom, there was little left to be frightened of. The look in her eyes was one of belief. Like she believed what I was saying. Like she believed that, despite all the horror she had lived through, a lobotomy was the ultimate stop on her freight train of nightmares. Like maybe she even believed in me.

"Okay, mister," she said after a long pause, "I don't know you from a wart on a frog, but I know you're no cop, judge, or spy and I don't think you work for the lousy bastards who run this snake pit. By sheer process of elimination, I'd say you're probably on the level. So, for whatever screwy reason you have for thinking you can bust us out of this hell hole, I guess I can at least go along with you. Christ, what can they do to me if it falls through? Ha! That's the damn irony of this place. What can they do? Let's get on with it. What did you say your name was?"

"Kovachs. But I'm here under the name of Mardonde."

"I'm sure you have your reasons. I'm here under an alias myself. My married name. Hasn't done me a whole lot of good, though."

"Yeah, I can tell."

Frances Farmer laughed and lit another cigarette.

"One of the nurses slips me three smokes every day. I told her I'd give her an autograph and a glossy for two cartons. The stupid broad went for it." She reached over and placed the tobacco in my mouth. "Here, you need this worse than I do."

I sat on the floor puffing the damn thing, smoke pouring into my eyes. I didn't care, I had to have those couple drags. Just like Bogart did when he was tied up on the floor of that roadhouse in **The Big Sleep** with Lauren Bacall passing him a smoke. I motioned for Frances Farmer to take the cigarette.

"Okay," I said. "Let's pool our information about this place. We're in a separate building. We get out of here, we're outside, maybe fifty yards from the main building. The distance between is a dirt court yard that is fenced in. How am I doing so far?"

"Right on the money."

"Good. I'd say it wouldn't be wise to go through the main building. Too many obstacles. If we get over the fence that closes in the court yard, where are we?"

"In trouble. Another three hundred yards away is a bigger fence that runs around the whole stinking place."

"I was afraid of that."

"And it is patrolled by a couple of guards. I think they carry rifles. I can't remember."

"Any gun turrets?"

"You mean, like in a prison?" The former actress stopped to correct herself. "Get a load of me. Like a prison. This is a goddamn prison. I must be getting soft. No, they don't have gun turrets."

"Okay, so we have two fences, a couple of bulls maybe toting rifles and an unknown number of orderlies to get past."

"Not very good odds, are they?"

"If they were you'd have busted out yourself long ago."

"You're telling me!"

"Okay. So that's what we'll have to do. It would be nice if we could just do a fast fade and slip away unnoticed, but that seems unlikely. We've got to go the old diversion route."

"What's that?"

"You know, create a commotion in one place so you can get away in the opposite direction."

"You've been to too many movies."

"Give me a chance, will you?"

"I'm sorry. So what kind of commotion did you have in mind?"

"You said something about soldiers from Fort Lewis coming in here and . . ."

"Don't remind me. Those bastards are going to make a run tonight."

"Good."

"What! You stinking creep, do you know what they do?"

"I'm sorry. I mean, good, that's our diversion."

"And just how do you figure that?"

"They sneak in from Lewis, right? I mean they don't sign the guest book and march through the front door."

"Yeah. So what?"

"So, that means a whole lot of people are in on it. Like the bulls who patrol the grounds. There's probably a convenient hole in the fence someplace."

"I get it. We can get out the way they come in. Through a hole in the fence."

"Well, it looks good on paper."

"Except we're not doing this on paper. And we don't exactly look like a couple of doughboys on furlough. Did you think about that? The guards aren't going to like it."

"You're right. That'll be the tricky part. We'll have to exchange clothes with two of them. And since they just arent likely to be crazy about the idea we'll have to be on our best and click like a seventeen-jewel Bulova watch."

"Okay, how do we do that?"

"Tell me how it works. I mean when the soldiers come here."

Frances Farmer looked away. She reached into the pocket of her smock and took out a single match and her last cigarette. She struck the match on the floor and lit the tobacco.

"Hell, I don't know why I get like this after so long. Like you said, I should be used to everything by now, right? The electric shock. I still have headaches and there are big gaps in my memory I don't ever expect to recover. And the hydrotherapy. You ever spent ten hours strapped in a tub of ice water up to your neck? First you scream until your voice goes away. And then you thrash your body until your muscles give out. All this while your mind goes blank from sheer terror and pain and you're reduced to a gibbering lunatic. I nearly bit off my lip the first time. And this is what they call therapy. Therapy, mind you!"

She took a long pull from the cigarette, filling her lungs with smoke. When she exhaled I could believe a lot more than smoke was coming out. She continued. "I guess it's no worse than being raped. I mean your body and mind violated and brutalized by mindless freaks. Some wear white coats, the others olive drab. But, you know, there is a difference. Maybe the treatment, the "therapy", is impersonal, while the rapes are a more private violation. I don't know."

I didn't know either. And I didn't know what to say

to this woman who had lived through it all for so many long years. A prisoner of war in her own country, her own state. It was one of those times that I was at a total loss for words, words that I could speak that would let her know that I cared, that I shared her pain and her rage, without sounding sentimental or condescending. The ditches of my eyelids filled with water. I told her it was the smoke from her cigarette. She smiled and continued.

"Okay. These goddamn orderlies bring the soldiers in. Generally about twenty of them. Mostly those dog faces just roam around until they find someone that strikes their fancy, then wrestle them to the ground like cattle. But most of the women don't put up a fight. I doubt if some of them even know what's happening to them. Anyway, I get special treatment, see. Being a movie star has its privileges, you know. There is a small staff room off the back end of the ward where the nurses and orderlies go to get away from this stinking mess. They take me in there. There are sometimes two or three of them. I hear one of the orderlies, a pig named Chatman, stands at the door taking money from the soldiers. I used to fight the bastards, but that was a long time ago. Now, I just try to think about other things." Her voice began to trail off. I had the information I needed so I didn't press her for any more details.

I spent the next few minutes offering what I judged to be the most plausible scenario for getting us out of Steilacoom. Getting out dressed as soldiers. It had a chance. Ever since Nixon and Chambers pulled that microfilm out of a pumpkin in Maryland I have believed in miracles. And it would take a miracle to pull this off. But we needed something a lot more than a lucky pumpkin.

CHAPTER 28

We talked a little more about the plan, such as it was. But as to the details, they would have to be developed on the spot. The G.I. raid from Fort Lewis, the separate room where they take Frances Farmer, the pimp orderly named Chatman — these were all factors that had to play out their roles, their routine of past ugliness, simply to trigger the plan. Then things had to run as smoothly as high octane ethyl just to get us on the other side of the violent ward door and into a fenced-in court yard.

But those were things not to think about. Faith was the best medicine in this situation. That and a large tablespoon of self-deception. I hoped we were prepared to swallow them both.

The actress got to her feet and left me. The idea was not to speak to each other until after the lights went out and the soldiers began arriving. The suspicious eye of a nurse or orderly seeing us spending too much time looking sane together could tip our hand and kill our chances of escape.

I spent the next several hours walking around the ward trying to avoid confrontations with the other inmates. To a few of them, eye contact was all it took to come over and bump you, start yelling in your face or try to be your friend for life. The ward was a large holding cell choked with people. The absence of fresh air coupled with the lack of physical space was suffocating. For many it had been this way day in and day out for years. Decades! No wonder they screamed out, struck their fellow inmates and laughed at nothing. The frustration of their immediate situation and the prospect of a lifetime of the same was enough to drive the sane stark raving mad. I could feel the process germinating within myself and I had been in stir only twenty-four hours.

After a period of aimless pacing, I noticed I was not exactly alone. I turned my head to see a man in a dirty gray canvas bag walking with me two steps behind. I tried not to notice him, but it wasn't easy.

"I've been watching you," he said. "Talking with that actress broad."

"Don't know what you mean pal," I replied with as little regard as I could dispense. "No actresses in here. Just us gooney birds."

"Don't play cute with me, man. I wrote the book."

I heard the faint sound of a faraway voice screaming with panic. It was my own. My heart began thumping like a rabbit's hind leg. I stared into the man's face for some kind of clue. He was young, about thirty, Negro and very angry. He had that same rage I saw in Frances Farmer.

"Look," he said, when I didn't say anything, "you're not crazy and neither is she."

"Well, that makes three of us, if you count yourself."

"Yeah. You can forget that wiseguy stuff. I know you're up to something and I want in."

"Don't know what you're talking about, pal. You got me confused with some other guy in a straight jacket."

"Damn it, man, I'm on your side. I want out of here and I think you have a plan."

"Just for the sake of argument, if I did have a plan,

as you call it, why should I include you in?"

"Because, just for the sake of argument, the three of us don't belong here and you know it. And the three of us know, ain't no court of law going to help us get out."

"Say, pal, just who are you, anyway? I mean how did you land up in this armless stir?"

"Like what's a nice guy like me doing in a lousy place like this?"

"I didn't say you were a nice guy."

"And I'm not. Being black and angry, they sort of go together. That's what got me here."

We walked as we talked. He told me he was a Merchant Marine during the war and sailed on the **Booker T. Washington**, the first integrated ship in naval history. And the first ship to be captained by a Negro commander.

The man continued to talk. "I guess I have always been angry in one way or another at the way Negro people are treated in this country. I grew up in Jim Crow Virginia. I spent a year at Howard University before the war. I discovered W.E.B. DuBois and began to think that it may not be white people but the system that is the cause of the problem.

"Then when I sailed on the **Booker T.** I got a chance to see democracy and fascism first hand. Like in Tunisia where I saw German prisoners of war guarding Arab workers building roads. And I saw American M.P.'s shoot starving kids on Italian docks who were trying to steal rotten bananas from American food stores. And I wasn't allowed in bars run by fascists or the Red Cross.

"Then, after saving the world for democracy I came home and got the same old discrimination. In some cases it was worse. I came out to L.A. and then

Seattle hoping it would be better. But it wasn't. Somewhere along the way I came to realize that it was only the resistance fighters and the crew of the **Booker T.** that treated Negroes fairly. And most of them were communists. I mean red flag revolutionary communists!

"Got me to thinking that maybe we weren't saving democracy after all during the war. I mean, where's the democracy for the colored people? Since the war ended, every time the black man stands up for his rights the papers say it's the communists behind the scenes making trouble. They also said it was the communists who were stirring up all the trouble in France and Italy. Hell, to my way of thinking it was the communists who were the ones that were really fighting fascism. The rest of them were just jive. The same goes for civil rights in this country. I don't know if that makes me a communist, but I got eyes and I know who is and who is isn't fighting fascism and racism."

The man, whose name was Clifton, said he became a militant, "a revolutionary hothead," as he himself put it, and since the war had been in one scrape after another, brawling with police, bosses and other outspoken rednecks. The incident that punched his ticket to Steilacoom was being stopped by a cop on a downtown Seattle street and getting pushed around one time too many for no good reason. Clifton laid him out with a couple hard rights to a glass jaw. He was wrapped in canvas and shipped to Steilacoom before the day was out.

"So, what do you say? " he said, concluding his story. "Am I in?"

I didn't say anything right away. We walked the length of the ward. "What if I say no? You turn us in?"

"Never been a snitch in my life. No, man, I wouldn't turn you in. But I might turn you inside out the first time I get out of this bag. I would make a point of it."

"I may be gone by then."

"Then again, you might not."

"I'm not saying I'm afraid of you, Clifton. I don't have the good sense to be frightened of anybody. But if you can follow my lead for the next couple hours you can join the team."

Clifton smiled for the first time since I met him. Probably for the first time in the two years since he'd been at Steilacoom. "Bossman," he said laughing, "you jes' says the word an' I be jumpin'."

If our hands had been free we would have shook them and slapped each other on the back.

I spent the next few minutes explaining the plan to Clifton. He knew no more about the grounds of Steilacoom than Frances Farmer. However, he did know the name of one of the guards, a bull named Chick. And, assuming we got that far, Clifton knew where the highways were. Highways that led away from the hell on Puget Sound.

CHAPTER 29

Dinner was another revolting spectacle of the institution administering humiliation and misery. A half hour later it was bedtime. Almost half the patients were strapped into their cots. Clifton and I, along with dozens of others, were assigned to the floor. When the lights went out a few minutes later the crying and babbling and gnashing of teeth began.

A short time after that Frances Farmer came to where I was lying helpless as a beached seal and propped me up against the wall. While she was cutting the straps to the strait jacket I told her about Clifton. She nodded affirmatively, but said nothing. Once free I went over and cut through Clifton's straps. We both kept the jackets on, replacing them very loosely. I told both my confederates that we were really freelancing this thing and if a breakdown occurred everybody was on his and her own.

Frances went back to her bed. Clifton and I whispered about the various contingencies that might arise in the next stage and how we might handle them. Then we separated.

Thirty minutes later I heard loud voices coming from outside the ward. Then a key turned in the lock of the door. The door swung open and fifteen to twenty men in uniform fell into the ward. They were loud, foul and drunk. There was enough light to take in everything, including the rank and campaign ribbons on the uniforms.

There were three white-jacketed orderlies who were orchestrating the intended gang rape. They were trying to quiet the doughboys and collect money from them at the same time.

The ward erupted when the inmates, aware of the intruders, began vocalizing their pleasure/displeasure. A few moments later the orderlies were joined by a man wearing a white coat that was longer than the rest. He looked like one of the doctors I had seen earlier at my staff observation, but he was wearing something that looked like a surgical mask, so I couldn't tell for sure. He and the orderlies went about the ward sedating some of the women inmates and a few of the more agitated men with hypodermic needles. It took only an instant. The din subsided some, but the situation remained on the thin edge of pandemonium.

Next, the men in the white coats began leading some of the soldiers to selected women. I saw one of them, the one described by Frances Farmer as Chatman, go over to her bed, flash a light in her eyes and then, pulling her up by the arm, lead her to the little room at the far end of the ward. He motioned for three soldiers to follow him. He called them by name.

That was my cue. I rose to my feet and started inching my way toward the room. I called out to Clifton thirty feet away. He knew what to do.

"Hey, Chatman," said the ex-sailor, walking up to the orderly who was standing in front of the door to the little room counting a fist full of paper money.

"What do you want, boy?" spit the muscle-bound Chatman. The man was large enough to have his own page in Jane's **Fighting Ships**.

"How 'bout a li'l action in there?" Clifton answered in his best Virginia drawl. "I ain't had me a piece of white meat in jes' ever so long." This inflamed the pimp, but that's the way Clifton wanted it. I could tell an old score was about to be settled.

"You crazy, nigger boy?" replied Chatman with a snarl. "You know this one's just for white men. Now get out of here before I break your goddamn back." He displayed a folded leather belt with a large metal buckle and slapped it against his thigh a few times to punctuate his remarks.

"You right, boss. Jes' thought I'd ask." Clifton turned around to walk away. The bull orderly smiled. In the next moment Clifton freed his arms from the strait jacket and spun around to face Chatman. A cocked right fist came out of nowhere and crashed into the orderly's face with a savage force of a tidal wave against an old wooden pier. The startled Chatman took the blow with his hands full of cash. He went flying backwards and was stopped only by the door and then just barely. Clifton rushed him and planted a boxer's combination of blows to his head and stomach as Chatman was sliding down the door.

I slipped out of my long-armed overcoat and joined Clifton at the door. I pulled him off his victim before he turned him into dog food. We picked up the unconscious Chatman and on the count of three pushed him through the unlocked door and into the room. There we found three very startled soldiers in various stages of undress. One had blood trickling from his face where Frances Farmer had hit him.

"Hey, you guys got to wait your turn," said one of them.

"The party's over, boys," I said.

"Hey, we paid good money for this," argued another.

"Yeah, where's Chatman? He can't do this," said the first soldier.

The conversation was growing stale. Clifton and I rushed the three of them. What ensued was a real pierside brawl. It was a pretty even match until Frances Farmer joined the fray. She unloaded a series of slaps and closed fist blows to one surprised soldier who went down like a wet noodle in a rain storm.

The fistivities were over almost before they started. The commotion, however, was bound to draw attention. The three of us changed clothes with the unconscious doughboys in double quick time.

Then there came a banging at the door. "Hey,

what's going on in there?" said a baritone voice. "Leave some for the rest of us."

"Yeah, hurry up in there," said a second, "we ain't got all night."

"Okay. Five more minutes," I said, trying to stall. "Give us a chance to get our money's worth."

"That you in there, Phil?" said the first voice.

"Yeah," I answered.

"Well, okay," said the baritone, "just hurry up, willya?"

"Five minutes," I repeated. I could hear the sound of feet walking away.

I turned to Clifton and Frances Farmer. "Now comes the tricky part. We've got to get to the ward door without drawing a crowd of belt-swingers."

"I say we rush them," Clifton offered.

"No, we'd never get half way. I'll take Chatman's keys and work my way to the door. I probably look more like a G.I. than either of you." They both nodded, agreeing with the obvious. "It'll take me a few minutes. Count to fifty then make a break for it. I'll be at the door. After that it'll be a can of corn. Only a pair of fifteen foot fences to shinny."

"Okay, get going," said the actress.

"Count fifty, then come out running," I said, reiterating the next step of the plan.

I opened the door and stepped out into the ward. It was louder than before. Several women were shrieking. Some male voices were telling them to shut up. Some others growled and moaned and yelled, agitated and excited by the evening's disruption. People were moving around the ward in erratic paths. Soldiers looking for the next body to mount; females darting away from and toward their pursuers; some male inmates pacing back and forth like caged animals; and some others following the soldiers, joining in the pursuit of the women. And the orderlies, now numbering two, and the man with the mask moving about unsuccessfully trying to keep everything under control.

No one noticed me as I walked unhurriedly toward the door. That is, until I was two-thirds the way there. One of the remaining orderlies came running over to me.

"What the hell is going on in there?" he demanded to know. "What do you mean hogging all the action? Hey, where's Chatman?"

I shrugged my shoulders and told him we were finished and he could send in a fresh team. The orderly wasn't satisfied.

"Where's Chatman," he repeated. "This thing's getting outta . . ." He didn't finish his sentence. His mouth dropped open. He was the white coat who opened my mouth with a belt buckle in the room where I had been strapped to the wooden chair.

"Hey, you're no damn soldier," he said regaining his voice. "You're . . ." He didn't get a chance to finish that sentence either. I gave him five folded knuckles across the lip. He went down like a medicine ball out the Tower of Pisa.

I was still twenty paces from the door when I turned and saw Clifton and Frances Farmer in the doorway of the small room. They drew a crowd almost immediately. They weren't fooling anybody. But they had the good sense to run like sixty before the doughboys knew exactly what to make of the situation.

I reached the door first and unlocked it. The only orderly left standing saw what was happening and flashed his light on me. When he realized I had the door keys and was making a break for it he sounded a mightly blast on a whistle that he was wearing around his neck. I didn't have to be told that was the signal for mayday.

Clifton and Frances Farmer raced for the door. The orderly ran to cut them off. They reached the open portal an instant before him. Clifton turned and slugged the orderly, planting him in his tracks. I slammed the door shut behind us and locked it. From the main building I could see lights snapping on. A claxon horn groaned, alerting everyone within a thousand yards of the jailbreak.

For the moment we were alone in the small courtyard that stood between the violent ward and the main wing of the asylum. The night was dark, damp and frigid, but the only thing on our collective minds was the fifteen foot high chain-link fence that enclosed the entire area.

But there was no time even to think of that. Five men in white coats came charging out the back door of the main wing. They were carrying strait jackets, leather belts and billy clubs.

I ran up to intercept their leader. "Get in there quick, pal. They've got a riot going on!"

The man stopped his small posse and took a long look at me. "Anyone escape?" he wanted to know.

"Hell, man, just us. And we're hightailing it back to Lewis. Don't want no part of this mess."

"What about them?" he said pointing to Clifton and Frances Farmer who were partially concealed by the darkness.

"Don't worry about them. Chatman is in there lying in a lake of blood! Better get in there before everybody gets killed!"

"Okay, hero," said the man sarcastically, gathering

up his charges and on to the rescue of his brethren in the violent ward. In a moment they disappeared behind the ward door.

"It's fence-climbing time," I said, herding my little squad to the end of the courtyard farthest from the violent ward. I cupped my hands for Frances Farmer to step in. I gave her a boost and she went up the fence slowly, but with determination. Clifton followed and reached the top before her. He reached out and grabbed her by the wrists and pulled her the rest of the way up. I was more than two-thirds of the way up when I heard voices coming from the direction of the violent ward. A beam of light crawled up my back.

"There they are!" someone called out.

"Phone the gate! Have them turn on the spot and get the dogs out!" said a second voice.

"Clifton! Frances!" I yelled. "We're going to have to make a run for the perimeter fence. There's bound to be a hole in it somewhere, but unless its got a neon exit sign we'll probably have to climb it. Get going!"

"Geronimo!" yelled Clifton, jumping from the top of the fence. I scrambled the rest of the way to the top. I could hear the pounding of a dozen feet closing in behind me. Frances Farmer was perched at the top of the fence, frozen.

"Jump, Frances! You've got to jump!" I hollered at her.

"I can't," she said. She was a shivering rack of flesh. Her physical condition, such as it was, was disputing her will to escape.

"It's the only way!" I pleaded. "Here, I'll help you."

She still refused to move. I reached behind her and gave her a push. She toppled forward. She reached out and grabbed the fence on her way down. It slowed her descent and helped break her fall. I jumped the fifteen feet, landing hard on my feet and pitching forward.

The beams from the orderlies' flashlights were in my eyes as I got to my feet. The posse was less than three dozen yards away.

Clifton must have seen us lying at the bottom of the fence. He came rushing back to help.

"Get out of here!" I screamed at him. "Get to the perimeter fence and find that hole! This is no time to be a hero!" Clifton didn't argue. He raced toward the fence that stood between us and freedom.

I went to Frances Farmer and helped her to her feet. She cried out with pain. It was her ankle.

"I can't make it, Kovachs! Leave me here! Save yourself!" I ignored her and began dragging her, hoping she would find the strength to run. After twenty yards she pulled herself free from my grip. "Let go of me damn it! I'm not going! Save yourself, you damn fool! They'll kill you if they catch you!"

The light from the orderlies' flashlights lit up her face. I searched it for some answers. I saw there was nothing that would change her resolve. I knew I would have to drag or pull her all the way to the perimeter fence. I also knew that wasn't possible. And I saw in her face something that said it was more than a sprained foot that was stopping her. It was **my** freedom that was in her eyes! By removing herself from the escape, she was rescuing me! There were tears on her cheeks.

"Go on, get out of here, you big dope! I don't want to spend the next twenty years staring at your ugly face."

I just stood there. Then she hauled off and slapped me.

"Get the goddamn hell out of here!" she bellowed in my face.

I could see the angry, murderous faces of the white-jacketed vigilantes approaching. Chatman was leading them. They were no more than twenty paces away. I grabbed Frances Farmer's hands and squeezed them. Then I embraced her. She allowed me a second and then pushed me away.

I turned and sprinted for Steilacoom's outer fence. I didn't look back. I heard Clifton yelling to me. Then shots rang out. I called back to Clifton. There was no response. I called out again. Only the shouts of my pursuers and the barking of vicious dogs answered.

I reached the fence and ran along it looking for him. The dogs, the angry voices and beams of light converged on me. I found the hole in the fence. I called out for Clifton one last time. I looked to the area where Frances Farmer was standing. It was swarming with white coats.

I raised my right hand and closed it into a fist and shook it into the night. "I'll be back!" I hollered. I doubt she heard me. Even if she did, it's doubtful she would have believed me. But it was something I had to say.

I turned and crawled through the opening in the fence and began running like my life depended on it.

CHAPTER 30

I ran as hard as I could for as long as I could. What was only minutes seemed like hours in a darkness illuminated only by the yellow sliver of a cloudy moon.

Trees and bushes jumped out of the night in an effort to tackle me as I whizzed by. Each one was a pursuing bull from Steilacoom trying to make the pinch. It made me run faster. Harder. Longer. The sound of my tortured breathing and the crunch and whoosh I made plowing through the thick grass was all that broke a night as still as its pretended innocence.

Thirty minutes, forty minutes, an hour later — I couldn't tell — I stopped to catch my breath. My ears pounded with a head-rattling thud. No sound obtained other than my own agonized breathing. No dogs, no bulls, no jeeps, no searchlights.

I squatted and grabbed my heels. I knew if I sat down in the soft thick grass I would certainly pass into an exhaustive unconsciousness.

I allowed myself only a few minutes, just long enough to let the dagger-sharp pain in my chest subside and push my pulse rate below two hundred. The precious time gave me the opportunity to get my bearings. I was at the point where I had to decide in what direction to flee.

Before the alternatives could be fully reviewed, I heard the undeniable sound of civilization — rubber tires grinding on pavement. I dove for cover and from a prickly clump of grass and weeds could see the twin beams of light bearing down on me. I lay as motionless as a dry twig. The lights were relentless. The vehicle to which they belonged drew closer. Three hundred yards, two hundred, one hundred, still closer.

I dropped my head to the cold ground and burrowed my nose into the moist earth. The vehicle's engine drew threateningly louder as it approached. Then it slowed down as if it were looking for an exact spot to stop and unload its cargo of slave catchers who would march over to my prostrate body and make an instantaneous decision to take me back or empty their weapons into my head.

I, on the other hand, couldn't run another step, regardless of the consequences. Instead, I bit hard on my lip and waited.

The vehicle's engine slowed gradually, ever gradually, as its lights grew brighter and closer. Then, without explanation, the whir of the engine quickened. My ears had developed perfect pitch while lying there in the grass. I could tell in an instant that, instead of slowing to a stop, the vehicle was resuming its earlier speed, and so, moving away from me. I listened to the high-pitched whine of its tires and the putting of its motor and was convinced they were growing fainter. In a moment there was no other sound but the night itself.

Confident that the vehicle wasn't coming back, I picked myself up and went to have a look. Slowly and gingerly I made my way beyond the sparse row of pines in the direction where I saw and heard the vehicle.

I stepped out of the bush and onto the berm of

highway! I had reached the highway, the glorious highway, the railroad to freedom! I immediately crossed the road and hung out my southbound thumb. A light rain began to fall. I welcomed it. Twenty minutes later a Nash pulled over. I ran down the highway to where it stopped. No chance any local authorities would be driving such an old, harmless looking bucket of bumpers. I opened the door and hopped in.

"Where you going, buddy?" said the driver, a man in his fifties, built like an Olympic Peninsula log.

"Frisco," I answered, "but anyplace down the road will be a help."

"Not going that far, but we'll get you to Portland, alright."

I climbed aboard without another word.

A mile or so later, the man turned to me. "Say, none of my business, but what's a soldier doing out on this God-forsaken stretch of road on a night like this? You go over the top, or something?"

"It's a long story, mister. You wouldn't have a smoke on you, would you?"

"Smoke a pipe, mainly, but I've got an old pack of Chesterfields on me." He reached into a pocket of his Pendleton shirt and produced the pack of butts and handed it to me. "Here, take as many as you want."

I took two. The man pushed in the dashboard lighter and in a moment I was inhaling the first drag on my own brand of smoke. It tasted like Christmas. I thanked the man and slid down a little in the seat. The rhythmic movement of the windshield wipers and their reassuring "whup-whup" captured and held my attention. My eyes stared blankly down the long, dark and blurry highway. Only an occasional road marker gave the void an earthly countenance. I took another drag on my Chesterfield.

My attempt to rescue Frances Farmer from the teeming bedlam of Steilacoom had failed. Period! What was to happen to her, I thought? No chance for a second escape. Should I go to the authorities? Ha! It was the authorities that put her away in the first place. There was not a bloody thing I could do. There was nobody to help.

Was she to remain the victim of fear, hostility and unspeakable torture the rest of her life? Would she pay for her "crimes against society" by having her brain cut away like a gangrenous limb? Would her soul continue to be punished hourly by an institutional savagery that even seeing, as I had, challenged believing?

And what about the other pathetic victims chained to the naked terror of Steilacoom? Were they, too, to be sentenced to a lifetime of hell? And Clifton. What about him? Was he lying on the ground back there, dead, in a pool of his own blood? Was a bullet to be the system's final punishment for his social felonies? Was asylum murder the wages for being a street fighter for human rights?

Places like Steilacoom, and they were to be found in nearly every major city in America, breed madness. The medical community, the "Healers," even the most noble-minded of them, are little more than keepers and conductors at best. And things didn't appear to be headed for any significant changes.

And what about us on the outside? Us, the living, for Frances Farmer and the others are but living corpses. Isn't there a touch of madness in the collective mind of a government that gives serious play to the idea of pulling the atomic trigger and reducing the world to a crisp cinder in its efforts to bluff the

Russians and beat back the rising tide of revolution? Are Truman, Marshall, and their industrial captains and their banker commandants insane to contemplate such a thing, or is it built into the system? A system grown old and decayed that stands trembling at the brink of a new age.

Was the article by General Spaatz the Harlem Kid read that night in the Glendale weeds an indication of what we can expect in the near future? A world war! Nothing is impossible. Maybe the bullet makers and bazooka tycoons will decide to turn a profit by sending all of us who survived the last war over to China and give us a second chance to come home wrapped in a flag. To some, I'm sure, that is a small price to pay for throttling communism.

And even if we survive the next few years, is the culture going to get the sharp knife of the political Dr. Freemans of the country? Hollywood has already been turned into a basket case and the schools and colleges are being given their own transorbital pruning that will sheer away any democratic memories.

The future looked grim to me. Grim as the Puget Sound night as the car hummed down the black tongue of asphalt toward Portland. What chance does Frances Farmer have, I murmured under my breath. What chance do any of us have?

"You a working man? said my benefactor, breaking the depressing silence. He reached over and offered me another cigarette.

"I've been around," I said still cautiously thinking of my past two days inside Steilacoom.

The driver shook it off. "Me, I'm a longshoreman in Portland. Say, you stiffs in Frisco are pretty tough cookies. That was some to-do in '34, wouldn't you say?"

"Yeah, I was there. It got pretty rough."

"Those were the days, weren't they? Stand up and fight. Union solidarity. Now the bosses are trying to smother us with this communist thing and Taft-Hartley. It's all a bunch of swamp water to me. Just another way they try to knock us off our pegs. But, hell, the war's over. They've got to pay! But they'd rather rub our noses in dirt than pay a fair day's wages. Cripes! Truman and those runny-nosed Congressmen who call theirselves Democrats. They're no better than the Republicans and they won't do a lick to stop Taft-Hartley from putting a rope around our necks. Hell no! We've got to fight them! Fight them every inch of the way! Don't you agree, buddy? Or are you with the bosses?"

I smiled, though my friend couldn't see my face. I snapped out of my trance. "No, I'm not with the bosses. And yeah, you're right. Dead right. We've got to fight them every inch of the way. Tooth and nail. This is a bad time for working people. Things are stacked to the ceiling in the other side's favor. But you're telling it right, we've got to roll up our sleeves and get in there and mix it up with them. They're not as all-fired tough as they'd like us to think. They can be had."

Out of the darkness came the lights of Portland. We stopped at a roadside beanery near the river. There was a rack of pocket books inside the door. I saw a copy of **The Little Sister**. With the change I found in the soldier's pants I picked it up for later. I wanted to see how Marlowe and Dolores Gonzales made out. Thoughts of another mysterious woman made my forehead warm. Despite all that had happened in the last forty-eight hours, I couldn't chase Helen from my mind. We had a political account to settle, not to mention the other things. And I knew if I didn't get down to L.A. soon it would eat at me for the rest of my life.

That was a second reason to get to L.A. The first was to inform certain people about Frances Farmer. That too would eat at me for a long time, whether I told anyone or not, whether they could do anything or not. But it was something I had to do. For the both of us.

I put the book in my hip pocket and joined my longshoreman benefactor at the counter. Over a couple cups of diner-house murk we began talking about John L. Lewis and the nationwide miners' strike in '43 that brought the federal government to heel. And the auto workers' walkout in '46, an explosion that was heard from coast to coast. It made us both feel good. And hopeful.

A SELECTED BIBLIOGRAPHY

Frances Farmer:

Anger, Kenneth, **Hollywood Babylon**. San Francisco: Straight Arrow Books, 1975.

Arnold, William, **Shadowland**. N.Y.: Jove, 1978.

Farmer, Frances, **Will There Really Be A Morning?** N.Y.: Dell, 1972.

Mental Asylums, psychosurgery:

Bowart, W.H. **Operation Mind Control**. N.Y.: Dell, 1978.

Breggin, Peter, "The Return of Lobotomy And Psychosurgery," **Congressional Record**, Feb. 24, 1972, pp 5567-5577.

Chavkin, Samuel, **The Mind Stealers**. Boston: Houghton Mifflin, 1978.

Deutsch, Albert, **The Shame of the States**. N.Y.: Harcourt & Brace, 1948.

Frank, Leonard Roy (editor), **The History of Shock Treatment**. San Francisco, 1978.

Freeman, Walter J. (articles)

"Transorbital Leucotomy: The Deep Frontal Cut," **Proceedings of the Royal Society of Medicine**, Sept. 12, 1949, pp 8-12.

"Transorbital Lobotomy," **American Journal of Psychosurgery**, Vol. 105, No. 10, pp 734-741.

"Psychosurgery," **American Journal of Psychiatry**. (1964) Vol. 121, pp 653-655.

(about) Glenn Frankel, series of articles in **The Washington Post**, April 6, 7, 8, 1980.

(book), and James Watts, **Psychosurgery**. Charles C. Thomas, 1950.

Cohen, Lucille, series of articles on conditions at Steilacoom, Seattle **Post-Intelligencer**, Feb. 18, 19, 24, 27, 1949.

Chorover, Stephen L., "The Pacification of the Brain," **Psychology Today**, May 1974. pp 59-70.

Kesey, Ken, **One Flew Over the Cuckoo's Nest**. N.Y.: Viking Press, 1962.

Szasz, Thomas, **The Myth of Mental Illness**. N.Y. Harper & Row, 1974.

(ed.) **The Age of Madness: The History of Involuntary Mental Hospitalization**. N.Y.: Doubleday Anchor, 1973.

Vallenstein, Elliot, **Brain Control**. N.Y.: Wiley, 1974.

Ward, Mary Jane, **The Snake Pit**. N.Y.: Signet, 1946.

Scheflin, Allan W., Edward M. Opton, **The Mind Manipulators**. N.Y.: Paddington Press, 1978.

Hollywood Blacklist period:

Belfrage, Cedrick, **The American Inquisition**. Indianapolis: Bobbs-Merrill, 1973.

Bessie, Alvah, **Inquisition in Eden**. N.Y.: Macmillan, 1965.

Caute, David, **The Great Fear: The Anti-Communist Purge Under Truman and Eisenhower**. N.Y.: Simon & Schuster, 1978.

Ceplair, Larry, Steven Englund, **The Inquisition in Hollywood**. N.Y.: Anchor/Doubleday, 1980.

Cogley, John, **Report on the Blacklisting**. (2 vol.) The Fund for the Republic, 1956.

Cook, Bruce, **Dalton Trumbo**. N.Y.: Charles Scribner's Sons, 1977.

Goulden, Joseph C., **The Best Years: 1945-1950.** N.Y.: Atheneum, 1976.

Hellman, Lillian, **Scoundrel Time**. Boston: Little, Brown, 1976.

Kahn, Gordon, **Hollywood on Trial**. N.Y.: Arno Press & **The New York Times**, 1972.

Kanfer, Stefan, **A Journal of the Plague Years**. N.Y.: Atheneum, 1973.

McWilliams, Carey, **Southern California Country**. N.Y.: Duell, Sloan & Pearce, 1946.

, **Witch Hunt: The Revival of Heresy**. Boston: Little, Brown, 1950.

Navasky, Victor, **Naming Names.** N.Y.: Penguin Books, 1981.

Trumbo, Dalton, **The Time of the Toad**. N.Y.: Perennial Library, 1972.